Matt looked up from the board and stood, his face reflecting his surprise. "Hello, Livvy."

The use of his old nickname for her stopped her cold. "I want to talk about what's going on between us."

"Between us? Have I missed something?" He smiled, and his brown eyes went warm. "No, I'd definitely know if there was something between us."

She straightened to her full height. "I expect you to stop making fun of me on the air. And I also expect you to keep your callers in line. I don't appreciate being held up to ridicule, even on that free-for-all you call a radio show."

"Well, you'd be a less tempting target if you didn't take yourself so damned seriously. It's just radio, Olivia. Not brain surgery. And no matter what you want to tell yourself, it's all about entertainment and ratings."

"That's no excuse for your behavior."

"Are you referring to my show or to what you assume to be my sex life? As I recall, at one time you had no problem with either."

The reminder carried the force of a slap. "I just can't believe you're still living in Never Land. Isn't it about time for you to grow up?"

He clutched at his chest, his tone still mocking, but there was something unreadable in his dark eyes. "Ah, Olivia. You wound me."

"I doubt it. But I'd like to."

She turned and walked carefully out of the studio . . . already searching for a weapon capable of blowing a hole in Matt Ransom's massive ego.

7 Days

and

7 Nights

Wendy Wax

BANTAM BOOKS

7 DAYS AND 7 NIGHTS
A Bantam Book / July 2003

Published by Bantam Dell
A Division of Random House, Inc.
New York, New York

Bantam Books and the rooster colophon are registered
trademarks of Random House, Inc.

ISBN 0-553-58613-0

Manufactured in the United States of America
Published simultaneously in Canada

OPM   10 9 8 7 6 5 4 3 2 1

Acknowledgments

I'd like to thank Jenni Grizzle, Karen Kendall, and Karen White, who help keep me sane and without whom I might have surrendered long ago. Ditto to Sandra Chastain, Deb Smith, and the other GRAN members, whose fertile brains helped birth the idea for this book.

Thanks, too, to Jeff Madsen, who already knows more about food and wine than I ever will. And to radio talk-show host Ian Punnett, for letting me watch him work and for telling me what could and couldn't happen. The words "not in my lifetime" still make me smile.

Any mistakes regarding food, wine, or the radio industry are mine, not theirs.

As always, I have to thank my sister, Cheri Madsen, for making me look like I actually paid attention during all those eighth-grade English classes. I'd also like to thank my editor, Wendy McCurdy, and her assistant, Anne Bohner, for their wonderful handling of my manuscript.

No acknowledgment would be complete without special thanks to my agent, Pam Strickler, who made this writer's dream come true.

"Sometimes I wonder if men and women really suit each other. Perhaps they should live next door and just visit now and then."

—Katharine Hepburn

7 Days
and
7 Nights

1

O livia Moore's day began with a cheating husband and went downhill from there.

This time the cheating husband didn't belong to her. Of course, he didn't belong to the wispy-voiced woman on the other end of the phone line, either—a fact Olivia, as host of WTLK Radio's *Liv Live*, felt compelled to point out.

"The man has a wife, Clarice."

"But . . ."

"No, no 'buts.' Let's recap the facts, shall we?"

Olivia ticked her points off on fingers that her audience could not see. "You've never been in his home, and you can't call him there. You don't go out together in public. He's never available on holidays. Your *dates* take place in hotel rooms."

The sniffling began on the other end of the line.

"What does this tell you, Clarice?"

More sniffles.

"This man is not available, Clarice, because he's married." Olivia's tone turned dry. "And unless you've been living on a desert island for the last year, you know that I've had some personal experience in this area."

Clarice stopped sniffling long enough to laugh a little.

"The bottom line here is, *he's* married, *you're* miserable, and his wife probably isn't turning cartwheels, either." Lord knew she hadn't been when she'd finally stopped pretending that nice, safe, dependable James was just working late.

"Married men do not belong in the dating pool. They're like catfish, Clarice. If you're unlucky enough to reel one in, you're honor-bound to either bash him against the side of the boat or throw him back."

Olivia settled her headphones more firmly in place and squinted out through the small rectangle of glass to the radio station control room beyond. The producer of her call-in advice show, Diane Lowe, cradled a phone between her ear and shoulder, her fingers flying across her computer keyboard as she typed in a list of callers waiting to go on the air with Olivia. After each name, she typed a brief summary of what he or she intended to say.

Scanning the monitor in front of her, Olivia noted four calls holding, two of them in agreement with her advice to Clarice. The other two, who'd never been married to a "catfish" or had the misfortune of dating one, thought Clarice should proceed more slowly.

Olivia drummed her fingers on the Formica tabletop and wondered how many Clarices her own ex-husband had dated. If you believed the tabloids, there had been truckloads of them. In the end, of course, the actual number hardly mattered; one or one million, the damage was the same.

Olivia sat up straighter, her thoughts leading her to ask, "Have you noticed that your boyfriend is the only one who seems to be enjoying himself?"

There was a sob. A hiccup. The blowing of a nose—all the more graphic for lack of accompanying video—and then a final sniffle.

"Can you hear me, Clarice?" Olivia leaned into the microphone. She could practically feel Clarice nodding her head.

"Yes."

"Good, because I want you to listen carefully."

A barely audible sniff, and then, "Okay."

"Get rid of the man, Clarice. Dump him. Throw him back. It doesn't matter what method you choose. *Just do it.*"

Olivia hit the "drop" button to kill the call and, without allowing herself time to stop and think, moved on to the next.

She let half of the women have their say, totally aware of the irony of her advising the "other woman" when she'd spent almost six months imagining fates worse than death for James's last fling. Then she moved on to a new caller with a new problem, hoping this one wouldn't hit quite so close to home.

"Rachel, hello. What's happening?"

"Hi, Olivia. It's, um, about my new boyfriend. And my, um . . . feet."

Olivia heard a snort of laughter from the control room, mercifully out of microphone range, and saw Diane shoot a triumphant fist into the air. Olivia felt the same fine rush of adrenaline; only in radio could the topic move from philandering to feet in less than fifteen seconds.

Olivia tucked a stray strand of hair firmly behind her ear and got down to work. For several minutes she extracted information from her embarrassed caller. In a husky voice Rachel described the new beefcake boyfriend who only laid hands on her aerobicized body long enough to get to her big toe.

Olivia made a mental note to devote a future program to foot and other fetishes. More calls came in, and she started contemplating a book on the subject. Idly, she considered titles. Maybe *Frenzied Feet*? or *Hung Up on Hangnails*?

Glancing down at her own feet in their cushy Aerosoles, she tried to remember how long it had been since her last pedicure.

Her schedule allowed exactly no spare time for either toe sucking or pampering. In the year since her headline-making divorce, she'd moved her radio call-in show, *Liv Live*, from Tampa, Florida, to WTLK in Atlanta and seen her audience expand exponentially.

The three hours on the air every morning were the most visible part of her day, but the articles she wrote on a regular basis and the fulfillment of her multi-book contract gobbled up what little free time remained. And that was without the promotional appearances the station insisted upon.

"Rachel, this isn't a particularly unusual fetish as fetishes go. And it's only a problem if it's a problem for you."

She stood up to pace the postage-stamp-sized room— a highly unsatisfying experience for a pacer of her magnitude—while the husky voice described what incredible shape her toes were now in and offered graphic detail about what her boyfriend liked to do to them.

The walls of the tiny room pressed inward as Olivia realized that her caller's feet were having a much better sex life than Olivia's entire body was.

She stopped pacing and waited out the moment of dead air while Rachel of the much-loved toes worked up to the real reason for her call.

"My boyfriend just took a job in the shoe department at Saks. He has his hands on other women's feet all the time." Her voice broke. "He comes home from work whistling every day."

Olivia bit down hard on the inside of her cheek and reminded herself that this was a legitimate problem to Rachel, one that deserved her full and serious consideration. Unfortunately, a glance through the window to the control room told her that neither her producer nor the news anchor getting ready to go on at the top of the hour felt any such obligation; they shook with silent laughter, their bodies doubled over with mirth.

Who could blame them? Her own self-control hung by the slimmest of threads. "You know, Rachel, as long as you have no reason to believe he's stepping out on you, I'd be careful not to jump to any conclusions. In fact, I suggest you keep your feet planted firmly on the ground and—"

Rachel dissolved into a fit of giggles while Olivia made one last stab at actual advice. "Remember, it's *your* feet, I mean, you, he runs home to every night."

The opening strains of the show's theme music in her headphones felt like a reprieve from the governor. Gratefully, Olivia leaned in to the microphone one last time and closed the show with her signature tag line. "I'm Dr. Olivia Moore, reminding you to live your life . . . *live*."

Olivia removed her headphones and gathered up the

notes now strewn across the table. Pushing the microphone back on its retractable arm, she began to clear her things out of the way. In the control room on the other side of the glass, she could see Diane doing the same.

Opening the door that separated them, Olivia popped her head into the control room. "Nice job today, Di. Thanks." A quick scan of the room's flat surfaces revealed no candy wrappers or cookie crumbs. The usual McMuffin smells were missing. "On a new diet?"

"Yeah. I just started the Everything-but-the-Crust Pizza Diet."

"Oh?" Olivia felt one eyebrow go up. Her producer approached both eating and dieting with equal enthusiasm.

"Today I get ten green olives, five slices of pepperoni, one slice of cheese, and all the anchovies I can eat."

"Wow." Olivia tried not to wince. She didn't have time for fad diet lectures or yet another attempt to persuade Diane to look at the emotional triggers behind her eating.

If she hurried, she'd just make it to her own lunch with the *Atlanta Leisure* reporter. With a wave, she backed through the door and into the hall where the Operations Manager's secretary lay in wait.

"Hey, Olivia. Loved the feet thing. T.J. asked if you could stop by his office on your way out."

"Can we make it another time, Anna? I've got less than twenty minutes to make it to an interview."

The pert brunette shrugged apologetically. The top of her head barely reached Olivia's shoulder. "Sorry. He told me not to let you get away. I don't think it'll take too long."

Resigned, Olivia followed Anna down the corridor past two other studios and another control room. They went through a heavy door that swung shut and locked behind them, then crossed the lobby to the station's general offices.

T.J. Lawrence smiled and stood when Olivia knocked on his open office door. The sunlight streaming through the window spotlighted his freshly shaved head and glinted off his wire-rimmed glasses. Olivia blinked at the brightness after her stint in the artificially lit studio and took the chair the OM offered.

T.J. was a bit of a maverick by current radio standards. In the corporate environment that now permeated the industry, his hands-on approach and personal commitment to local production made him a rarity. It also commanded fierce loyalty from the people who worked for him.

It had been T.J. who'd talked Olivia into moving her show to WTLK, and T.J. who'd put the station and its resources firmly behind her during the media feeding frenzy that followed her divorce.

In a market where more and more stations relied on prepackaged syndicated programs, he continued to produce and promote local programming, building his on-air talent and staying personally involved in the direction of their shows. As a rule, he was head strategist and chief cheerleader.

Today, T.J.'s smile lacked its usual wattage, and his warm brown eyes looked troubled. Olivia settled into her chair and looked up at the man perched on the desk in front of her. "What's the problem, T.J.?"

He studied her for a moment as if weighing his words. When he folded his arms across his chest and then crossed his long legs at the ankles, Olivia shifted uncomfortably in her seat. As body language went, his was not promising.

"I know you're in a hurry, so I'll spare you the gory details. The problem, as always, is the corporate office in Detroit." He paused and shook his head in disgust. "Normally, I can handle the suits. But this time when I got out my whip and chair, they refused to back off."

The picture of T.J. in lion-taming spandex notwithstanding, Olivia found herself wishing they *were* in the big top so that T.J. could cage those mangy business types, or at least throw the beasts some . . . dead meat. Uh-oh. The image of *Liv Live* as a hunk of raw sirloin dangling above razor-sharp teeth was not a particularly pleasant one.

Olivia stood and walked to the window, where she stared down at the lunchtime traffic inching along Peachtree Street. T.J. joined her there, and for a long moment they stood side by side watching the antlike activity seven stories below. "*Liv Live's* not in jeopardy, is it?"

T.J. ran a hand over the dome of his head and sighed. "I'm afraid I'm going to have to take a hard look at it."

"Why is that?"

"It's one of our most expensive shows. It and *Guy Talk* pull the biggest audiences and have the most export potential, but they're also the most costly to produce. You and Matt Ransom are WTLK's highest-paid talent. Based solely on the bottom line, your shows are roughly equivalent."

"How can anyone compare *Liv Live* to *Guy Talk*? They don't even belong on the same planet."

"Yes, well, that's pretty much what Matt said. But WTLK is owned by people who started out marketing dog food, Olivia. To them, one can is pretty much like the next."

"How do the dog food people expect you to handle this problem?"

"Basically, they've informed me that I can't afford both Alpo and Gravy Train. Both of your contracts are up for renewal. They're sending the consultant down. I may have to give one of you up."

2

_____

Olivia made the drive to Figaro, Atlanta's trendi-est new Italian restaurant, in record time. Screeching into valet parking, tossing her keys to the attendant, and hurrying around the car toward the canopied entrance, she arrived for her appointment out of breath and totally out of sorts. She hated being late or unprepared, and at the moment she was both. She also hated being inter-viewed—which left her zero for three. And that was without T.J.'s bombshell thrown in for good measure.

The reporter from *Atlanta Leisure* stood as the maitre d' ushered Olivia to the table. He was young and self-consciously hip in a black T-shirt under a black unstruc-tured jacket. A noticeable amount of gel forced the hair above his forehead up in little spikes, and although he looked relatively harmless, the red warning light in Olivia's head flashed just the same.

She'd acquired the red light and other survival tech-niques when the media decided a radio therapist whose own marriage had crashed and burned made great head-lines.

Keeping her current motto, "Never forget the potential

for disaster," firmly in mind, she chatted amiably with the twenty-something reporter. When he pulled out a small tape recorder, turned it on, and placed it on the table between them, she didn't bat an eyelash, but the tiny hairs on the back of her neck stood on end.

"Do you mind?"

"No, no, of course not," she said as the flashing red light in her head strobed brighter.

For the first fifteen minutes or so, he stuck to the safe and predictable. Yes, she loved Atlanta. Yes, she was thrilled at the buzz about her show's syndication potential. No, she didn't think being divorced disqualified her from advising others. A Gen X Dr. Laura? No, she hadn't thought of herself in quite that way. After all, she wasn't preaching morality, but trying to help women stand up for themselves.

More like a Dear Abby, then, with Gloria Steinem tendencies? Though that description came a lot closer to the mark, Olivia didn't come out and say so. Between bites, she bobbed and weaved, trying to duck both the pigeon-holes and pitfalls. And all the time, she thought about the decision T.J. would be making.

She was waiting for the question about how Tampa, the city where *Liv Live* had been born, compared to Atlanta, when the tone of the interview began to change.

They'd just finished their Caesar salads, and she was in the middle of dipping a hunk of crusty Italian bread in seasoned olive oil, when her companion brought up the one name guaranteed to kill her appetite.

"*Atlanta Leisure* named your colleague, Matt Ransom, Bachelor of the Year again this morning. As a therapist, what do you think makes him so appealing to women?"

He stared at her expectantly, his sheep's clothing beginning to slip, but Olivia was busy sorting through her real feelings for a socially acceptable response.

"Well," she hedged, "if there's one thing I've learned from my listeners, it's that there's no accounting for what women find attractive in men."

"So, you don't find the host of *Guy Talk* attractive?"

Unfortunately, only a blind woman could get away with calling Matt Ransom unattractive. Olivia tried not to squirm as her brain reached into its memory banks to replay her first glimpse of Matt years ago at WZNA. Then, as now, he was movie star handsome. In fact, he bore an uncanny resemblance to the actor George Clooney. Though taller and broader, Ransom possessed the same close-cropped dark hair going gray at the temples, the same brown eyes under thick dark brows, and the same sort of perfectly chiseled features over a square-cut jaw.

Personally, Olivia found him too good-looking, too argumentative, too egotistical . . . too . . . everything. Eight years ago in Chicago he'd ground every one of her romantic illusions into dust, but this hardly seemed the time or place to say so. "I didn't say that."

"Do you think he deserves the title 'Bachelor of the Year'?"

Olivia took a sip of water and swallowed. Matt Ransom was thirty-six going on twenty and wouldn't recognize a committed relationship if it bit him on the . . .

Olivia looked up, caught the feral gleam in the reporter's eye, and knew how Little Red Riding Hood must have felt.

"I honestly can't think of anyone who deserves the title

more. Mr. Ransom brings a whole new meaning to the definition of bachelorhood."

"And the sniping on air and in interviews? What's the problem with you two?"

She cocked her head and squinted at the reporter. *You mean, besides the fact that I'm a trained therapist dealing with interpersonal issues that impact my listeners' lives, and he's a seat-of-the-pants rabble-rouser who explores burning issues like why women can't fathom football?*

Or how about the fact that working with him again dredges up memories I've spent eight years trying to bury, and today I found out that one of us is about to knock the other off WTLK?

Olivia managed a smile. "Just a little on-air hijinks. Mr. Ransom's show draws a large male audience; mine is predominantly female. Sometimes there's some . . . banter. It doesn't mean anything."

The reporter grinned and gleefully shed the last stitch of sheep's clothing. "So you weren't bothered by the article in which he referred to you as"—the wolf actually looked down to check his notes—" 'an insurgent in the war between the sexes'?"

Olivia slipped a last crust of bread into her mouth and tried not to choke on it. She chewed carefully for a moment before speaking. "Well, I was somewhat surprised that Ransom acknowledged there was a war on when his side is losing so badly. I'm even more surprised that a man who admits to frequenting bars named after female body parts knows what the word 'insurgent' means."

"But you're not upset that the host of *Guy Talk* named you Killjoy of the Year? Or that a good twenty minutes of his show last night featured callers laying odds on how long it's been since you last had sex?"

Olivia felt her jaw drop at this latest affront. She covered by dabbing at the corner of her mouth with her napkin and reminding herself that some questions didn't deserve answers. Since signing on at WTLK ten months ago, she'd been very careful to keep her interaction with Matt purely professional, but the Bachelor of the Year obviously felt no such compunction.

"Do you have a rebuttal for Mr. Ransom or his listeners?"

Olivia continued chewing her food carefully and forced herself to think. Not too long ago, a reporter had asked her to sum up a woman's greatest obstacle to happiness in five words or less, and she'd made headlines by doing it in one. "Men," she'd said.

Then she'd rethought her answer and added the word "sex." Those two subjects, and her willingness to tackle them on the air, had sent her ratings soaring.

Olivia had no intention of being railroaded into making a remark she'd regret. Nor did she intend to let Matt Ransom destroy her again—personally or professionally. If she kept her head, she could come out of this interview with her dignity intact and maybe even an advantage in the coming battle.

"No comment, Dr. Moore?"

Olivia set her napkin on the table and pushed her plate gently away. She met the wolf's eyes and raised a queenly eyebrow in return, speaking clearly and calmly for the benefit of the small tape recorder sitting on the table between them.

"While I have great respect for Mr. Ransom's show— what little I've heard of it—if he ever decides to tackle weightier subjects like real life and relationships, I might be able to help him out."

The wolf's fangs disappeared into a pleased smile. He stopped eating, picked up his notepad, and started scribbling.

Olivia knew when to make an exit. Slipping her purse over her shoulder, she thanked her host for lunch, slid her chair back from the table, and stood. Pausing with her hands on the back of the chair, she nodded toward the notebook and tape recorder and flashed her best smile. "I do hope you'll feel free to quote me on that."

"This is *Guy Talk*, where a guy can be a guy. And it's 11 P.M. on a Freefall Friday, which means no topic and no rules. Give me a call at 1-555-GUY-TALK. I *always* have an opinion. It's a guy thing."

Switching his microphone off, Matt Ransom leaned back in his chair, put his long legs up on the table in front of him, and clasped his hands behind his head to wait out the five-minute commercial break. With just an hour to go before midnight, the station was close to empty, which made it just the way he liked it.

Two minutes later, he tossed a Nerf ball at the basketball hoop duct-taped to the wall and smiled when it swished through. He shot the next one left-handed, the one after that with his eyes closed.

Satisfied, he reached for the mug of lukewarm coffee more from force of habit than from a need for caffeine. He was a night owl, always had been, and preferred working late, when things were looser and less structured.

At one minute until air, he made a few notes about a

topic for next Monday's show and let his thoughts wander to the previous night's program. He'd begun by posing the question, "Why can't men and women share a TV remote?" planning to segue into a discussion of the elemental differences between males and females, a topic custom-made for his particular brand of humor.

Instead, the show had digressed into a trashing of couples' counseling, which had led to another caller's caustic evaluation of therapy in general, which had ultimately led to the topic of WTLK's very own Dr. Olivia Moore.

Even he, who normally had no problem following the flow, had been a little surprised at how quickly her name had come up and how strongly his callers, mostly male, felt about her. In loud voices they objected to her pro-female stance and the male bashing that often accompanied it, but they couldn't seem to stop talking about her.

He was fairly certain he wasn't the one responsible for bringing up Olivia's sex life, or the imagined lack of one. But once the subject was raised, he'd had a devil of a time getting off it. He winced as he remembered the jokes and innuendo.

Almost as bad as his callers' fixation with the earnest Dr. Moore was the way they kept trying to get him to rehash and counter her advice. Hell, even if he had the least bit of respect for or belief in counseling, he had no interest in providing it to his listeners. He was in the entertainment business, and his show was designed for mental stimulation—not rehabilitation.

At ten seconds to air, he hunkered deeper into his seat and took one last shot at the hoop. The coffee had grown stale, and his aim was faulty. The digital clock on the wall provided his countdown, and on cue, he said, "This is *Guy Talk*, where a guy can be a guy. I'm Matt Ransom."

"Hey, Matt."

Matt recognized the deep drawl of one of his regular callers, a long-haul trucker who'd picked up his lifelong nickname as a linebacker for the University of Georgia Bulldogs. "Hi, Dawg. How ya doin'?"

"Not so great. My girlfriend, JoBeth, wants to get married."

"Aw, hell, Dawg. This is not Relationships Anonymous."

"I'm sorry, man, but I've got to talk to somebody."

"Can't we talk about football? Or maybe the relative merits of owning versus leasing a vehicle?"

"I need some help here, Matt. JoBeth's been listening to that Dr. Olivia. I need somebody on my side."

Matt looked to his producer, Ben, for assistance, but the coward refused to look him in the eye. A check of his monitor showed only one caller waiting. There wasn't a commercial break in sight.

"All right, all right. What seems to be the problem?"

"Well, *I* don't think there is a problem. But JoBeth keeps going on about her biological clock. Says it's time to settle down and start a family."

"Why don't you just tell her you need some time? I'm sure she doesn't want to rush into anything. How long have you been dating?"

"Three years."

"Three years? Good Lord. How long does it take to figure out whether you want to be with somebody?"

"That's what *she* said. And aren't you the one to talk?

How many times have you been named Bachelor of the Year, now, Ransom?"

"A few."

Dawg snorted. "Not exactly settling down and making any life-altering commitments yourself, are you?"

"Nope."

"How come your girlfriends aren't calling in on that show to complain?"

"Because I don't give them anything to complain about. I'm honest. I tell them right up front what they can expect, namely a good time, but I don't pretend I'm offering anything more than that."

"And that works for you?"

"Always has. Let me put it this way, Dawg: Real guys need to be real clear. Then there's no problem."

"Well, it's a little late for that now. JoBeth's a fine woman and all, but I'm just not ready to do the marriage thing again."

"I hear you, Dawg. But I'll tell you, it's a whole lot easier to say that up front instead of later in self-defense. You've put yourself in the middle of a classic no-win situation. Whatever you do now, you're pretty much screwed."

Matt terminated the call and glanced at the clock, relieved to discover it was almost time for a commercial break. He took one of the holding calls, listened to some more less-than-macho whimpering, and dumped the rest, signaling Ben he was ready to move on.

This was what came of telling men they were supposed to have a sensitive side; it made them wimpy. He didn't like it one bit.

At long last Matt heard the strains of his theme music. He needed this break, and when he came back on the air he wasn't going to allow any more whining. Matt looked through the small plate-glass window, glared at Ben on general principle, and then leaned in to the microphone. "This is *Guy Talk* . . . not Dear Abby. If you've got something manly to say, give me a call. It's a Freefall Friday."

At the all-clear signal, Matt stood, removed his headphones, and headed out of the studio. He made it past the control room, down the corridor, and through the security door before slowing down. The last two days were enough to spoil a man's good time. First, T.J. had to go and share his budget dilemma with him, and now his audience was trying to turn him into some kind of Donahue. Sheesh.

As far as Matt was concerned, the best relationships were every bit as uncomplicated as he'd said. Two people got together, they enjoyed each other's company, and they moved on when it stopped being fun. If you didn't get too close, no one got too hurt. He'd been living that philosophy successfully all his adult life, with the exception of one long-ago assault on his heartstrings, and he saw no reason to reconsider that philosophy now.

He stopped in front of a publicity photo someone had tacked up on the bulletin board and studied Olivia Moore, Ph.D. Funny how completely she'd managed to intrude into his life, once again. Not only was her show beginning to change the face of his own, but according to T.J., Olivia was now the competition. One of their shows could go.

He narrowed his gaze and contemplated the likeness more closely. She'd grown sleeker, more sophisticated, but physically Olivia hadn't changed much since Chicago. Her cheekbones still angled dramatically upward on either side of the straight, slightly pointed nose, while her lips remained too full for the determined chin underneath. Her silky blonde hair fell straight to the shoulder like it always had, and her wide-set green eyes continued to glitter with wicked intelligence.

And she still turned him on without even trying.

Matt poured himself a last cup of hours-old coffee, zapped it back to life in the microwave, and headed toward the control room, his mind full of Olivia. When the time came for T.J. to make his choice, he'd be strangely sorry to see her go.

Yep. He'd miss her all right. He'd also miss the surge in listener response that resulted every time he ruffled her feathers on the air.

B

_____

JoBeth Namey sorted through the basket of dirty clothes on the laundry room floor. Spinning the washer's control knob, she started a stream of hot water and propped up the lid of the machine. Then she added a cup of liquid detergent and watched the water turn sudsy before feeding the contents of the basket into the washer one article at a time.

Dawg's T-shirts were as industrial-sized as the man who wore them, and so were his jockey shorts. JoBeth dangled a pair of white cotton briefs above the soapy water, blushing as she remembered how urgently she'd tugged them off him the night before. A sigh escaped her at the memory of his lovemaking and the contentment she'd felt cradled in his arms afterward—a contentment that had disintegrated when she awoke to overhear him discussing her on the air with Matt Ransom.

JoBeth felt a fresh wave of humiliation and an equally unwelcome pang of despair. Earl Wayne Rollins II was not the first man she'd ever had a relationship with, but she'd assumed he'd be the last. She loved him, that was the hard, cold truth of it, and he kept saying he loved her.

But the ticking of her biological clock had begun to drown out those words of love.

She wanted . . . Lord, she wanted children and a family of her own. Not the empty keeping-up-appearances sort she'd grown up in, but the real thing fueled by real feelings and emotional commitment. Being forced to lobby for a marriage proposal made her feel like an article of clothing destined for the clearance rack—not worth the original, retail price.

JoBeth dropped the lid on the washer and bent to pull a load of blue jeans out of the dryer.

"JoBeth, you downstairs?"

Silently she pulled clothes out of the dryer and folded each one in turn, carefully separating hers and Dawg's into neatly stacked piles.

Dawg came up behind her and wrapped his arms around her. His touch, as always, was surprisingly gentle for such a big man. "Mornin', sweetheart."

Normally she would have turned, gone up on tiptoe, and pressed her body up against the solid wall of Dawg Rollins's chest, but today she held herself stiff.

"What's wrong?" He nuzzled the back of her neck and locked his forearms together just under her collarbone. In a minute he'd be slipping his fingers under her pajama top and making her tingle all over again. "We don't have anywhere we need to be just yet. Why don't you come on back to bed?"

Holding her body rigid, she pulled away and turned to look up into the rugged angles of his face. He had a good ten inches on her and close to a hundred pounds, but she refused to feel small. Righteous indignation bubbled in her veins, and she enjoyed his start of surprise when she placed a hand in the center of his chest and pushed him back a step.

"You have got more nerve than the whole state of Texas."

Golden-gray stubble covered Dawg's cheeks, and his blue eyes shone with good humor. He actually smiled.

"You went on the radio last night and told the whole of Atlanta that you don't want to marry me."

His smile fled.

"How do you think that makes me feel?"

"Well, now, I—"

"That was a rhetorical question, Dawg. You are not supposed to answer."

"But, JoBeth, I—"

"I'm in love with you. And you keep saying you're in love with me."

"I am, JoBeth. You know I—"

"No." She pointed a finger at him, cautioning him not to speak. "Don't you dare say it right now. I'm tired of hearing words that go nowhere."

"But JoBeth, honey . . ."

She stopped him with a look.

"I'm forty-one, Dawg. I can't keep hanging around while you think this through. Who knows how many good eggs I have left?"

Dawg opened his mouth as if to speak, but now, when she yearned for a response, no words came out. They just faced each other in the overheated laundry room with the sounds of the washer and dryer underscoring the silence that stretched between them.

His blue eyes turned apologetic, and he looked almost as miserable as she felt. Realizing she was close to tears, she ducked under his arm and escaped upstairs. Yanking on a pair of jeans and a T-shirt, JoBeth swiped at her eyes and reflected on the irony of her situation. Four years ago she'd walked away from a marriage proposal because she couldn't settle for a man who didn't make her pulse pound or her heart race.

Now she had more pulse pounding and heart racing than she could shake a stick at, but it looked like it would take an act of God to convince the man she loved to marry her.

With her Monday morning show behind her, Olivia went in search of Matt. Braced for confrontation, she strode toward the production studio where Matt was recording commercials, determined to establish ground rules for the remainder of their time together at WTLK.

She'd been wrong not to acknowledge what had happened between them in Chicago. While she had no intention of making their past common knowledge, letting it simmer in silence between them had proven a bad idea. She hadn't realized how hard it would be to work with Matt again, but now that she knew, well, she'd just have to find a way to set things straight.

The glowing red light above the studio door indicated Matt's microphone was open, so she stopped outside and studied her nemesis through the rectangle of glass.

As she watched, he leaned forward in to the microphone, his attention split between the typewritten copy and the digital timer beside it, and read the copy aloud. His body language declared him both focused and relaxed. Olivia was neither, because even through the wall of a sealed room, Matt Ransom still had the power to un-nerve her.

She'd been a twenty-one-year-old intern when WZNA's sexy afternoon disc jockey had singled her out. He'd been worldly; she'd been painfully inexperienced. He'd offered a good time; she'd fallen completely and em-barrassingly in love. And if she'd been ill prepared for the advent of their relationship, she'd been even less equipped to handle its sudden end.

Her experience with Matt had marked and changed her. Never again did she give herself so freely or trust so blindly. Even her choice of husband could be traced to the lessons she'd learned from Matt.

Now, eight years later, it was hard to fathom how she could have fallen so deeply for a man she'd barely known. It was even harder to understand why a part of her still wanted to believe there was more to Matt Ransom than a sexy smile and easy charm.

Watching him work, she told herself that she felt only disdain for a man who plowed through women like a farmer did a field, but she could still remember every detail of his lovemaking. Just as she remembered what it felt like to have the full force of his personality focused solely on her.

The red light flashed off, and Olivia reached for the doorknob. Quickly, before she could lose her nerve, she turned it and opened the door.

Matt looked up from the audio board and stood, his face reflecting his surprise. "Hello, Livvy."

The use of his old nickname for her stopped her cold. It took several long seconds to recover and an enormous amount of will not to drop her gaze. Stepping forward, she pulled the door shut behind her, trying not to notice how small the space was and how completely he filled it. "I want to talk about what's going on between us."

"Between us? Have I missed something?" He smiled, and his brown eyes went warm. "No, I'd definitely know if there was something between us."

She felt the heat steal up her neck to warm her cheeks and fought the urge to fall back a step.

"It's amazing, given what you do for a living, Olivia, but talking about sex still makes you blush." He didn't wait for a reply. "We were talking about sex, weren't we?"

The smug amusement in his voice straightened her spine. "*You* may have been, but then, that's standard operating procedure for you, isn't it? I'm not here to trade double entendres, Matt, and I have no interest in wasting time on sexual innuendo."

"No, let's not ever waste time. And let's not enjoy ourselves too much, either. Wouldn't want to appear *too* human."

She felt a fine, hot flash of anger.

Raising her chin, she said, "Until T.J. clarifies our situation, we need to strive for a little professionalism. You remember what that is, don't you?"

"Remember it? I taught it to you. Along with quite a few other things."

Olivia flushed at the blatant reminder. She opened her mouth to respond, but had to swallow her retort when a knock sounded on the door. She turned as the door swung outward to reveal a very young, very beautiful female.

"Hope I'm not interrupting." The girl's gaze swept over

Olivia. "You promised me lunch, Matt. Are you almost done?"

"Olivia, this is Cherie. She just started in the sales department. Cherie, Dr. Olivia Moore."

Cherie's face glowed with obvious adoration. For Matt. "It's a pleasure to meet you, Dr. O. I'm a big fan." The girl's respectful tone placed Olivia squarely in the ancient-crone-not-to-be-considered-competition category—not a place a woman approaching thirty wanted to be.

Olivia forced a smile. "Thank you, Cherie, it's a pleasure to meet you, too. But I'm not quite finished with Matt yet." Assuring herself she had not just made a Freudian slip, Olivia waited for the young woman to duck back out the door. Then she turned to face Matt again, fortified by the knowledge that Matt, like her father, would always be surrounded by Cheries.

She straightened to her full height. Matt Ransom was nothing more than a colleague—and according to T.J., a temporary one. All she required from him was professional courtesy and a little respect. "I expect you to stop making fun of me on the air. And I also expect you to keep your callers in line. I don't appreciate being held up to ridicule, even on that free-for-all you call a radio show."

The glint of amusement disappeared from Matt's eyes. "Well, you'd be a less tempting target if you didn't take yourself so damned seriously."

"I beg your pardon?"

"It's just radio, Olivia. Not brain surgery. And no matter what you want to tell yourself, it's all about entertainment and ratings."

"That's no excuse for your behavior." Belatedly she

realized that her gaze had strayed to the young woman waiting on the other side of the plate glass.

Matt followed Olivia's gaze. "Are you referring to my show or to what you assume to be my sex life? As I recall, at one time you had no problem with either."

The reminder carried the force of a slap. What a mistake it had been to try to reason with him. "I don't give a fig about your sex life. I'm not one of your groupies anymore, Matt. And I don't think every word that spills out of your mouth is gospel. I just can't believe you're still living in Never Land. Isn't it about time for you to grow up?"

He clutched at his chest, his tone still mocking, but there was something unreadable in his dark eyes. "Ah, Olivia. You wound me."

"I doubt it. But I'd like to."

With that, she turned and walked carefully out of the studio, past the waiting Cherie and down the hallway, her brain already searching for a weapon capable of blowing a hole in Matt Ransom's massive ego.

"Good morning, everyone, and welcome to the Tuesday edition of *Liv Live*. Today we're going to do something a little different."

She caught Diane's surprised glance and gave her a thumbs-up. Butterflies threw themselves against the walls of her stomach, but she didn't let them deter her.

"Instead of starting off with your individual issues like we usually do, we're going to talk about a problem that plagues lots of relationships. It's kind of a *guy* thing." She paused for emphasis. "Dan Kiley wrote a book about it in the eighties, but I'm convinced it's still a problem in the new millennium."

Diane took the first call as Olivia explained. "The Peter Pan Syndrome refers to the problem many men have growing up. Like the mythical Peter, they want to fly through life without ever having to accept adult responsibility."

Olivia smiled. "I'll describe typical Peter Pan behavior, and you let me know if you know anyone like that. I'm especially interested in hearing how this kind of behavior has affected your life."

Olivia glanced down at her notes, though she didn't need them. She could describe this man in her sleep.

"He's attractive, lots of fun, and knows how to show a woman a good time. He's probably a serial dater, staying with one woman until she starts making noises about commitment. Chances are he's got it down to a science. You know, that whole 'just let them know what to expect up front' business that he uses to rationalize his inability to sustain a long-term relationship. Bottom line, this guy has plenty going for him—unless you're interested in 'happily ever after.'

"When someone wants to discuss real feelings, he looks for a less threatening topic." She paused for emphasis. "Like football or car leasing versus buying. The last thing he wants is a serious discussion about anything personal."

Olivia caught Diane's eye through the rectangle of glass, and the two women shared a smile as Olivia took her first call.

"Hello, JoBeth. Do you know a Peter Pan?"

"Oh, yeah. I've been living with one. Dawg, that's my

boyfriend, he qualifies big time. And so does his hero, Matt Ransom."

Olivia couldn't believe her luck. She hadn't expected to hit pay dirt so quickly.

"Matt Ransom, really?" She tried to sound surprised, but didn't think she was that great an actress. "What makes you think your boyfriend and Matt Ransom are Peter Pans?" She felt a twinge of guilt at letting her caller do the dirty work.

"Well, Dawg thinks Ransom walks on water. Especially since Matt got named Bachelor of the Year for about the hundredth time. Whenever I see a picture of him in the paper, he's with a different woman, and I don't think I've ever heard so much as a rumor about him settling down. Does that qualify him?"

Big time. "Gee, JoBeth, I guess it does."

"I just don't understand it. Dawg and I have so much in common. I thought we wanted the same things. But when I told him I wanted to get married, he looked at me like I'd just told him I had the plague or something. Why would he react that way, Dr. O?"

She was going to have to put this woman on the payroll. "Well, JoBeth, according to Kiley, it's all about fear. These men feel inadequate"—she enunciated the word carefully—"and they are deathly afraid of little old us and having to grow up. I'm going to take a few more calls, and then we'll discuss how to deal with these Peters."

"Is it going to require bashing and throwing them back? I'm not sure I could do that to Dawg."

"Don't you worry about Dawg, JoBeth. We're going to try a little tough love on that boy. But first let's see what some of our other callers have to say."

The morning flew. Not surprisingly, everyone knew or had been involved with a man who belonged in Never Land. And Matt Ransom's name came up a gratifying number of times. As Atlanta's reigning Bachelor of the Year and host of the ultra-macho *Guy Talk*, he was a highly visible example. Olivia continued to feign surprise whenever his name came up, and she refrained from male bashing herself, but she felt vindicated just the same.

In conclusion, she offered some additional insight into the syndrome and invited anyone with serious concerns to log on to her website to see Kiley's original questionnaire.

To be fair, she doubted Matt, with the level of success he'd achieved, would fit Kiley's profile, but she didn't feel compelled to share that opinion with her listeners.

As promised, during the last few minutes of the show, Diane got JoBeth back on the line. Olivia imagined both Dawg and his hero would take exception to the advice she offered.

"JoBeth, not knowing the reasons behind your boyfriend's unwillingness to commit, I can only make suggestions based on his behavior. If you love Dawg and want to marry him, then you need to make him understand that his refusal to marry you could cause him to lose you. It's not a threat or an ultimatum, though I imagine he'll call it that. It's exercising your rights and standing up for yourself. If you want a committed relationship and he doesn't, then you owe it to yourself to get back out there where you can meet someone who does. If he refuses to set a date, move out."

"Move out?"

"Yes, and for God's sake stop having sex with him."

"No sex?"

"The truth is that even today the old adage holds true: Most men will not buy the cow if the milk is free."

Olivia caught the startled expression on Diane's face and winked. "We're talking no more free milk, JoBeth. Not a drop."

Olivia glanced up at the digital clock, amazed at how quickly the morning had gone. She felt incredibly good, as if a weight had been lifted from her shoulders.

"Thanks to everyone who shared their Peter Pan stories. It's time to ask for and receive what you want, ladies; making yourself happy is no fairy tale. JoBeth, let me know what happens with Dawg. I'll be looking forward to hearing from you."

The theme music sounded especially sweet in her ears today. As it built and flared, she smiled once again and bid her audience farewell.

"Thanks for being with me today. I'm Dr. Olivia Moore, reminding you to live your life . . . *live*."

4

Matt signed on Tuesday night determined to avoid advice-giving at all costs. He planned to do what he did best—rouse the guys, shock a little bit, encourage spirited discussion. He'd already wasted more time than he'd meant to thinking about Olivia Moore. He wasn't going to let her infringe on his show, too. At least that's what he believed until he took his first call.

"Hello, Peter." The caller was male, his voice unfamiliar.

"I'm sorry?"

"Is this the unable-to-commit-or-grow-up Peter Pan? The one currently residing in Never Land?"

Shit. Maybe his listeners did need counseling. "This is Matt. And you're on *Guy Talk*. What's all this about Peter Pan?"

"You're going to have to start listening to morning radio. You were a big hit on *Liv Live* this morning."

"Me? On *Liv Live*?"

"You betcha."

Matt peered through the glass at Ben, who held up a cassette tape as if it were a time bomb. His producer typed him a message: "It's addressed to Peter P. It was in your office mailbox."

The next few calls went much the same, but no one really offered answers until Dawg called in. "Hi, Matt. Rough day, huh?"

"Not until recently. What's going on, Dawg? I seem to be the last to know."

"Well, they had a field day with you on *Liv Live* this morning. Dr. O talked about something called the Peter Pan Syndrome, and then she asked people to describe Peter Pans they knew. A whole bunch of women described you—I think some of them were old girlfriends who weren't as comfortable with your up-front warning as you thought." Apparently even Dawg couldn't resist getting in a dig tonight.

"JoBeth described me. She used my name and everything—I heard part of it on my run to Montgomery— and then she left a message on my cell phone saying that if I wanted any more milk I was going to have to buy the cow. Danged if I know what she meant by that."

"Women can be downright mysterious, all right."

"And mean, too. You shoulda heard some of the things they said about you."

Matt teetered between anger and amusement. On the one hand, he didn't particularly relish being likened to a cartoon character like Peter Pan. On the other, what in the world had gotten into prim and proper, play-by-the-rules Olivia Moore? He could hardly wait to listen to the tape of her show. There was nothing like a worthy adversary to make the game more interesting.

A week later the score was tied and bets were being placed on the winner. Though few at the station thought she'd topped her Peter Pan program, it was generally acknowledged that Olivia had shed her white gloves and had a good shot at the title.

Matt had gotten in a few licks of his own, including a show devoted to the kinds of hang-ups that drove people into the counseling profession. Far from scientific, it had digressed into a comedic free-for-all that left callers stacked up waiting to go on the air.

Today's joint meeting of the staffs of *Liv Live* and *Guy Talk* was the first of its kind, and those already seated around the conference table seemed distinctly wary. Sauntering in with only moments to spare, Matt chose an empty seat directly next to Olivia and made a show of making himself comfortable.

When all eyes were on them, he nodded amiably, scooted his chair even closer, and took her hand in his. "I don't believe we've been introduced. The name is Peter. But you can call me Pan. And you would be ... Wendy? ... Tinker Bell?" He flashed a smile that managed to be both brazen and boyish.

Embarrassed, Olivia tried to pull her hand free. When that didn't work, she forced an equally cocky smile to her lips. "Nope, just a concerned mental health professional trying to help the lost boys find their way home."

He smiled appreciatively and turned her hand over, examining it closely. "No hook, I see, though I detect a few claws." He bent down to kiss her palm like a courtier of old, and whispered so only she could hear, "You can take me home anytime."

His lips were warm and intimate against her skin.

Olivia gave up on subtlety and set about retrieving her hand one digit at a time. Once free, she turned her attention to the Operations Manager, who looked surprisingly happy for someone experiencing a budget crisis.

"Okay," T.J. said. "Now that we all have our hands to ourselves, we can get started." He cleared his throat and leaned forward. "As you all know, we've had the company consultant down from Detroit looking at audience reaction to both of your shows."

Everyone groaned. But as T.J. continued, the reason for his good humor became evident. In radio, as in television, the larger the audience, the more the station could charge for both commercial time and the right for other stations to air their programs. "We won't have the total picture until we get the final book at the end of the ratings period, but from what we can determine, your little 'squabble' is already having a measurable impact."

T.J. smoothed a hand over his bald head. "Every time you talk about each other on the air, your approval ratings shoot up."

"Oh, great," Olivia said. "Why don't I just examine one of Matt's psychological issues on every show? He's bound to have enough of them to fill a couple years' worth of programming."

"Look who's talking." Matt's snort of laughter was less than flattering. "Listening to my audience rant about you hasn't been any picnic, either. For somebody who's supposed to help others, you've got quite a few peculiarities of your own. Not," he added hastily, "that I have any interest in taking up any more time talking about them on my show."

"Children, children, save it for on air." T.J. sat back in

his chair and studied Matt and Olivia. "I mean that literally."

Matt shook his head in disgust. "Oh, right. What are you going to do, put us on the air and let us duke it out? We're not trained animals, T.J. I, for one, am not willing to spar with Olivia on cue."

"No?" T.J. continued to study them carefully. "That's too bad, because our promotions department has come up with a way to capitalize on your little 'feud' and do some good for the community at the same time."

Matt lounged in the chair beside her, but his negligent pose was at odds with the waves of energy rolling off him. For once they were in accord. She, too, had a bad feeling about the direction of this conversation.

T.J. turned to the Promotion Director, newly acquired from a sister station in Boston. "Charles, why don't you fill everyone in."

Charles Crankower ran his elegant fingers through his perfectly styled blond hair. In an environment known for its informality, he was painfully pressed and stiffly correct. Those who didn't care for him—and their number was growing—expended considerable energy trying to spot the stick they claimed must be stuck up his butt. So far, no one had managed to locate or extract it.

"Actually, the idea is stunningly simple, yet complex." Charles crossed one knife-edged trouser leg over the other and steepled manicured fingers on the table in front of him. His voice was a rich baritone, the accent cultured.

"As you probably know, the Muscular Dystrophy Association conducts a 'jail and bail' fund-raiser each year."

They all nodded warily, trying to figure out where Charles was headed.

"Well, the Third Harvest Food Bank approached us about attempting something similar, though the bail would be paid in food rather than monetary donations. They need help replenishing their pantries."

"So they want to pretend to lock us up somewhere and have our listeners donate food to get us out?" Matt's tone was clearly skeptical. "I don't see how this ties in to what's happening with Olivia and me."

"Yes, well, we've come up with a slightly different twist." He unsteepled his fingers, rested his elbows on the conference table, and smiled. It was the most animated Olivia had ever seen him, and she didn't care for it one bit.

"We want to lock you up together in a kind of *Big Brother/Survivor* situation. For a week." If Crankower noticed their shocked expressions, he chose not to acknowledge them. "The idea is to set it up so that you can both do your shows all week from the site. And we'll have a Webcam feeding live to the Internet so your listeners can actually watch you anytime they choose. During the week they can vote for their favorite host and pledge food at the same time. As far as the public is concerned, whoever raises the most food and votes wins."

"Wins what?" Matt's tone was dry as the Sahara.

Charles shifted carefully in his seat, but he didn't falter. "T.J. will address that in just a moment, but the ultimate prize, of course, is increased exposure and enhanced ratings."

There was a long silence before Charles pressed on. "Given your audiences, we assume donations will fall along gender lines. In essence, we expect a true battle between the sexes." Charles smiled and bowed his head slightly, as if expecting applause.

"You're kidding, right?" Matt shifted his gaze from Charles to T.J., barely sparing a glance for Olivia.

"No, I'm not."

"Let me see if I've got this right. You want to lock us up for a week and see who's still standing at the end?" Matt's tone still smacked of disbelief, but as Olivia watched, a glint of mischief stole into his dark eyes, lightening them considerably. "I assume we can't vote each other out?"

T.J. laughed. "No, no voting out. No eating of rats. The apartment will be completely equipped with all the creature comforts. In fact, your sponsors are already vying with each other to stock the place with their products. It's an incredible promotional opportunity."

Olivia finally found her voice. "You spoke to sponsors before you talked to us?"

Charles swallowed, but held his ground. "We wanted to see whether the idea would fly before we bothered you with the details." He smiled again. By Crankower standards, the man was positively glowing. "Virtually everyone's on board. They absolutely love this idea."

"That's because no one is suggesting they spend a week with this character." She shoved a thumb in Matt's direction. "I'm not going to do this, T.J. I'm not going to be stuck in a confined space with a maniac for a week while a national audience watches through a—a peephole. Torture is illegal in this country."

Matt grinned. "You're hurting my feelings, Olivia. Just think how much quality time we'd have together. Why, we could really get to know each other."

"I don't want to know you better. I'm sorry I know you as well as I do."

"You just keep slinging those arrows, don't you? I hate to sound immodest, Olivia, but there are women who would kill for the opportunity you're being offered. Unless, of course, you're afraid to be alone with me?"

"Afraid of you?" She was terrified, but not of him. "Don't flatter yourself. I just think it's stupid." Olivia turned to Diane for support, but her producer shrugged apologetically.

"I hate to say this, Olivia, but it really is a great idea. You saw what happened with the Peter Pan thing. We're looking at a huge ratings kiss here, and major press coverage."

Matt's producer agreed. "It's a win-win situation. The food bank gets food and publicity, you both get big numbers—everybody wins. All you have to do is put on a bit of a show. Tangle with each other a little." Ben grinned. "That shouldn't be a problem for you two."

Diane scribbled a few notes and then addressed Charles. "There will be some private areas not covered by the camera, right?"

"Yes." Charles pulled out a floor plan of one of the smallest apartments Olivia had ever seen. "The two bedrooms and the bathroom are unwired, though the hall between them will be visible. So, if either one of them feels the urge to kill, there's a place to retreat and cool down. Obviously, though, we're counting on a certain amount of hostility."

"Hostility is not a problem. But I'd rather donate the money than go through this ridiculous charade." There was too much history here, and too much old heartache.

Olivia shuddered at the idea of being trapped for a week with a man she couldn't stand . . . and wasn't sure she could resist. The fact that she'd turn thirty during the week they'd earmarked for the promotion smacked of cruel and unusual punishment.

She studied Matt's profile, strong and sure, and thought about how easily he unnerved her. Her gaze settled on his cocky grin, and every synapse in her brain screamed out a warning. "I'm sorry, T.J., but I just can't see myself doing this."

T.J. looked Olivia straight in the eye, his gaze never wavering. "You're perfectly free to say no to this, Olivia. I wouldn't dream of forcing you to be a part of the promotion."

Olivia's sigh of relief died on her lips as T.J. continued. "Of course, if you don't participate, Matt will end up with his own weeklong remote."

Olivia silently weighed her options. Letting Matt gain a promotional advantage seemed a lot smarter than spending a week alone with him in a sardine-sized apartment. But then, almost anything would be smarter than that. Unfortunately, T.J. didn't seem to be finished with her yet. He said, "And of course I'm planning to use this remote to help me make my decision between your shows. The favorite-host vote and food donations will be the most visible popularity indicators, but corporate's a lot more interested in audience attitudes."

The pause that followed was so pregnant Olivia feared it might be carrying twins.

"The consultant's coming back during the remote to conduct a series of focus groups and a targeted phone survey to get a better handle on how our listeners really feel about the two of you. First he'll measure P1 response—the listeners who already consider WTLK their preferred station. But then, and this is key, he'll be taking a thorough measurement of P2's—the listeners who consider us their secondary choice. Converting them to P1's is a very big deal."

It sounded like a bad game of bingo, but Olivia understood that audience preference was what it all came down to.

"At the end of the week," T.J. concluded, "I should have what I need to make an informed decision. If you're not in on the remote, it's going to be a very uneven playing field."

Olivia sat back in her chair, stunned and silent, listening to the excited chatter around her. She felt Matt's gaze on her and turned in her seat to face him. As usual, his eyes were too warm and his smile too knowing.

Agreeing to Charles's scheme would be a mistake of epic proportions. If she were half as assertive as she advised her listeners to be, she'd stand up and commit hari-kari before she allowed herself to consider a promotion as outlandish as the one Charles had just put before them.

Matt leaned in closer, and the blood whooshed through her veins with the force of a tsunami. The sooner she said no, the better.

It didn't matter what Matt or anyone else thought. Before she'd say yes to a plan as potentially dangerous as this one, they'd be holding the Winter Olympics in hell.

5

_____

Does it feel cold in here to you?" Olivia stood inside the doorway of the apartment, trying not to hear the front door click shut behind her. Or the dead bolt slamming into place. Or Crankower's footsteps echoing down the empty hallway toward that final elevator ride to freedom.

She reached for the thermostat and adjusted the dial, even though she knew the chill cutting through her had little to do with the temperature and everything to do with the panic that gripped her.

Taking an exploratory step into the room, Olivia set her suitcase on the floor and let her gaze wander around the living area. What she saw did nothing to calm her nerves.

To the left was an upside-down U of a kitchen in varying shades of beige. Its eat-in counter jutted back toward the front door, and a wooden dinette set sat next to it. A postage-stamp window above the sink admitted a dollop of daylight.

Straight ahead of the entryway, a gap in the apartment's longest wall led to the bedrooms and bath. To the right of the gap, two nubby brown sofas formed an L around a mission-style cocktail table and faced a bulging entertainment armoire on top of which perched the eyeball-shaped camera that would document their every move.

Glimmers of daylight teased through French doors set into the far wall, and next to them stood a portable punching bag with a caricature of Matt's face emblazoned on it.

Squeezed in between the front door and the armoire, a desk with computer, audio mixer, and telephone had been set up as a temporary audio console. Matt leaned across her to punch a series of keys on the computer, and seconds later, everything in the camera's path appeared on both the computer monitor and the television screen.

"Smile, Olivia. It's show time." Matt's mouth brushed against her ear, and his warm breath tickled her neck.

Determined to ignore him, Olivia peered at the television screen. She could see herself and Matt in the foreground with the kitchen and bedroom area behind them, but because of the wide angle required to cover the whole space, subtle movement and fine detail were lost. As a test, she raised one hand and waggled all five fingers at the camera. A glance at the monitor confirmed what she'd hoped—though the raised hand was obvious, what it was doing was not.

The lack of audio was another blessing. Since sound would only be broadcast during their shows, they wouldn't have to guard their words as closely as their actions. Olivia took a step back from Matt. "I'm going to put my things away. Do you have a bedroom preference?"

Matt's lips parted in a grin, and Olivia realized she did,

in fact, need to choose her words with care. "Let me re-phrase that. Do you care which bedroom you sleep in?"

His dark eyes glittered.

"Never mind." Olivia picked up her suitcase and strode across the room to the first door on the left. "I'll take this one." Then she sailed through the bedroom door.

The bedroom, like the rest of the apartment, had a certain minimalist quality. Which was to say it was small and sparsely furnished. After laying her suitcase on a luggage stand she found in the closet, she sat on the edge of the queen-size bed and contemplated the Victoria's Secret bag that someone had placed in its center. Fifteen minutes alone with Matt and she was tripping over her tongue; adding lingerie to the equation seemed decidedly . . . stupid.

Wary, she reached into the bright pink tissue paper and pulled out the skimpiest black satin nightgown she'd ever seen. Feather light and boasting more slits than satin, it came with an equally skimpy thong. She had just lifted the tiny triangle of material gingerly between two fingers when she heard Matt's voice coming from the doorway.

"Olivia . . ." Whatever Matt had been planning to say died on his lips at the sight of the thong dangling from her fingertips.

She crammed the slip of satin back into the bag, and turned to face him.

"You seem to have picked the right room," he said.

Olivia refused to show any embarrassment. "What, no goodies in yours?" she asked.

"I got cologne and green plaid pajamas." He leaned nonchalantly against the doorjamb. "The sponsor was planning to send you a matching pair, but I told them you belonged in black satin . . . or nothing at all. Looks like they sent the best of both." His gaze swept over her body. "Too bad you don't have the nerve to wear the black number on the air."

"I didn't build my career strutting around in black satin."

"A real shame. You could score two, maybe three rating points with the thong, Olivia, and I don't think I could bring myself to object."

"Very sporting of you. But I have every intention of beating you with all my clothes on." She opened the nightstand drawer and shoved the pink and white bag inside. "In my experience, most people prefer their therapists dressed."

One dark eyebrow sketched upward. "Yeah. Don't ya just hate those naked counseling sessions? So hard to maintain eye contact."

Unable to stop herself, Olivia laughed out loud. She'd forgotten how on target Matt's humor could be. And how handsome he was when his smile leaped up and lit his eyes. Her laughter faded and she fell silent under his regard. It was time to get out of this room and back on a professional footing. Now. She rose and walked toward him.

Matt didn't move when she stopped just inches from where he stood. Instead, he looked down at her with eyes that were frankly assessing.

"Was there something you needed?" Olivia asked.

"Mmm-hmm."

Still he didn't budge. Olivia's pulse rate kicked up. It was impossible not to be aware of his broad shoulders brushing the doorjamb, and his muscled chest pulling the black T-shirt taut. She resisted the urge to let her gaze drop lower, below the silver belt buckle and down the faded blue jeans that rode his slim hips.

"And you're in my room because . . ."

If he was surprised at her tone, he didn't show it. "You have," he glanced down at his watch, "about ten minutes until you go on the air. Diane wants to set levels."

"Oh." Less than thirty minutes in his company and she'd already forgotten why she was here. "If you'll excuse me?"

With a cocky bow he stepped back to allow her to pass.

Sitting down at the microphone, Olivia put on her headphones. "I'm here, Di. Let me know when you've got what you need."

Matt still lounged in her bedroom doorway, coffee cup in hand, watching her with interest. Everything about this place was too close and too intimate, including Matt Ransom. Clearly, it would be up to her to maintain some distance between them.

"Testing. Testing. This is Olivia Moore broadcasting live from the smallest apartment on Earth." She dragged her thoughts from Matt. "How's the dieting, Di?"

"Great. I just switched to the All-the-Sushi-All-the-Time Diet. It's supposed to burn the fat right off you."

"You know, I can help you with this food thing. These extreme diets are not—"

"Yeah, thanks, boss. But I really think this one will do it. I'm good for level. Do you need anything in there?"

"How about a new roommate and a couple thousand more square feet?"

Diane laughed. "Wish I could deliver on that."

"I'd settle for a plate glass window with you on the other side." She and Diane had been together since the first *Liv Live* in Tampa, and her presence would have gone a long way toward restoring Olivia's equilibrium.

She glanced over at Matt, who still lounged in the bedroom doorway, and wondered who she was kidding. Real peace of mind would require more than Diane or additional square footage. A continent or two placed directly between her and Matt Ransom ought to do it.

Matt watched Olivia start her show, while his mind painted pictures of the no-nonsense woman before him clad in the no-holds-barred black satin. The good doctor could square her shoulders and march away from him all she pleased. In the end, the contest would be won by the person who managed to harness and control the raw current that surged between them. Olivia might choose to dabble in denial, but he preferred to acknowledge the truth: They were sitting on a powder keg of sexual attraction, and he was itching to light the fuse.

Wandering into the kitchen, he rifled through cupboards and listened as Olivia advised her callers. A peek in the pantry confirmed that Crankower had delivered on their sponsors' promises. The pots and pans came from Williams-Sonoma, the produce from Diangelo's, the imported foods from Gourmet to Go. A case of his favorite wines sat on the counter waiting to be unpacked, and two six-packs of Newcastle were already chilling in the fridge. All in all, everything a man required for a civilized existence was on hand.

His roommate appeared to have simpler tastes. From

what he could see, she intended to subsist on peanut butter and jelly sandwiches with occasional infusions of chocolate chip cookies. Her refrigerated goods consisted of two packages of processed American cheese food, a quart of skim milk, and a case of Diet Coke. If she'd requested anything remotely resembling a fruit or vegetable, he hadn't stumbled across it. In fact, for a doctor, she seemed woefully unconcerned with the basic cornerstones of good nutrition.

Matt walked back through the living area to observe Olivia more closely. When she bent over to retrieve a slip of paper, he couldn't help noticing how nicely she filled out her jeans. Her legs were long, her rear perfectly padded. As she settled back into her chair, his gaze traveled up the lean length of her to the high, full breasts that strained against the cream-colored T-shirt. If she was undernourished, she was hiding it beneath some pretty impressive curves.

Crossing to the seating area, Matt plopped down on the sofa and put his feet up on the cocktail table. It didn't take him long to decide that Olivia Moore was not deficient in vitamins or anything else that mattered. In fact, she was such fun to watch that he gave himself up to the pleasure of it.

Her white teeth tugged at her full bottom lip, and her green eyes radiated concern as she listened to a caller's problem. When she leaned forward to make a note on the pad in front of her, a curtain of blonde silk swirled over one slim shoulder and hid her features from view.

His pleasure was short-lived. Olivia's hands stilled and her voice sputtered out and died. Then she looked up and, for a full ten seconds, watched him watch her. When she finally spoke, it was to put her caller on hold for the commercial break. "What in the world are you doing?"

"Who, me?" He pointed a finger at his chest and checked the room as if looking for another culprit.

"Of course you. Why are you sitting there? I'm in the middle of a show."

"Where else would I be, Olivia? I've had too much coffee to take a nap, and I'm not about to spend three hours in the bathroom."

"Well, you can't just sit there and watch me."

"Because?"

"Because I don't like it."

"We have 850 square feet of living space. My options are limited. You're going to have to do better than that."

"Okay. You're interfering with my concentration."

"Then concentrate harder." He glanced up at the TV monitor and saw them squared off against each other. The Webcam might not broadcast their audio, but no one watching could miss the adversarial body language.

Olivia took off her headphones and stood. "I'm not kidding, Matt. You cannot just sit there and stare at me while I'm working."

"Fine. I'll read." He yanked his briefcase off the nearby chair and rifled through it, ultimately taking out a dog-eared copy of the *Sports Illustrated* Swimsuit Issue that he'd brought along just to annoy her. He also pulled out his own headphones, the ones with the cord long enough to allow full range of the living area, plugged them into the control panel, and sat back down on the sofa, raising the magazine up in front of his face with a flourish. When the silence continued, he lowered the magazine and peered over it. Olivia still stood there, headphones in hand, her mouth open in surprise.

She was very cute when she was stunned.

"I believe I hear your cue."

"What?"

"I said, you're on the air, Olivia." He pointed to his headphones. "It's time to talk to those people who call in and ask you questions. You know . . . your listeners?"

He gave her a wink, the raunchiest one he could come up with. "If you don't get back to work, you're going to be trailing so far behind me by the end of the week that you'll have to wear that thong." Confident that he'd offered the perfect incentive, Matt raised the open magazine in front of his face once again.

How he managed to stifle his laughter and feign interest in the magazine for the remainder of her shift, he didn't know. Olivia pointedly ignored him, which he chose to interpret as an indication of her interest in him. But his musings were cut short by the tremulous tone of Olivia's final caller.

"Dr. O? I did what you said."

"What's that, JoBeth?"

Matt's ears perked up. JoBeth was the name of Dawg's girlfriend.

"I told Dawg that I wanted to get married, *again*. And he told me I was ruining a perfectly good relationship."

"Then what?" Olivia's tone was calm and soothing, in stark contrast to JoBeth's quiet distress.

"Then he wanted some, um, milk, and I told him he'd have to find himself another cow."

"Good for you, JoBeth. You did the right thing."

"It didn't feel right, or good."

"What happened then?"

"He said he didn't understand a word I was saying, and that if I didn't want to be with him, no one was forcing me to stay."

Matt turned a page of the magazine, but his attention was riveted on the drama being played out on the air.

Olivia waited out a long pause and then said, "What did you do?"

"I moved out. I left him." JoBeth's voice vibrated with regret, and Matt took the opportunity to steal a glance over his magazine at Olivia. She sat very still, and the triumphant smile he'd expected to see on her face was absent.

"I love him, Dr. O. I thought we'd be spending the rest of our lives together."

"I know, JoBeth. Sometimes doing the right thing hurts." Olivia closed her eyes briefly, then opened them, her look momentarily far away. "Now you just have to hang tough. And if that Dawg doesn't come through, then you'll go out and find someone who can appreciate you enough to commit. That's my best advice. You stay in touch. I want to know how it's going, okay?"

"Okay."

Olivia gathered her notes as she launched into her sign-off. "And for the rest of you out there, keep those food pledges coming. You can post them on the station website at the same time you vote for your favorite host. Or you can call the station and make your pledge. Thanks for tuning in. I'm Dr. Olivia Moore, reminding you to live your life . . . *live*."

Olivia removed her headphones, shoved her notes into a folder, and stood up. She knew just how JoBeth felt.

It was hard to walk away from someone you loved, and even harder to walk away from someone you wanted to love you.

Lost in thought, she stepped into the kitchen to search for something to eat and started when she felt Matt's hand on her wrist.

"Are you happy?"

"I beg your pardon?"

"Do you feel good about the advice you just gave that poor woman?"

"I don't know which poor woman you're referring to, unless you mean one of the naked ones you've been ogling for the last forty-five minutes."

"I'm talking about JoBeth and all that bullshit about cows and free milk."

"It may be bullshit to you, but to that woman it's a question of self-preservation. I'm entirely comfortable with the advice I gave her. If it weren't for irresponsible men like you and that Dawg she's in love with, maintaining self-respect wouldn't be so damned difficult."

They glared at each other, neither willing to look away first. After a long moment, Olivia drew a calming breath and pulled her wrist out of his grasp. She'd known all along that the only way to survive the week was by maintaining her distance. Turning her back on him, she retrieved her briefcase from the floor next to the console and pulled out a sheaf of papers.

Coming to stand in front of him, she waved them in his face. "I've taken the liberty of drawing up some suggestions for our time together."

She saw him bite back a laugh and watched the insulting glint of amusement steal into his eyes.

"I'll be glad to read them to you, if necessary. They don't have as many pictures as your usual reading material."

She handed the pages over one at a time, practically nailing them to his chest with her finger. "This is a bathroom schedule. I've blocked out the mornings for myself, since I have to be up and on the air by nine o'clock. I wasn't sure what time of day you liked to shower, so I left your side blank."

When he didn't comment, she continued. "I usually just grab a sandwich or something, but I'm willing to make extra for you and leave it in the fridge so we can eat in shifts. That way we won't be tripping over each other in the kitchen."

He studied her from beneath sable lashes most women would kill for.

"I figured whoever ate last could handle cleanup. Obviously, on this chart you're 'M' and I'm 'O.' "

"Obviously."

"We should probably work out a schedule for the television, too. There are only a few programs I watch regularly." She handed him a blank form and cleared her throat. "I've gone ahead and divided the living area into two sections so that we each have a place to sit and relax without intruding on the other."

Matt walked the three steps to the refrigerator and took out a beer. Bringing it back to the living room, he took the diagram she handed him—the one with a dotted line down the middle of the sofa—took a long sip of beer, and sat right in the middle of her section. Then he put his feet on "her" half of the cocktail table and looked up into her eyes. "Tell me, Olivia, just what is it about me that scares you so?" He took another swig of beer while he considered her from beneath hooded eyes.

"Don't flatter yourself, Matt. I just want to be sure you understand what's acceptable. Take dressing and undressing, for example."

"You're planning to tell me when to dress and undress?" He set his beer down and flipped through the sheaf of papers. "I can't wait to see this diagram."

"There is no visual aid because there's only one rule: If you're not dressed, you need to be behind closed doors. In a word, no flashing." Lord knew she didn't need the temptation.

"Well, you've certainly spent a lot of energy thinking all this out, Olivia. It's very . . . industrious of you." He paused. "I'll be sure and give your suggestions the consideration they deserve."

He folded the sheaf of papers in half, doubled them over once more, and shoved the whole wad into the back pocket of his jeans. Then he cocked his head in her direction and said, "I guess getting you to put on that thong would be out of the question right now?"

6

Lunchtime at the Magnolia Diner was no time for
deep thought, a fact JoBeth appreciated at this particular point in her life. She'd already wasted an inordinate
amount of time worrying over her relationship with
Dawg Rollins, and an embarrassing amount in tears
since she'd moved out two days ago. Crying over her dis-
appointments was a luxury she'd never before allowed
herself, and she wasn't wild about the idea now. She
might not have a whole lot else, but she'd always had her
pride.

Hefting her loaded tray high over one shoulder, JoBeth
snatched up a fresh pot of coffee with her free hand and
backed through the swinging door. Before she swung
around to face her waiting customers, she found and put
on her brightest smile. A good waitress didn't bring her
personal problems to work. And she didn't slack off because some fool man had gone and mangled her heart.

"Hey, Bert." One-handed, she set the tray on a serving
stand and commenced to dole out the food, refilling coffee mugs as she worked her way around the table of four.
"How's that new grandbaby of yours?"

"Just fine, darlin'. Head looks kind of like a bowling ball to me, but my Darcy's real proud of him."

"That's great." JoBeth fought off a brief stab of envy at Darcy's good fortune. "You tell her to bring that boy in here soon. I want to have a look at him."

"You know I will."

Whipping her order pad out of the front pocket of her starched white apron, JoBeth pulled a gnarled pencil from behind her ear and moved on to the next table.

"Hey, Homer, Myra. You gonna have the fried chicken today?" She scribbled out their ticket and slipped her pencil back behind her ear as she contemplated the white-haired McCauleys holding hands in their favorite booth. JoBeth tried to imagine herself and Dawg snuggling in a corner booth somewhere thirty or forty years from now, but the picture just wouldn't come.

Blinking back tears, she swapped the coffeepot for a pitcher of sweet tea and leaned over to pour the elderly couple's drinks. "You leave some room for dessert now, you hear? Ina made her strawberry rhubarb pie today."

With calm precision, JoBeth worked her tables, taking orders, refilling drinks, chatting up the regulars. There was comfort in the routine tasks, satisfaction in the occasional appreciative glance sent her way. Her fortieth birthday had come and gone, but L'Oréal kept her short red curls free of the evil gray intruders, and she liked to believe that the fine lines now radiating outward from the corners of her eyes lent character to what she'd always thought of as a too-cute face. Smoothing a hand down her hip, she paused to straighten her apron and give herself a pep talk.

There would be life after Dawg Rollins, just as there'd

been life during those long years of caring for her parents, and life after they died.

She had lots of good years ahead, years she could spend on herself now, if she chose. Plenty of time to get the college degree she'd always dreamed of and to turn the tiny house she'd inherited into a home. If Dawg didn't want to be with her while she did those things, she'd do them alone or take Dr. O's advice and find someone who didn't just say he loved her, but proved it. Someone who wanted to have a child with her before it was time to check into a nursing home.

The bell on the front door jangled, and awareness crept up JoBeth's spine. Even before she turned to look, she knew it was Dawg. Her heart raced like it always did at her first sight of him, but she made a point not to show it.

Why, after three years together, the big lug still made her palms sweat and heart pound, she didn't know. Earl Wayne Rollins, Jr., looked like what he was: an aging ex-linebacker with a profile created at the bottom of a ten-man pileup. His blond hair, shot through with gray, was in full retreat, and his athlete's physique had begun to lose its battle with middle age.

JoBeth wiped her palms on the short skirt of her uniform and stood her ground as he approached.

"JoBeth."

She managed a polite nod before forcing herself to turn and go about her work, but she breathed a small sigh of relief when he had the good sense to bypass his usual seat in her section.

From the corner of her eye, she watched him chitchat with Jackie at the register and say something amusing to Emmylou at the counter where he took a vacant stool.

JoBeth frowned. Dawg sure didn't look like a man who'd lost the love of his life. And he sure as hell didn't appear to be nursing any broken heart.

JoBeth's fingers clenched on the handle of the iced tea pitcher as Emmylou batted her eyelashes at Dawg and leaned across the counter to display her double D's. When Emmylou turned and strutted her stuff back to the kitchen, Dawg's eyes were practically glued to the blonde's behind.

Putting down the pitcher, JoBeth walked through the counter opening, brushing past Dawg. Without a word, she opened the pie case, yanked the strawberry rhubarb off its shelf, and cut two large slices for the McCauleys, leaving the remainder on the counter. Emmylou served up Dawg's Mile High Burger, with a wide toothy smile on the side.

The big lummox winked and tucked into his burger, unaware of how close to death he'd strayed. He chewed with relish for a while, then put down his burger to take a big swig of tea.

JoBeth delivered the McCauleys' desserts and came back to face Dawg across the counter, the strawberry rhubarb in front of her.

"Hi, JoBeth. You're looking mighty fine."

"Feeling fine," she lied. "Never felt better."

They studied each other, taking silent stock, and she felt her damned heart kick up again. Her insides went all warm and soft under his regard, and her pulse skittered just beneath her skin. Unconsciously, her hands wrapped around the pie plate.

"Aw, hell, JoBeth." His voice was quiet and full of a lot of things she couldn't put a finger on. "When are you going to get over all this marriage nonsense and come on back home?"

" 'Scuse me?"

"The house is empty without you."

JoBeth swallowed. She wanted to take Dawg's head and cradle it against her bosom. Or slam it against the wall. It was a difficult choice.

"Don't you talk to me about empty. I'm about as alone in this world as it's possible to be right now. But I'm not looking for company. I want someone to share my life with. In my book that requires a Justice of the Peace."

"Now, JoBeth, if you'd just calm down and come on home, I'm sure—"

"I'm not coming back, Dawg. We're not kids, and I'm not interested in being your live-in girlfriend anymore."

"Aw, JoBeth, honey."

"Don't you 'JoBeth honey' me. And don't you come into my place of work and ogle other women."

"But you're the one who moved out. You're the one who said—"

"I know exactly what I said. You don't have to throw it back in my face. You're the one who doesn't seem to be getting the point." Her fingers picked nervously at the fluted edge of the pie plate.

"Oh, I get the point all right. It's just like Matt Ransom said. My big mistake was not being clear up front. I love you, JoBeth, but I don't want to get married. I've been married, and it's not the picnic you seem to think it is."

A hush fell over the diner as the last of the lunch crowd gave up the pretense of eating. JoBeth pried her gaze from Dawg's for a slow scan of the room. Even the McCauleys were staring in shocked amazement at her and Dawg. Emmylou tittered out loud.

"Well, now you've managed to humiliate me in person." Was that her voice going all shrill and quivery? "Why don't you just take out an ad in the damn paper—'JoBeth Namey gives great milk but she's not worth marrying.'"

Dawg shot her a look of such wounded outrage that she almost managed to get herself under control. If he'd apologized then, or offered one ounce of reassurance that he'd never thought of her that way, she might have been able to avoid what came next. But keeping quiet had never been Dawg's strong suit.

"Now that is about the stupidest thing I've ever heard you say."

"Stupid? Now you're calling me stupid?" Her hands stilled. Embarrassment spiked up her spine, fueling her anger, which was a lot easier to deal with than the hurt and desperation she'd been feeling. Then he got that annoying look on his face, the one that said he was the calm, rational one, and she was some harebrained female, and her hands wrapped tighter around the aluminum pie plate.

"The stupidest thing I ever did was waste three years loving you." The next thing she knew, she was hefting the pie plate in her right hand, savoring its weight. "But I sure do hate to leave you without something to remember me by."

A smart man would have backed off then, or at least put some distance between himself and an angry woman with a partially cocked pie, but Dawg just sat there glaring back at her, his face only inches from what remained of the strawberry rhubarb.

"Do what you gotta do, JoBeth. You are not making a lick of sense anyhow. And you haven't been since you started calling that Dr. O."

She knew better, really she did. It wasn't going to solve anything, and it certainly wasn't going to win her any waitressing awards. But a herd of wild animals couldn't have made her put the pie down at this point.

She heard a collective gasp as she lifted the pie and pushed it firmly into the middle of Dawg's irritating face. No one spoke as she ground the pie back and forth with the heel of her hand until the flaky brown crust worked its way into the grooves of his face.

Dawg sat completely still. He barely blinked as the red-colored goo began to drip down his chin. For a minute she half expected him to stick his tongue out for a taste like they did on TV, but he didn't move a muscle.

Momentarily stunned by what she'd done, JoBeth froze, too. The silence ended just as suddenly as it had begun. The buzz of excitement built around her but it was once-removed, like something that was happening to someone else. She could barely think, let alone come up with an appropriately cutting remark. And instead of the elation she expected, she felt only regret . . . and the insistent welling of tears she refused to shed.

JoBeth placed the empty pie plate down on the counter in front of her. Then she untied her apron and laid it gently on the Formica next to it.

A dull ache settled around her heart as she faced the man she'd hoped to grow old with, but it was too late now for regrets. She straightened slowly and looked

Dawg Rollins straight in the eye—the one not currently covered with crust.

With a small smile and an apologetic shrug, she pulled her order pad from her pocket and passed it over to Emmylou. She didn't think she'd have any trouble getting the rest of the afternoon off.

"I'm sure Em'll clean you up, Dawg. And I'll take care of your tab." She paused for a second to survey the damage she'd done before offering her parting shot. "But it looks like dessert's on you."

7

Matt wiped steam from the bathroom mirror. Still humming the tune he couldn't seem to push out of his head, he lathered his face and then shaved in time to the mental beat. A slash of deodorant, a splash of after-shave, and he was set.

With the towel tucked around his hips, he left the steamy warmth of the bathroom. From the hallway he spotted Olivia behind the kitchen counter, knife aloft, and spent a moment or two imagining just what sort of meal she might be making with the provisions she'd laid in.

Olivia kept her head down and her gaze on the counter, but the stiffness of her shoulders and the rigid tilt of her head revealed her awareness of him. He almost felt sorry for her, trapped as she was with a man who knew just how much heat simmered beneath her cool fa-cade.

A gentleman would allow her to pretend indifference. But no one had ever accused him of being a gentleman.

In his bedroom he dropped the towel and dressed quickly, then padded, barefoot, out to the living room.

Olivia looked up from her seat at the kitchen table.

"What're you eating?"

Olivia stopped in mid chew. He waited patiently while she swallowed and then took a sip of her Diet Coke. She dabbed delicately at the corner of her mouth with her napkin, as if she were dining in a five-star establishment.

"Peanut butter and jelly. I made an extra sandwich if you're hungry."

"That's what you're having for dinner?"

"Um-hmm."

"Peanut butter and jelly."

"That's right."

"For dinner."

"Yep." She dropped the last bite into her mouth, chewed it thoroughly, and swallowed. "Is this a problem for you?"

"No. I've just never met anyone over the age of ten who would consider that an actual meal."

"And I suppose you're a connoisseur?"

"Well, I know the difference between PB&J and . . . dinner. But if your taste buds are willing to settle, who am I to criticize?"

"Who indeed?"

"So is this what you eat every night, or are Monday nights special?"

"What are you, the food police?" She dabbed once more at her mouth and then got up to throw her napkin away, erasing all evidence of her meal.

Matt shrugged. "I'd just hate to see you waste away on my watch."

Olivia went to the pantry and pulled out a bag of chocolate chip cookies. He watched as she removed one cylinder, opened the plastic casing, and took out three cookies. Replacing the bag, she moved over to the counter, munching happily. "I'm hardly wasting away. And I'm sure even you have heard of comfort food. Lots of people like to eat foods that remind them of their childhoods."

"Not me. I prefer my comforts grown-up. And without chocolate bits." He leered at her—just in case she hadn't caught his meaning.

She bit daintily into a cookie and ignored him. Pointedly.

Undaunted, Matt began to assemble ingredients for his dinner. From the fridge he pulled wrapped packages containing paper-thin medallions of veal and sliced mushrooms. From the case of wine, he selected a Barolo and pulled two wineglasses out of the cupboard.

Olivia finished the final chocolate chip cookie and slid onto a barstool.

"Can I pour you a glass?"

"You're going to drink before you go on the air?"

"Absolutely."

"But . . ."

"But what? I have roughly three and a half hours until I go on, I don't have to drive to work, and I'm not planning to operate any heavy machinery."

"But . . ."

"We don't have any heavy machinery here, do we?"

She studied him from beneath spiky lashes. Her eyes were a lovely shade of green flecked with tiny shards of hazel. And they were not amused.

Since she hadn't exactly refused, Matt poured a generous glass of wine for both of them and set hers in front of her. He swirled the heavy red liquid and sniffed appreciatively before taking a satisfying sip of his own. Then he started to cook.

Within minutes he had dredged the veal in flour and had butter melting in a large sauté pan.

Olivia eyed him suspiciously. "What are you doing?"

"Making dinner."

"Dinner?"

"Um-hmm."

"You cook?"

"That's right." Without taking his gaze off her, he emptied the mushrooms into the waiting butter.

"But you're using flour and . . ." She peered over the counter at the ingredients he'd assembled. "And mushrooms and . . . and *utensils* . . ." She pronounced the last word as if it were foreign and didn't quite fit on her tongue.

"Yep." He allowed himself a small smile but held a tight rein on his laughter. "Too bad you've already eaten. I make a mean veal marsala."

"Veal marsala." Her voice was little more than a whisper. "You're making veal marsala?"

Olivia looked as if she'd just discovered the world was actually flat after all, and he couldn't resist passing the perfectly sautéed mushrooms under her nose as he removed them from the pan and set them aside. She sniffed audibly, a reflex action that told him she'd probably cave in and join him if he asked her again.

Which left him feeling smug, in charge, and completely in control. Until Olivia licked her lips. He watched, fascinated, as the tip of her tongue darted out and worked its way across the bow of her mouth. His own hunger spiked, though it had nothing to do with the meal he was preparing.

She took a sip from her glass, and then she ran her tongue over her lips once again. They were wet and dewy with wine, and Matt considered volunteering to dry them off with his own. He glanced up quickly but caught no hint of malice or sexual intent in her eyes. They were, however, full of hunger and lust—all of it focused on his veal marsala.

Matt put pasta in a pot of boiling water and broke up a loaf of Italian bread. For a few minutes he cooked in silence, sipping his wine while he contemplated the situation. However attractive he found Olivia, no matter what the sight of her tongue skimming over her lips did to him, she was the competition. Only one of them would walk out of this apartment with a radio show on WTLK. And while he doubted he'd be on the street for long, he had no intention of coming in second.

Feeding Olivia would be like offering aid to the enemy. He wanted her off balance and uncertain. Could he use food and drink to help achieve that end?

He drained the linguini, put a large helping on the plate next to the veal, and then topped the cutlets with marsala sauce. The aroma made his mouth water.

Matt slid his plate across the counter, topped off both their wines, and moved around to claim the stool next to Olivia's. Her entire body tilted precariously toward his plate, and her eyes were locked on the result of his culinary efforts.

"Gosh, I feel bad eating in front of you like this." He tried to look truly apologetic, but it was hard to pull it off when she looked as if she might land face first in the center of his veal.

He waited for her to say something. A little polite begging and the second helping could be hers, but she just closed her eyes and breathed deeply, no doubt committing the smell of veal marsala to memory for replay during her next PB&J extravaganza.

"No, no. Don't be silly," she said. "I'm, uh, just going to finish my wine and watch the food, I mean . . . tube, for a bit. You go right ahead and meat . . . I mean, eat."

Matt clinked his wineglass against hers and took a healthy sip, enjoying the flush of embarrassment that rushed up her cheeks at the obvious Freudian slip. He watched her as he slipped a forkful of veal and mushroom into his mouth, and had the satisfaction of seeing her wince with envy. His cooking had thrown her off balance, which was exactly the way he wanted her. Surely he had enough resources at his disposal to keep Olivia Moore permanently off kilter. All he had to do was identify them.

Her green eyes clouded under his perusal. She took a sip of wine, swallowed it, and stole a surreptitious glance at his plate, as if to reassure herself she wasn't imagining things. "Did you know how to cook in Chicago?"

"Hmm?"

"When we knew each other in Chicago, did you already know how to cook like this?"

He couldn't remember sharing a single meal with her, though he knew there'd been many. What he remembered was her earnest innocence and the joy with which she'd given herself to him.

"Did I *have* a kitchen back then?"

He could tell from the stain spreading across her cheeks and the way she shifted in her chair that her memories were no more food related than his.

He watched her worry her bottom lip with her teeth and realized he'd been overlooking the obvious. As an experiment, Matt leaned in closer and let his lips brush against her ear. "I couldn't tell you where or what we ate in Chicago, but I remember exactly how *you* tasted, Olivia."

He paused for a moment, waiting for a reaction, and sure enough, her eyes fluttered closed. Encouraged, he continued. "I'll never forget how cool and smooth your skin used to feel under my tongue."

Matt reached a hand out to brush his knuckle down the curve of her cheek. "And I remember the little sounds you used to make when I was inside you. And how you used to sink your nails into my back when you were ready to come."

He used the truth and their memories to probe beneath the cool exterior, hoping to find the woman who had once dwelt inside. "Do you remember?"

Olivia's eyes were suddenly wary. Unsure whether she was about to turn tail and run or round on him with teeth bared, Matt turned and glanced up at the Webcam monitor. What he saw there at first stopped him cold and then filled him with delight. He cocked his head and studied the video image a moment longer while he considered the possibilities.

The shot revealed the mostly empty bottle of wine, the two wineglasses, and himself and Dr. O engaged in what appeared to be an intimate tête-à-tête. The average viewer would see only what was framed in the camera, and that didn't include the snarl springing to Olivia's lips or the warning glint stealing into her eyes.

"Nice try, Matt."

She uncrossed her long legs and sat up straighter on her stool. The steely look she sent him made him grateful that Mother Nature hadn't seen fit to endow her with the defense mechanisms of either the skunk or the porcupine. With the Webcam and its misleading image in the forefront of his mind, he maintained the illusion of intimacy by staying put.

"Don't think you're going to use what was between us, Matt. I already regret that we ever had a past, and I'm going to do everything in my power to make sure we don't have a future."

He put a hand out to cup the back of her neck and used his thumb to caress her cheek once more. She tensed at his touch, but he ignored it, keeping his voice low and his body language intentionally intimate. "You go ahead and give it your best shot, Olivia. But I still remember every delicious thing about you, and as you may have noticed, I've learned a thing or two about good food over the last eight years."

"You really think you're every woman's fantasy, don't you? You've been listening to your own show too long. I am not even remotely tempted."

"Liar." Even to his ears, the word sounded suspiciously like a caress. Matt smiled as Olivia slipped out from beneath his hand. He couldn't help admiring the picture she presented as she made her exit—striding across the living room with her head held high and her shoulders thrown back. She sat on the edge of the couch, her posture painfully correct, and picked up the TV remote like a queen reaching for her scepter. Very carefully she tuned CNN in and, he suspected, the disturbing Matt Ransom out.

Being dismissed didn't bother Matt in the least. He'd noticed the way Olivia had responded to him.

If he wanted to come out of this week the victor, undermining his opponent's formidable powers of self-control would certainly give him an advantage.

It was time to bring out the big guns, time to lay siege to Dr. Moore's castle of calm. Thanks to his friend the Webcam, he now knew exactly how to breach her defenses.

All he had to do was make history repeat itself.

8

In the WTLK control room, Charles Crankower studied the Webcam monitor with interest. At the audio board, with his back to Charles, Matt's producer, Ben Markum, set up for the night's show. Olivia's producer stood next to him discussing some problem with the on-hold system that she wanted fixed before morning. Charles tuned them both out to concentrate on the drama unfolding on the screen.

Matt and Olivia sat at the counter with a bottle of wine between them. They looked much cozier than he would have expected, and as he watched, Matt not only reached out and cupped the back of the doctor's neck, but caressed her cheek with his hand. Charles waited for Matt to either kiss her or get smacked, but neither happened.

A glance out of the corner of his eye confirmed that the couple on the screen now had Ben's and Diane's attention, too. In silence, the three of them watched Olivia storm off to the couch while Matt cleaned up the kitchen, and he knew he wasn't the only one wondering what in the hell was going on.

When Matt moved to sit down at the audio board,

Olivia passed by him without a glance, and all three of them watched her bedroom door close behind her.

Charles was still puzzling over what he'd seen as Matt put on his headphones, propped his feet up on the audio table, and leaned back in his chair.

"What do you think, Ben?" Charles started at the sound of Matt's voice booming over the control room speakers. "How long do you think it'll take me to have her eating out of my hand?"

Ben looked over his shoulder at Diane and Charles. "Hey, Matt, there's, uh . . ."

Matt laughed. "Forget about eating out of my hand. I'll bet you a hundred bucks I'll have her flat on her back before the end of the week."

Diane Lowe froze, while Ben hurried to cut his boss off. "Matt, this isn't a good time to . . ."

Ben put on his headphones and shut off the control room speaker, turning the conversation private. After aiming a withering glare at Ben, Diane stormed out of the room, but Charles just sat there thinking about the possibilities. This promotion was his brainchild, and he intended to use it to prove he could handle things at WTLK without interference from the corporate office. What better way to preserve his autonomy than with a local promotion that garnered national attention?

Charles smiled at the thought, because anything resembling a relationship between the proper Dr. Moore and the alley cat Matt Ransom would warrant that kind of attention. It was his job to make sure of it.

At 9:45 P.M. Olivia locked her bedroom door, slid between crisp, cool sheets, and congratulated herself on surviving her first day of captivity. She'd taken a few hits, but she was still alive. For a good five minutes she reveled in her newly appreciated privacy, breathing the quiet into her being and attempting to exhale the anxiety.

Snuggling deep under the covers, she breathed in the good thoughts and tried to breathe out the bad. She could do this, of course she could. All she needed was a good night's sleep.

Olivia closed her eyes and tried to drift off, but her brain refused to shut down. Old memories, the very ones she'd spent most of the evening trying to block, rose up to taunt her: the feel of Matt Ransom's skin against hers, the merging of his body into hers, the utter contentment of drifting off to sleep in the shelter of his arms.

She breathed in and she breathed out until she was huffing and puffing like the Big Bad Wolf, but sleep eluded her. With a groan, Olivia sat up in bed, clicked on the radio, and tuned in *Guy Talk*.

"Thanks for the donation, man. Remember, you can donate food or money, and you can donate it in the name of guys everywhere. To find out how we're stacking up against the ladies, just log onto our website for an up-to-the-minute tally."

A prerecorded chanting of "Go men, go men, donate" done to the foot-stomping rhythm of "We will, we will, rock you" played out full blast as Matt engineered a one-man pep rally.

The chant continued for several seconds and then faded out. The next thing she heard was the unexpected sound of waves washing up on the shore. If she'd had any thoughts of falling asleep while she listened to Matt's show, his next words quashed them.

"I had a chance to listen to *Liv Live* this morning, fellas."

The sound of canned gasps and murmurs rose, then fell as Matt continued. "Yeah, I know, I know. The woman is way too preoccupied with life's harsh realities."

Another wave rolled into shore, and the surf pounded. A gull cawed.

"I prefer a little fantasy in my life. Tonight I'm going to show you how to add some to yours."

Olivia let out the breath she held and abandoned the in-and-out thing. Like a conductor staring into the headlights of an oncoming train, she closed her eyes and braced for the crash.

"Pretend for a minute that you're shipwrecked on a deserted island. You've got warm trade winds, a lovely little inlet for swimming and fishing, and unlike Tom Hanks, you do not have to form an intimate relationship with a rubber product. You get to choose both your companions and your supplies. This is, after all, your fantasy."

Reggae music snuck up full and then lowered to background volume. Gulls called again and mingled with the subtle rhythm of waves lapping gently on the shore. Olivia could almost feel the sun on her back as Matt continued.

"It's a gorgeous day. The sand is like powdered sugar. The sea is that bright blue-green color it gets when the sun is dancing on top of it. I can see a shipping channel off in the distance, so I know when I'm ready to be rescued everything will get worked out. No pressure, just a great escape."

His voice was as powerful and warm as a deep-tissue

massage, and Olivia began to relax despite herself. What could happen on an island getaway?

The soft strains of "Don't Worry Be Happy" joined the audio mix and then disappeared beneath the mesmerizing timbre of Matt Ransom's voice.

"I walk down the beach and discover two crates that have come in on the tide. One of them holds twenty-four jars of beluga caviar packed in ice. The other is a case of Guinness with an opener attached."

The happy island music cranked up and then faded back under.

"As I set the crates under a palm tree near the entrance to a cave, I spot the only other people on the island—you can have a maximum of three companions, guys. In my case, they're Heidi, Lourdes, and Veronica—a blonde, a brunette, and a redhead—who look absolutely exquisite in the only article of clothing they've brought with them: thong bikini bottoms."

Male sighs of ecstasy mingled with the island sound effects. Then came several seconds of teasing feminine laughter.

Alone in her room, Olivia gritted her teeth.

"Okay, guys, that's my scenario, but everyone gets to create his own."

Matt paused and then brought the soft feminine laughter up once more.

Olivia was just getting ready to write off the whole thing as a waste of time when Dawg came on the air. She recognized his name from her conversations with JoBeth, and she wasn't surprised to discover that he spoke like a good ole Southern boy—and an unhappy one at that.

"Hey, Matt."

"Dawg. Did you call to pledge food or to visit Fantasy Island?"

"Well, I wanted to pledge some milk for the food drive, but I'm not getting any of that anymore."

Olivia caught herself smiling at Matt's puzzled silence.

"JoBeth moved out. She's left me."

"I'm sorry to hear it, man. You definitely deserve a getaway. Who do you want to take with you?"

"JoBeth. She's the only one I want on my island, but thanks to you and that Dr. O, she doesn't want to have anything to do with me."

"We're talking Fantasy Island, Dawg. You don't need to invite JoBeth . . . or anyone else you actually know. I'd consider Miss March. Her last pictorial tells me she knows exactly how *not* to dress for an island vacation."

"Matt, I don't think you're listening. JoBeth has moved out. And not only that, she'll barely talk to me. Threw a damn pie in my face when I tried to get her to come back home."

Olivia sat up in bed, intrigued, but Matt refused to be drawn into Dawg's reality.

"I'll say this one more time, Dawg, because I like you and you've been calling in to the show for a while. This is not Relationships R Us. You can call Dr. O in the morning if you have to, but the only advice I'm going to give you is this: Suck it up, man. Stop whining. There are probably two million women in Atlanta. Pick another one. Women are like buses. If you miss one, another will be along any minute."

Olivia felt her spine stiffen. She heard none of Dawg's protests or Matt's flip responses as he moved on to the next caller. She remembered all too well how easily Matt had switched buses in Chicago, though she couldn't understand why the memory still hurt.

Olivia burrowed back down beneath the covers. She wanted to be in her own bed. She wanted her life back. She also wanted to be asleep right this very minute and not lying here wondering whether Matt Ransom really remembered exactly how she had tasted eight years ago.

Olivia reached over to snap off the radio, but something perverse inside her made her keep listening.

"I've got Jason on the air. Who are you with, Jason, and what have you brought with you?"

"Wow. I can't believe I got through. I listen to your show all the time."

"Thanks, Jason. Does your mother know you're up this late?"

Jason laughed, but Matt was right. The caller sounded distinctly pubescent.

"Tell us what's happening on your island."

Jason cleared his throat nervously. "Well, I, um, spend the first day just hanging out drinking beer."

"You can imagine yourself under a palm tree drinking until you puke if you want to, Jason, but I'm not sure this will appeal to our other listeners. So . . ."

"Wait. A raft is floating toward my island."

"A raft?"

"Yeah. It's just a bunch of trees lashed together with a little lean-to on one corner. And there's some kind of material rigged on a really tall branch for a sail."

"That's nice, Jason. But what about the occupants?"

"Well, at first I can't tell if there's anyone on the raft or not. But then I spot this really long pair of legs sticking out of the lean-to."

There was a pause and Olivia imagined she could hear the boy's Adam's apple bob up and down.

"It's a woman."

"Very good, Jason. You have real potential. Who is she?"

"I can't tell yet. But when she comes out and stands up, I can tell that she's really tall, you know. Like an Amazon."

"Ah, a Xena, Warrior Princess, fantasy."

"Well, she's tall like her, but she's blonde. And it's really weird, but there's something familiar about her, you know?"

"What do you mean?"

"Well, she's naked except for this little, like, animal skin between her legs. And she's tan. All over." Jason's voice went up another octave.

"This would be from floating on the raft without clothing?" Matt's tone was dry.

"Yeah, I guess. Anyway, she steps off the raft onto the beach and I can see that she's in really incredible shape, but older. You know, like thirty or something."

"That old, huh?"

Jason totally missed Matt's sarcasm, but as a woman turning thirty in a matter of days, Olivia was not amused.

"So I can't believe this is happening, and I—"

"Jason, please. Just tell us who the woman is. Believe me, at this point, that's all anyone wants to know."

"Well, that's the really strange thing, you know? Because when she gets closer I recognize her."

"And?"

"And, well, I hope it's okay to say this."

"Don't worry, Jason. As long as it's not obscene, you're okay with—"

"It's that head doctor you're locked up with. The one you call Dr. O."

"Why, of all the . . ." Olivia muttered as she sat straight up in bed. She flipped on the light and swung her legs over the side.

Matt's shout of laughter filled her ears. He laughed for a good thirty seconds until Olivia pictured tears running down his face.

"Boy, Jason. I have to hand it to you. I didn't even see it coming."

Yeah, right. Olivia sprang out of bed. In two strides she had her hand on the doorknob.

"What a fertile imagination you have, son. And a thing for older women, too. I can just picture how flattered Dr. Moore will be when she discovers she's every boy's fantasy."

The reggae music swelled up and then faded underneath Matt's voice. "Thanks for sharing, Jason. You've given us all something really . . . special . . . to think about. This is *Guy Talk*, where a guy can be a guy."

When she heard the first commercial come up, Olivia yanked open her bedroom door. Unwilling to get too close to the Webcam, she stood in the doorway and hissed, "What do you think you're doing?"

Matt looked up from the audio board. "Olivia?"

"No, it's Xena, Warrior Princess. Come here."

He got up, walked around the equipment, and came to stand in front of her door. "Nice pajamas." Reaching out a hand, he traced a part of the design with his finger. "Are those sheep?"

Olivia slapped his hand away. "How dare you set that boy up to talk about me that way?"

"You think I arranged that?"

"I know you did. And I won't stand for it."

"This is talk radio, Olivia. People say things. I did not put those words in that boy's mouth." He laughed. "But I really wish I had."

The blood thrummed through her veins, urging her to wipe the smile off his face. "Your show is a complete and utter travesty. For your information, women are not buses to be *ridden* at will. Your advice to that poor Dawg was completely insulting. And if you ever hold me up to that kind of ridicule again, I'll—"

"Listen, I hate to interrupt, but I'm back on in thirty seconds. Why don't you come on out and tell my listeners how you feel?"

His hand clamped around her wrist. "Come on. You can give Jason a piece of your mind and tell the world that you've never been on a raft naked in your life."

Amusement tugged at the corners of his mouth. "And be sure to stand right in front of the camera so they can see the pretty pink and blue sheep on your jammies."

The challenge in his eyes was unmistakable. He wanted her out there in her sheep pajamas trying to defend herself against a ridiculous teenage fantasy. Which was all the reason she needed not to.

"Good Lord, you piss me off."

"I know." He offered her a smug, lopsided smile that she wanted to rip right off his face. "It's one of my greatest assets."

9

JoBeth waved goodbye to her daddy's La-Z-Boy recliner.

"We sure do appreciate the donation, JoBeth. This'll help make the group room a whole lot cozier."

JoBeth watched the pickup back out of the driveway and make a right out of the small Lawrenceville neighborhood. She knew exactly what Horace Namey would have said about his prized possession serving out the rest of its usefulness under rear ends at the Union Mission Halfway House, and the thought of his outrage provided the first real smile she'd managed in days.

She walked back into the tiny house. The living room was empty except for the few pieces she'd claimed for herself. She ran a hand over the old pine sideboard that had belonged to her great-grandmother and let her gaze linger on the bun-footed curio cabinet that now held the best of her mother's Depression glass. Dropping into the rocker she'd dragged in from the front porch, she surveyed the beginnings of the room's transformation with pride.

The baseboards and trim gleamed under a fresh coat

of white paint, and the corners and edges of the room's longest wall carried a first coat of apple green. She planned to finish painting the living room today and start on the kitchen tomorrow. JoBeth found comfort in the logical progression of the work and fully intended to deal with her inheritance the same way she'd learned to deal with her life—one day at a time.

Originally, she'd thought she was fixing up the house to sell and had imagined the proceeds as a kind of dowry she'd bring to her marriage to Dawg, her contribution to their life together. Now there would be no life together, and there was no reason to sell. She'd fix the house up for herself, get one of those home equity loans so that she could see some of the world or go to college full-time. She'd spent her twenties running around wild, and most of her thirties taking care of her parents. It was more than time to start looking after herself, like Dr. Olivia said.

JoBeth turned the baseball cap backward on her head to keep the brim out of her way and rolled up the bottoms of her overalls so they wouldn't end up apple green. The smell of fresh paint battled the old, more familiar smells of cigarette smoke and medicine, vanquishing them in the same way the pretty pastel green drowned out the dingy undercoat of white.

She moved the ladder onto the newspaper that lined the edges of the room, and hooked on the aluminum paint tray. After climbing the first few rungs, she dipped her roller into the paint.

As she reached for the wall, the screen door creaked open, then slammed shut. Before she could turn, boots clumped across the hardwood floor and came to a stop behind her. She recognized the footsteps even before she heard Dawg's voice.

"Hey, JoBeth."

She didn't turn or pause in her painting. She just tapped the excess paint off the roller and began to apply it to the wall.

"Need a hand?"

She extended the roller smoothly upward, then brought it back down. "No, thanks."

"I, uh, just wanted to see how you were doing."

"I'm fine." She lifted the roller out of the pan, reached for the wall without tapping off the extra paint, and felt a glob land on her cheek. The back of her free hand found the glob and turned it into a smear.

"It looks a lot bigger here without all your folks' stuff in it."

"Yep." Hurt warred with anger, and JoBeth stoked the latter, afraid of what would happen if she showed the least bit of weakness. She needed Dawg out of here now, before she caved in and let him see just how miserable she was without him.

"Mind if I take a look around?"

"It's a free country."

She heard his boots clump down the adjoining hallway, heard a door creak open, and heard the sound grow muffled by carpet. With an iron grip on the roller, she continued spreading paint on the wall, keeping her movements slow and controlled until Dawg clumped back and stopped directly behind her.

"You're sleeping on a mattress on the floor?"

"Um-hmm."

"You'd rather sleep on the floor than stay with me?"

Feeling the crackle of his anger in the air about her, JoBeth set the roller in the pan and backed down the ladder. Once her feet touched the floor, she had no choice but to turn and meet his gaze. Schooling her paint-streaked features into a casual expression, she turned her face up to his. Dawg hadn't bothered to mask his feelings, so she was forced to stare into his storm cloud of a face, all dark and seething with disbelief.

He ran a ham-sized hand through his hair and then shoved it into the pocket of his jeans. "I told you you could have my spare room until you got things taken care of here."

"I don't need your spare room when I have a perfectly good house sitting right here." She inhaled the rugged spice of his aftershave and felt herself drawn to the massive body she knew so well. Alarmed, she pushed by him and came to a halt a good foot and a half away, where resisting him would be easier.

"But what about us, JoBeth? How can you walk away from three years?"

"I'm not the one turning my back on what we've had, Dawg Rollins."

"Aw, honey." He reached out toward her, clearly intending to scoop her up into one of his big, brawny embraces, the kind that had always made her feel so safe and protected. If she let him get his hands on her, she knew she'd be lost.

"Look, I'm sorry about the pie thing yesterday. I didn't care for the way Emmylou was behaving, and I took it out on you. You have every right to rub up against anyone you want to."

Dawg grunted and shook his head, but he didn't tell

her he didn't want Emmylou, or that he was ready to settle down and get married.

"I'm too old to play games, Dawg. I love you, but I expect I'll get over it." She felt a tear slide down the side of
her cheek to mingle with the apple green paint, and before she could stop it, another one slid through the mess.

"Aw, hell, JoBeth." Dawg drew her into his arms and
cradled her against the soft cotton T-shirt that stretched
across his rock-hard chest.

For all his great strength, his touch was remarkably
gentle. As unwilling as he was to make a commitment,
he'd never been shy about showing his affection. She
closed her eyes to hold back the longing when he placed a
kiss on the top of her baseball cap and used his big fingers
to tuck a stray lock of hair behind her ear.

"Lord, but you are one hardheaded woman. I cannot
for the life of me figure out why you are so hell-bent on
getting married. It's just words and a piece of paper,
JoBeth. And you are tossing everything away to get
them."

He put a finger under her chin and lifted her face up to
his. She knew she must look ridiculous with the paint
running down her face and the ugly tears welling out of
her eyes, but she saw only tenderness reflected in his.
When he joined his lips to hers, it was with a sweetness
that made her heart ache inside her chest.

To JoBeth's way of thinking, you signed the piece of
paper and spoke the words because the other person
brought out the best in you; because you were more with
them than you could ever be on your own. It proved you
meant to stick when it would be easier to give up.

But she didn't know how to explain that to Dawg, any

more than she could explain how important it was to make the commitment out of love and not the stifling sense of duty that had held her parents' marriage together.

She wanted to lift her arms up around Dawg's neck and whisper her love for him, but she couldn't give in now. Nor could she follow him back home with her tail between her legs, grateful for whatever scraps of commitment he was willing to toss her way.

He released her lips but held her gaze with his. "You know where to find me when you come to your senses, JoBeth."

"And you know where to find me," she countered. "But I really can't say for how long."

Olivia prowled the apartment like a caged animal. From his seat at the kitchen table, Matt watched her pace off the confines of their prison, past the couch to peer out the French doors of the balcony, back to the tiny kitchen to stare out the postage-stamp window at the brick wall beyond.

For a while he just enjoyed the long-legged grace of her, the swirl of blonde hair teasing against slim shoulders, and the way the occasional ray of sunlight caught her hair and separated it into a hundred different shades of gold.

She ignored him as she paced, her gaze skimming over him, then moving away.

"It is a bit tight in here, isn't it?"

She continued to pace. "A bit tight? I have *clothes* bigger than this apartment."

She turned her back on him and strode over to the television armoire, not even sparing a glance for the camera perched on top. "I'd give anything to head out for a run right now. Just a little one. I'd come back."

"Yeah, I'll mention your idea to T.J. and Charles. Maybe they'll let me out after my show for a couple of drinks. I'd come back, too."

Her snort of laughter was not at all flattering, but she did stop pacing. "Do you think it's possible to accrue time out for good behavior?"

Her desperation added a sparkle to her green eyes that Matt found oddly endearing.

"Or maybe we're just going to be stuck in here until we're so old it doesn't matter anymore."

"Ah, ah, ah." He wagged his finger at her. "I believe you're allowing your glass to become half empty rather than half full. It's just a week out of your life, Olivia."

"At the end of which, one of us, preferably you, will be out of a show."

Matt shrugged and stood. "You have to admit it does add a certain . . . piquancy to the whole situation."

He walked around the table to stand beside her. He moved a little closer, intentionally invading her space, and watched her eyes glaze over. It was obvious Olivia wanted to step back and put more space between them, but she held her ground. "You'll forgive me for saying so, but you seem a little tense."

She averted her gaze. "Tense? Me?" She shook her head and offered what he supposed was meant to be a smile.

"Turn around." He took hold of her shoulders and spun her around. Without asking permission, he began to massage her neck. When she tried to pull away, he pulled out his trump card. "You don't want our viewers to think you're afraid of me, do you, Liv?"

Olivia stopped struggling, but she didn't relax.

He worked his way down the graceful column of her neck. "Jesus, Olivia, you feel stiff enough to break in half." *Who said they had nothing in common?* "This much physical tension is not good for a person."

A quick glance up at the monitor told him that, once again, he and Olivia looked decidedly cozy. But then the viewing audience couldn't feel what he felt beneath his constantly moving hands. Olivia was as tightly strung as a bow, and he knew it was only pride that kept her from jerking away. Working his way down her throat one last time, Matt brought his hands to rest on the nape of her neck and thought about making her quiver.

With strong fingers, he kneaded her warm, taut flesh. And suddenly he was remembering details he'd put out of his mind long ago: the feel of her supple body shifting under his, the delicious length of her thighs wrapping around him, her hands on his buttocks urging him inside.

Olivia didn't relax under his ministrations, but she *did* respond.

And, damn it, so did he. He willed himself into submission, offered himself some very direct words of discouragement, but crucial body parts didn't seem to be listening. In fact, he seemed to have gone completely deaf below the waist.

If there was one thing he'd always been able to count on, it was his self-control. Not that he'd needed to call on it all that often, of course, but it had always been there at the ready. He was fairly certain of this.

Now he was the one taking a step back, carefully separating his front from Olivia's behind before she encountered the evidence of what touching her did to him. It would never do to let her hold it against him the way he'd been planning to hold it against her.

He turned Olivia around to face him and saw her eyes narrow with suspicion. "What are you doing?"

"Just trying to help you relax."

"You want to help me relax?"

"Um-hmm." *Relaxed and sloppy and no longer in control would be just about perfect. As long as he didn't find himself in the same condition.* He nodded toward the couch. "Of course, it's easier to do that horizontally than vertically."

"Gee, how tempting. I've always dreamed of performing nude before a national audience."

"I'm here, Livvy. Willing and able to make that dream come true."

"An incredibly generous offer, Matt. But I don't think I need to be quite that relaxed. Any other ideas?"

"Feel like hitting something?"

She tilted her head at him and cocked an eyebrow. "Absolutely. Are you volunteering?"

"In a way." He pulled the punching bag away from the wall and dragged it to the patch of space between the dining and living areas. "It's not quite as effective as sex, but it will release some of the same, er, energy."

The caricature of his face stared out at them from the side of the bag. Beneath it were the words PLACE FIST HERE.

Olivia smiled. "Great target. Very motivating."

Matt worked the gloves onto her hands, careful to keep his distance as he laced them up.

"Right." He aimed her at the bag and pulled the gloves

up in front of her face, the right slightly above the left, in the classic fighter's stance. "I hope this won't be too complicated for you."

"Why don't you use real small words like you do on your show while I listen real carefully? Maybe we'll get lucky."

"*Touché.*" He moved beside her and raised her gloves. "Okay. First you're going to jab with your right hand, but you want to keep your left up where it is in a defensive position."

Olivia put her right arm out and connected with the bag.

"Not bad. But you need to do it like you mean it. A real quick extension and a hard jab before you pull back."

She jabbed harder, making solid contact with the picture of his face.

"Ouch. Very impressive."

She smiled and took a bow.

"Okay, champ. Why don't you try that with your left, now? Take it across your body at an angle, like this," he pulled her glove forward, "and jab hard."

Olivia followed his instructions and clipped the side of his caricature's face.

He knew he should move around behind her to better help guide her punches, but was reluctant to get too close to the delicious backside. It would be a hell of a lot easier to use his body to unsettle her if his own weren't so eager to take the bit in its teeth.

Matt stayed where he was as she began to dance around on the balls of her feet. Something about the way she held her body gave him the sense that she'd done this before.

"How's this?" She jabbed harder, pummeling the bag with both gloves, working into a barrage of blows. Right after left, then two quick lefts and another right.

"I feel like the crotchety old trainer in *Rocky*." He hummed the movie's theme music as he directed her attack on the bag and earned an unguarded flash of white teeth.

Her arms were tanned and gently muscled, and her full breasts bobbled beneath the sleeveless T-shirt that had come untucked at the waist. He liked watching her body move. Whether pacing or punching, she had a natural grace that drew his eye and definitely held his attention.

Matt stepped in closer and crouched over a bit, intrigued by the rotation of her hips as she moved from foot to foot. Her belly was flat, and there was an occasional flash of smooth skin as her T-shirt rose with her movements. The way she bobbed and weaved struck a chord in the back of his mind.

"That's it. Now you're cooking."

He forgot both his plans and her flying fists as her hair came loose from its clip and swirled seductively around her shoulders. In fact, he was at exactly breast height and getting quite a jiggly eyeful when he saw her body start to whip around and heard the beginning of her breathless warning.

"Matt, watch out for—"

And then he heard nothing but the resounding thud of her foot connecting with the side of his jaw, followed by the slap of his body hitting the floor.

And then there was silence, followed by a merciful layer of dark.

10

———

"Ṉone of your publicity mentions a former career as an assassin." Matt lay flat on the floor where Olivia's kick had sent him.

"Are you all right?"

He turned his head toward her and slowly opened his eyes. "What in the hell did you hit me with?"

"Try not to talk." Olivia squatted down next to him and pressed a dishtowel stuffed with ice against his jaw.

Pushing her hand away, Matt pulled himself into a sitting position and ran a hand tentatively along the side of his jaw. When it reached the big tender spot, he winced.

"Jesus, Olivia. What happened?"

"Here. Hold this on it." She placed the makeshift ice pack in his hand and directed it toward his face, noting the grimace when cold met throbbing skin. "It was a spinning hook kick. I didn't see you bend over."

"You're a kickboxer?"

"Well, I'm not a professional or anything." She put a hand out to stop him when he started to remove the ice. "Keep the cold pack on it, Matt. You're going to have a big-time bruise as it is."

She stood and took a step away.

"How long have you been kickboxing?"

"I was only on the amateur circuit for a couple of years."

"Oh. Well. That must be why I'm still alive." He leaned back so that his shoulders rested against the back of the sofa and drew his knees up in front of him. "How long was I out?"

It was Olivia's turn to wince.

He closed his eyes and sighed. "You don't need to spare my feelings now, Olivia. The station's recording the Webcam feed twenty-four hours a day. They're probably already rerunning the KO in slow motion."

"You were only out for about a minute. Not all that long."

"Oh, great. I was afraid this was going to be embarrassing or something."

"Do you want me to call a doctor?"

"No, I don't want you to call a doctor." He moved as if to stand, but seemed to reconsider. "I thought you were a runner."

"I was until it got too hard to go out and sweat in public. You'd be surprised what my listeners have decided I should and shouldn't do."

"Yeah. I bet they feel real good about your ability to tear men apart with your feet. Aren't people in the helping professions supposed to be nonviolent? I mean, what did you do, get a doctorate in psychology and a master's in martial arts?"

The phone rang, eliminating the need for a response, and Olivia left him propped against the couch while she went to answer.

"Oh, hello, Charles." She walked the cordless phone back toward Matt. "No, he's fine. No, you don't need to call 911." She covered the mouthpiece with one hand and looked down at Matt. "He wants to send in the paramedics. Someone told him that might warrant a segment on *Real Life Rescues*."

She handed him the phone and then stood beside him to eavesdrop.

"No, Charles. Don't call anyone. I'm fine. Olivia just kicked the shit out of my face. It's no big deal." He started to grin up at her, but the grin turned into a grimace of pain. He moved the ice to another spot on his jaw. "Yes, if anyone's going to hurt anyone again, we'll be sure to call you first." Matt rolled his eyes, a move that didn't require the use of his jaw. "Yes, I promise. Yes, I'll get up off the floor now. Goodbye, Charles."

Matt turned the phone off and rose slowly from the carpet. "He wasn't happy about not being able to promo our altercation, and he doesn't want me sitting on the floor. Evidently my pain and suffering aren't visible enough from down here."

He walked around to the front of the couch and plopped himself down on it, offering a jaunty wave to the Webcam as he went. "Charles is becoming quite the tyrant, isn't he?"

Olivia sat down on the edge of the couch and pressed the ice back against Matt's jaw. "And why not? He's got us performing like a couple of trained apes, while he's out there poking sticks through the bars of our cage."

"Well, this monkey's thirsty. How about a cold one from the fridge?"

"I guess I did more damage than I realized. Aren't your arms and legs working?"

"My injuries are not all visible. You coldcocked me in front of a live audience. Just think of the dent you put in my masculine pride. We're talking major emotional pain and suffering." He kept his expression tragic, but there was an unholy twinkle in his eye. "I'd say you owe me some special treatment."

Olivia went to the refrigerator and extracted a Newcastle, which she presented to him with a flourish. "For you, Your Injured Highness."

Matt took a long pull on the beer. "Ahh, I think I feel my wounds beginning to mend already." He took another sip and set the bottle on the table beside him as Olivia turned to go. "But I also hear my stomach rumbling. I was going to make linguini with clam sauce, but I'm not sure I have the strength."

Olivia turned back to face Matt. "You're asking me to make you dinner?"

"Well, I do need to rest up for my show, and I'm going to have to eat to produce energy for all those hours of talk."

"You don't seem to be having any trouble running your mouth right now."

"I know there must be at least a flicker of guilt buried under your unconcerned facade." He leaned forward so that she could plump the pillow behind his head and then settled back into the couch with a grateful sigh.

"Thanks. You don't mind if I put on the Braves game while you whip up a little something, do you? They're playing the Cardinals."

Without waiting for an answer, Matt pointed the

remote at the TV and tuned in the game. Then he reapplied the ice to his jaw and reached for the beer with his free hand. She saw him smile as he crossed his long legs at the ankle and settled in to watch.

Without a word, Olivia made her way to the kitchen. She did in fact feel guilty about knocking him out, but if he was thinking linguini with anything, he was in for a disappointment.

While Matt lolled on the couch, Olivia foraged in the kitchen. Ten minutes later she laid his dinner tray on the cocktail table.

Matt eyed his meal with interest. "Gee, I haven't had grilled cheese and tomato soup since elementary school. Can we have cookies and milk for dessert?"

"If you behave yourself, I might part with a few of my Chips Ahoy. But only because you're injured."

"I guess I'll have to mind my manners, then, won't I?" He lifted one golden brown triangle to his lips and took a healthy bite. Then he took a long pull on the beer. "Maddux is pitching. The count's two balls, one strike."

Olivia wouldn't have minded watching the game, but she never actually got the chance to sit down. First she cooked another grilled cheese—this time made with sourdough bread and a fat slice of tomato at Matt's request. Then she fetched aspirin and water to combat the throbbing he said he felt in his jaw, though it didn't seem to stop him from voicing an ever-increasing list of demands.

While she contemplated the possibility of taping his mouth shut in the guise of first aid, he wolfed down a whole sleeve of her chocolate chip cookies and started on a second bottle of beer.

She had just taken a first bite of her own long-cold

sandwich when Matt held up the makeshift ice pack and waved it in her direction.

"If you're not too busy?" He handed her the plastic bag that she'd tucked inside a dishtowel. "My ice seems to be melting."

"Funny what a blast of hot air can do." Olivia snatched the baggie out of Matt's hand and went to the freezer to refill it.

"Oh, and while you're up, I was thinking that—"

"No." She slammed the freezer shut. "No more thinking. No more food and drink. No more requests."

"Why, Olivia, what happened to your bedside manner? I'm going to have to call the nurse's union about your attitude."

Olivia stalked back to the couch. "I'll bring you the phone if you'd like to call an ambulance or a cab, but I will not bring you one more ridiculous thing."

Standing over him, she lifted the bag full of ice, positioned it precisely, and when she had his complete attention, dropped it directly into his crotch.

"This is *Guy Talk.* You're on the air."

"What's going on in that apartment, Matt? How could you let the doctor get the drop on you like that?"

"Ding, ding, ding, ding. You are the one thousandth person to call and ask that very same question. In a moment, our announcer will tell you what you've won. In the meantime, I have a question of my own: What were you doing watching us on the Internet in the middle of the afternoon? Does your boss know you're visiting non-work-related websites during business hours?"

"I hate to disappoint you, Ransom, but I caught it on *Atlanta Alive*. They ran it in slo-mo about twelve times just before the six o'clock report."

Matt raised the ice pack to his jaw. "Great. So all of Atlanta has seen it, huh?"

"And then some. Your own station's promoting the hell out of it. They're talking about offering a poster of Dr. O's foot hitting your jaw as part of a giveaway. Do you have any idea how I could get one?"

"Not in this lifetime." Matt dropped the call and punched up the next.

"This is *Guy Talk*. You're on the air."

"Matt, you're not looking so good at the moment, buddy."

"I'm okay."

"Maybe, but you're giving us guys a bad name. I couldn't believe it when I saw you hit the floor. I'm donating a carton of Wheaties in your name. And half a dozen cans of spinach."

"Gee, thanks."

"You're welcome. And if you'd like a little free advice, you ought to dismantle the punching bag while she's asleep. The boxing gloves definitely belong in the dumpster."

"Yeah. Great plan. And maybe I can glue her feet to the floor to give myself an extra advantage, huh?" Matt dropped the call just as Olivia wandered out of her bedroom and headed for the kitchen. "Wimps, all of you," he finished. "Sometimes you just have to take it on the chin . . . or jaw, like a man."

Without a word, Olivia picked up her headphones, plugged them into the board, and walked into the kitchen to put a kettle on to boil. He'd just opened his mouth to comment when he noticed the new message scrolling across his monitor. Instead of the usual caller name and opinion, his producer had simply typed "va-va-va-voom." Matt put the mystery caller on the air.

"You're on *Guy Talk*. But if you're calling to harass me about kissing the carpet, I'm not interested."

"Oh, I wouldn't do that." The voice was female and sultry, not his usual brand of caller at all. "I'm actually calling to offer my sympathies."

Matt sat up straighter in his seat. "Sympathy? Now that's been in short supply tonight."

"I sure do hope your jaw is feeling better, Matt. And I'll tell you something else. If I were locked up with a big, strong hunk of man like you, I wouldn't be wasting my energy on a punching bag."

He cut his gaze toward the kitchen and caught a glimpse of Olivia standing stock-still, her hand outstretched toward the kettle.

"Now that's exactly what I was telling the good doctor before she laid me low." He leaned in closer to the microphone and let his tone grow as intimate as his caller's. "You'd never knock a guy out, would you?"

"Oh, no. I prefer to *tire* my men out."

Matt kept his gaze trained on Olivia, who was still doing her statue imitation despite the now-howling teakettle.

"It's good to hear there are women out there who still know how to *be* women."

He bit back a grin as Olivia's jaw clenched.

"Why, thank you. I do pride myself on knowing how to treat a man." The caller's voice was close to a purr. If he wasn't mistaken, Olivia looked ready to roar.

"I bet you wouldn't have to be forced into cooking a meal or pampering a fellow a bit, either."

"You're right about that. I think men deserve all kinds of attention. And if you make it out of that apartment in one piece, I'd like to give you some. Um, attention, that is."

Olivia snatched the kettle off the stove and the whistling stopped abruptly.

Matt kept a watchful eye on Olivia—and the boiling water—as he ended the call with, "Now there's an offer no man in his right mind would refuse. You check in with me anytime you feel like it."

He could read the anger in Olivia's eyes as he rose from his chair at the audio console and leaned down toward the microphone. "This is *Guy Talk,* where a guy can be a guy. Call me."

Matt flipped his microphone off and stepped around the console. "You look ready to deck someone . . . again. I hope you're not expecting me to turn the other cheek?"

"I can't bear to hear women talk as if their entire mission in life is to make some man happy. And you, of course, lapped it up as if it were your due."

"It was a harmless flirtation, Livvy. Men and women have been talking to each other that way since Eve tempted Adam. I don't think she meant any more by it than I did. It was just a little wordplay."

"Hmmph. Foreplay is more like it."

He moved closer, intentionally invading her space. "Jealous, Livvy? I have plenty of wordplay to go around. Hell, we could kill a little time looking up new definitions in the dictionary."

"Are you ever serious?"

"Are you always?"

They stared at each other for a long moment, neither budging. Olivia's eyes still sparked with anger; they'd deepened to a verdant green that made him think of primeval forests.

"You need to lighten up, Olivia. I happen to know first-hand that life is way too short to waste it sweating the small stuff. And in the end, it's all small stuff."

"Now there's a convenient philosophy for a man who refuses to grow up. I assume you'll forgive me if I don't consider *my* show or *my* career small stuff."

She folded her arms in front of her chest and tilted her chin up another notch. "If this is all so insignificant to you, why don't you just concede right now, Matt? Call a halt to this whole charade and move your show someplace else. You were pretty hot in Chicago, as I recall."

"I'm not conceding a damn thing. But I'm sorely tempted to teach you how to enjoy yourself. Without the ability to relax and enjoy, all the success in the world isn't going to do a thing for you."

"Thank you so much, Professor Ransom, for that introduction to Fun and Frolic 101. I'm sure you're qualified to teach at the graduate level."

Matt looked down into Olivia's face. Her eyes glittered in challenge, and her tone dripped scorn. He kept his own tone light because he knew just how much it would piss her off. "I've never met anyone who needed tutoring in the subject as much as you do, Olivia." He let a small smile play around the corners of his mouth and gave her an impudent wink for good measure. "I'm thinking I may have to design some sort of crash course."

11

Olivia didn't see Matt again until the next afternoon. She was staring out the French doors at the tiny park across the apartment parking lot when she heard a noise behind her.

His jaw looked slightly puffy, but otherwise he seemed none the worse for his encounter with her foot. He tipped a Coke can at her in greeting. "Morning."

"It's way past morning."

"So it is." Matt seemed unconcerned with the distinction.

"How's your jaw?"

He ran a hand down the smoothly shaven side of his face, pausing momentarily over the point of impact. "I'll survive as long as you keep your feet to yourself."

Matt's gaze strayed to the jar of peanut butter sitting on the counter. "I see you've dined."

"Do you have something against peanut butter and jelly?"

"No. I just hate to see you go through life undernourished." He yawned and scratched at his midsection. "Mind if I turn on the TV?"

"TV?" Olivia glanced down at her watch. "But there's nothing on right now but the—"

"Soaps." He checked his watch. "It's too late for *All My Children*, but *One Life to Live* will be on in a few minutes. *General Hospital* comes on at three."

Olivia could feel the disbelief etched all over her face, but there was no way Matt Ransom watched daytime television.

He flicked on the set.

"You watch soap operas?"

"Um-hmm."

"Soap operas, as in 'My mother slept with your father and you're my second stepbrother twice removed so we shouldn't be having this affair' soap operas?"

"Well, I don't remember that exact story line, but that's the basic idea."

"When did this happen?"

Matt laughed. "It's not a disease, Olivia, or a sign of mental deficiency. I've been watching *General Hospital* since we . . . I was twelve. I discovered some of the other shows later in life. I work until two in the morning, go to sleep about four, and get up around noon." He shrugged. "I watch soap operas in the afternoon."

He moved over to the sofa, once again sitting right in the middle of the area she'd designated for herself, and picked up the remote. "*GH* doesn't start for another hour, but we can watch *One Life to Live* or *As the World Turns*." He turned to her as if asking nothing more surprising than how she took her coffee. "Which would you prefer?"

Matt propped his feet up on the cocktail table and settled back into the couch, patting the space beside him.

"Come sit down. If you leave the remote to me, we can watch both of them."

Olivia eyed Matt suspiciously. "You're kidding, right?"

"No. Come on."

She knew he was going to spring something on her or find a way to make her look bad, because this just couldn't be true. "You're telling me that Atlanta's 'Hundred-Time Bachelor of the Year, Mr. Macho Guy Talk,' is a closet soapie?"

"There's nothing closet about me, Olivia. I'm hooked. Have been since I watched my first episode back in '78. That's when Bobbie Spencer brought her big brother Luke to Port Charles to try to land Laura in reform school."

Olivia took a seat, though not quite so close as the one Matt had indicated. "You started watching *General Hospital* when you were twelve."

"Pretty much."

"Because?"

"Because our older sister didn't get home until fifteen minutes after the show started, and she paid me a dollar to watch the beginning and fill her in on what she missed."

"You must have amassed a small fortune by now."

Matt threw back his head and laughed, and Olivia caught herself wanting to join in. It was all so wonderfully absurd.

"So why are you still watching?"

"Well, when I was about fifteen, I discovered what a great pick-up tool it was. Just me and the girls discussing who was cheating on whom." He looked incredibly pleased with himself.

"And you still need pick-up material?"

His smile was slow and sensual, the brown of his eyes turning as warm as a tumbler full of whiskey. Suddenly, it felt as if someone had sucked all the air out of the apartment. "Not usually. Now it's just a great escape. After all those hours of talk, it feels good to be brain-dead for a while."

"I wasn't aware you used your brain all that much in your work."

Matt didn't bite or react to the barb, but leaned in closer until she could feel the warmth of his breath tickling her cheek. "Don't you ever want to shut that overworked brain of yours down, Olivia? You know, just turn it off and enjoy yourself?"

It must have been the power of suggestion. Or maybe it was how close he was and how husky his voice had gone—as if it were completely weighted down with sex—but Olivia felt her normally nimble thoughts slow to a crawl. Then her vision blurred around the edges and the air turned hot and thick with something she did not want to identify.

"Don't think, Olivia. Just feel."

He lowered his lips to hers and kissed her—a soft, gentle joining that took her completely by surprise. The breath caught in her throat, and her pulse fluttered like butterfly wings beneath her skin.

Cradling the back of her head in the palm of his hand, he drew her closer and deepened the kiss, his gentleness giving way to something more urgent.

She wanted to do just as he'd instructed, wanted to lose herself in his touch, wanted to let him make love to her once more, wanted to forget about the silly competition between them.

Competition. Olivia's body stilled, only this time it was due not to desire but to dismay. She was sitting on a couch in plain view of their audience, being kissed by Matt Ransom. In another second she'd be kissing him back. She had a very clear idea of the kind of reaction the focus group would have to that.

"Olivia?"

"Why, you . . ." Appalled, she pulled back. Her brain, still struggling to get back up to speed, couldn't come up with anything bad enough to call him.

Matt's eyes lit with amusement. "I was just trying to help you relax."

"If I want to relax, I'll take up yoga."

What she wanted to do was slap his smug, handsome face. Hard. In front of the world. So that no one would know just how much she'd wanted him to kiss her. Her hand itched to make contact, but she'd already perpetrated too much violence in the last twenty-four hours, and she didn't intend to win her time slot by maiming her opponent—no matter how much he deserved it.

Olivia retreated to the other couch. "I don't know what you're trying to do here, but it's not going to work."

"I'm not trying to *do* anything. You looked like you needed to be kissed, so I kissed you. Let's not make a big deal out of it."

"We're not going to make *anything* out of it. And in the future, I'll decide when I need to be kissed. And by whom." Olivia crossed her arms in front of her chest and glared at Matt.

From his seat on the opposite couch, he winked and

offered her a mock salute. "All right, then. When you're ready to be kissed, you just let me know. I've been waiting for more than twenty years for all the loose ends to get tied up on *General Hospital*. I think I can wait a day or two for you to beg for a kiss."

Olivia picked up the phone and speed-dialed the station. Though she and Matt were allowed free access to their producers, up until now she'd only called Diane to discuss business. At the moment, however, thoughts of her show were running a distant second to the need for human contact with someone other than Matt Ransom. Someone in the real world. Someone she could trust.

"Hi, Di."

"Oh. Hi, Olivia. Great show this morning."

"Thanks."

There was an expectant pause, during which Olivia wracked her brain for a topic of conversation.

"How's the new diet going?"

Diane sighed. "I've lost roughly one tenth of one pound, and if I eat another piece of raw fish I'm going to have to apply for a job at SeaWorld. *In* the tank."

"You know, if you'd just give up on these crazy diets and let me help you explore why you're using food to—"

"I know, boss, I know. I just keep thinking one of them will actually work." Her laugh was rueful. "So what can I do for you?"

"A jailbreak would be nice."

"Hey, I'll be outside at dawn with an extra horse if that's what you want."

The idea of escaping was all too appealing. She

drummed her fingers on the table, not ready to hang up, but unable to come up with a legitimate reason to stay on the line.

"So, um, is there something in particular you wanted to talk to me about?" Diane asked.

Olivia felt like a mountain climber dangling off the side of a cliff clutching her lifeline. If she hung up, would she go careening down the side of the mountain?

"You know, if you ever really need out of there, all you have to do is—"

"No. Don't even go there, Di. Quitting is not an option."

"Okay, then. What would you like to talk about? The show? The weather? Kissing Matt Ransom?"

Olivia groaned. "I was hoping no one had noticed."

"I can think of a whole lot of adjectives that could be applied to that kiss, but unnoticeable isn't one of them."

Diane's curiosity hummed across the phone line, and suddenly a free fall down the mountainside seemed safer than pursuing this particular line of conversation.

"Yes, well. I think I'm going to have to go now, Di."

"You're going to hang up without telling me how it felt?"

"Afraid so." She lifted a hand and waggled it toward the Webcam.

"Not even a few descriptive words for those of us who've always wondered?"

"Sorry."

"I don't suppose you'd consider describing his veal marsala?"

Matt drizzled lemon butter over the pompano fillets and wrapped them in parchment. Yellow rice simmered on the stove, and a bottle of chardonnay sat open on the counter. An Anita Baker CD infused the room with an intimate warmth.

It was 7:00 P.M., three hours after the conclusion of *General Hospital*, which Olivia had watched, spellbound, and pretended not to enjoy. He'd prepped for his show, worked out on the bag a bit, and taken a cold shower—a blessed relief after spending most of the afternoon in an unexpected and unwelcome state of arousal.

As soon as his lips had touched Olivia's, he'd realized his mistake. Within minutes, what had begun as a calculated maneuver to unnerve Olivia and keep the audience tuned in had turned into a humbling struggle for self-control. She should be sued for hiding all that heat and turbulence under that cool, touch-me-not exterior. It would take real agility for him to keep fanning the flames without getting burned.

Backing away from the refrigerator, Matt turned to find Olivia studying him from the other side of the counter. Her smile was wary, but she sniffed appreciatively.

"It's pompano *en papillote*. There's enough for two if you're hungry."

Her smile warmed. "Gee, I don't know. I was really looking forward to my usual peanut butter and jelly."

"I'm not going to tie you to the chair and force-feed you, but if you want to set the table, you're welcome to join me."

"Okay." Maintaining the maximum possible distance,

Olivia set the table and took a seat on the opposite side of the counter.

Matt slid a glass of wine toward her, and they drank for a moment in silence. Olivia sat on the very edge of her barstool, as if she expected him to lunge across the counter and drag her into his arms at any moment. Whether the idea intrigued or appalled her he couldn't tell, but it sent his thoughts scurrying back to the kiss he'd stolen earlier.

He stirred the rice, and put a salad together, while his brain replayed the feel of her lips against his. It took a considerable effort to keep his responses to Olivia's questions even.

"How long did you stay at WZNA after I left?"

Matt pulled the fish out of the oven. "I did afternoons there for another two years, and then I took over morning drive."

"The King of Darkness made chitchat and played music at 6 A.M.?"

"It wasn't pretty. I only made it a year and a half before my body clock shorted out."

"Then what?"

He stood and shrugged. "Then I stopped fighting Mother Nature and moved to late night talk."

"Not a blatantly upward move."

"No." He forced his thoughts back to the choices he'd made in Chicago. "When I approached the Program Director about doing a guys-only talk show, he couldn't believe I wanted to give up morning drive for what he assumed would be perpetual obscurity."

Olivia carried their wineglasses to the table, and they started on their salads. "*Guy Talk* was obscure for about five minutes, as I recall." She took a bite of salad and chewed appreciatively. "Weren't you pulling a fifty share within the first six months?"

"Yeah." Matt speared a piece of romaine. "As it turned out, I really liked the talk thing."

He removed her empty salad plate and replaced it with a serving of pompano and rice, slicing open the parchment as she watched.

Olivia closed her eyes and breathed in deeply. "Oh, God, Matt. This smells heavenly."

Her first mouthful of fish and rice produced a sigh of ecstasy. She took a second bite and a third, and he suspected she'd never again see peanut butter and jelly in the same light.

He let her wash it all down with a long sip of wine before picking up the conversation. "You've made some history yourself."

Her laugh was rueful. "Yeah, most of it because I married a guy who couldn't keep his pants zipped. Therapists are supposed to know better." She speared him with her gaze, and her tone turned dry. "I seem to have a weakness for men just like my father."

He sliced open his own parchment but didn't lift his fork. "I didn't cheat on you, Livvy. It's not cheating if there's no commitment."

"Ahhh, we're going for the *technical* definition of fidelity. I guess I've been remembering it wrong all these years."

"You were barely out of college. Neither of us was ready to make a commitment."

"No. One of us wasn't ready. The other never had a chance to express her opinion."

He tasted the rice and fish, but no longer felt like savoring the meal. It struck him that they'd never had this conversation, and he wasn't wild about having it now. Olivia had gotten too close, and he'd moved on. End of story—except for the eight years he'd spent trying to erase her memory. For the first time, he allowed himself to wonder how long it had taken her to forget about him. "Olivia, you were a baby. You needed to go back to school and get your doctorate, not hang out in Chicago with the likes of me."

"So you said. Repeatedly. And evidently it wasn't just me you didn't want to commit to."

He saw some emotion he couldn't identify sweep over her face and watched her shake it off.

"But why are you still doing the hit-and-run thing, Matt? What is it about real intimacy that frightens you so?"

"I do believe you're getting ready to try and analyze me."

She took another sip of wine and ate for a few minutes in silence. When she spoke, it was with an intentional lightness. "Hey, we've got eons of time ahead of us. If you're ready to seek help, I'm available." She scooped up a last morsel of fish with her fork and turned an impudent smile on him. "If you keep cooking, I'll waive my hourly fee. That's a real bargain when you consider I get two hundred an hour for private consultation."

"Right. So you're going to, what, peel me like an onion and expose all my innermost feelings to our listening audience in exchange for three square meals a day?"

"Gee, when you put it like that, I can hardly wait to get started."

Matt stood and carried his plate to the kitchen, and

Olivia followed suit. Together they piled dirty pots, pans, and dishes in the sink while he rummaged in the cabinet underneath for cleaning supplies. "I'm stunned by the generosity of your offer, Olivia. I don't know why I didn't think of it myself."

He tossed the rubber gloves at her and spun her around to face the mound of dirty dishware. "But this is the only expertise I need from you at the moment."

12

Chinkapin Lanes roared on Wednesday nights.
Packed to capacity for the weekly Couples League, the
fifties-era bowling alley shook with sound in a way its
more modern competitors did not. Balls thundered
down wooden lanes, pins crashed madly against each
other, and music blared from an antiquated audio system
that actually shook, rattled, and rolled. Despite the din,
or perhaps because of it, men and women let their
hair down at the Chinkapin. It was said there were
Wednesday-night teams that had outlasted many mar-
riages.

This Wednesday was the first in more than three years
that Dawg Rollins arrived at Chinkapin Couples League
alone. He'd missed driving over with JoBeth, missed her
droll recap of her day at the diner, and her interest in the
details of his. He'd come early as usual, had placed the
usual beer and pizza order, and stowed his bowling bag
under the seat, but it just didn't feel like Wednesday night
without JoBeth at his side.

If she'd arrived with him, JoBeth would already be
making funny comments about who was hitting on

whom and sharing odd news stories she'd found in the newspaper. Instead, Dawg chatted quietly with the captain of the other team while he waited for the rest of his team to arrive. And while he chatted he wondered how JoBeth's day had gone and whether she'd caught herself wondering about his.

"Hey, Paul. Hey, Emmylou."

"Hey, handsome." Emmylou gave him a wink and a hug and added what looked like a whole new wiggle to her walk. While he and Paul watched, she turned her back on them and bent from the waist to retrieve her ball from her bag. Dawg found himself holding his breath as her flowered capris stretched even tighter across her lush backside, testing the limits of fabric science and treating them both to an awesome floral display.

"Kinda makes a guy wish he was a bumblebee, doesn't it?" Paul's gaze never wavered from Emmylou's flower-covered rear end.

"I can see how the idea of pollination might pop up," Dawg replied.

"Of course, some of us are free to think about the birds and the bees all we like." Paul thumped himself on the chest and turned sympathetic eyes on Dawg. "Others of us would just be asking for trouble."

"Is that right?"

"You keep eyeing Emmylou's backside that way and JoBeth's gonna end up on death row for murder one. And I'm not sure which one of you she'll blow away first."

Dawg rubbed his jaw. "JoBeth does tend to get a bit jealous, doesn't she?"

"I think that's kind of like saying the *Titanic* ran into an ice cube." Paul set his ball down on the ball return and fished his shoes out of his bag. "That woman does not like to see anyone else's hands on you." His gaze narrowed. "You have an awfully strange look on your face, Dawg. I hope you're not getting ready to do anything too stupid."

"Me? Do something stupid?"

Paul glanced around the alley and his brow furrowed. "Say, where is JoBeth?"

"She decided to drive herself tonight. She'll be along any minute." He avoided Paul's gaze and busied himself with retying his bowling shoe.

"Have I mentioned how sorry I am that I screwed things up so bad with Dorie?"

Dawg sighed. "Not in the last two minutes."

"Good. I mean, I'm glad JoBeth brought Emmylou in so we could field a team and all, but I sure would like to be bowling with Dorie again." He dropped his voice. "I miss the shit out of her."

"Yeah?" Dawg had no intention of telling his friend how badly he'd screwed up his own relationship. And he didn't intend to give up on JoBeth Namey just yet, either.

Paul's words ricocheted around his brain.

"Yeah." Paul drummed nervous fingers on the table and then mercifully changed the topic. "You ordered the beer yet?"

"It's on the way."

"Well, thank God for that." They both watched Emmylou's backside rotate over to the other alley, where she stopped to talk to a member of the opposing team. "I had a hell of a day."

Dawg dragged his thoughts from Emmylou's rear end and its place in his plans. Paul was an electrician whose clientele included residents of the more affluent suburbs in north Fulton County. "What happened?"

"You remember that customer I told you about up in Alpharetta?"

"The one that keeps coming to the door in a see-through nightie?"

"That's the one." Paul slid onto the banquette across from Dawg and leaned closer, his voice dropping to a whisper. "Today I go out there about 10 A.M. to install recessed lighting in the basement."

"And?"

"And she's not only wearing the see-through nightie, but she insists on going up the ladder to show me where to put the fixtures." He paused dramatically. "She didn't have a stitch on underneath."

"You're kidding."

"Nope. I thought I was going to swallow my tongue."

"Shame on you, Paul Willard."

Both of their heads jerked up at the sound of JoBeth's voice. Paul turned three shades of red, and Dawg suspected he looked just as guilty.

"Lord, JoBeth, you could give a guy a heart attack sneaking up on him that way."

"I'm surprised you didn't have one earlier, P.W., ogling your customer that way." She wagged a finger at the two of them. "And the poor woman unable to afford underwear . . ."

Paul hooted with laughter while Dawg watched JoBeth remove her ball from her bowling bag with the same clean, economical movements she applied to everything she did. He kept his tone purposefully light, like hers, as he responded. "Maybe you should offer her a discount so she can buy some before your next visit."

"Or maybe Paul should stop swallowing his tongue and take some sort of action." JoBeth's tone was still light, but it was clear they were no longer talking about Paul's customer.

Dawg looked down at JoBeth just as she looked up at him. They stood still, gazes locked, while Paul's swung back and forth between them. "Yeah, JoBeth, sure. And what if I decide to be this woman's boy toy? How would you feel about that?"

JoBeth didn't turn around. She just kept staring right into Dawg's eyes.

"Right. Well. It looks like the beer's here," Paul continued.

He got no response.

"And the other team's about ready to start."

Neither Dawg nor JoBeth moved a muscle.

"Fine. I'll, uh, go coach Emmylou a bit. I don't think she's ever been up against Todd's bunch before." Paul backed away from them slowly, a puzzled frown on his face.

"You really think Paul should be jumping some strange woman's bones?" Dawg asked.

"No. But he's a free agent, and it's obviously what the woman wants. For some reason she's just not coming out and saying so."

"Unlike you."

"I've always been direct. When did it start bothering you?"

Dawg shrugged. He was in no mood to rehash her ultimatum, but he was ready to demonstrate her plan's fatal flaw. "So what exactly do you see happening now?"

"Well, I guess we both get out there and meet new people."

"Okay." Dawg shrugged again, careful to keep his expression casual.

"Okay, what?"

"Okay, I'm ready to get started, if you are." He didn't allow himself to smile at her stunned expression. Instead, he aimed an obvious glance at Emmylou's backside and let his gaze run up the blonde's body to linger on her breasts. Then he turned back to JoBeth, who seemed to be grinding her teeth. "There's no time like the present."

By the middle of the second game, JoBeth couldn't decide which irritated her more—the way Emmylou managed to shake and wiggle her incredibly large behind at every opportunity, or the fact that Dawg obviously relished the show.

If Dawg had always been aware of Emmylou's way-too-obvious charms, he'd been smart enough to hide it. Until tonight. Now he appeared to be president of the Emmylou fan club and kept shouting things like, "Nice frame, Em. Try to release it like I showed you."

Midway through the first game, Dawg had started coaching Emmylou. During a break in play, with the whole damn alley looking on, he'd pulled her backside to his front and led her through the approach and release of the ball—not once but several times. Neither the hands-on demonstration nor the verbal coaching appeared to be doing much for Emmylou's game, but it was having a decided effect on JoBeth's.

During the third or fourth frame, she'd begun picturing Emmylou's face on the headpin. Now, every time she got up to bowl, she tried to knock the woman's block off. Her last two turns had been strikes, and she couldn't seem to bowl anything less than a spare.

Beyond annoyed, JoBeth waited for Emmylou to finish her turn. It took the big-haired blonde two tries to knock down five pins, but you'd have thought she'd just won a spot on the pro tour the way Dawg was grinning at her.

"Thatta way, Emmylou. I swear you're a natural," he shouted.

With a triumphant smile on her face, Emmylou stepped off the alley and brushed past JoBeth. Like a country-fried Marilyn Monroe, she led with her bust and let her flower-covered fanny jut out behind as she made her way toward Dawg.

JoBeth looked down at her hands. She flexed them for just a moment, imagining the feel of them wrapped around Dawg's twenty-inch neck. She looked up to meet his knowing gaze and decided she'd settle for another strawberry rhubarb pie—as long as it had a small-caliber pistol baked inside.

At the score table, Emmylou draped herself over Dawg, turning sideways to sandwich his left shoulder between her doughy breasts like a ham caught between two slices of rye.

"How was that, Dawgie?" The woman's voice had gone Marilyn too, all breathy and suggestive.

JoBeth wanted to puke.

"Perfect, Em. Your game is definitely improving."

Dawg let his hand slip down to cup Emmylou's backside—the one JoBeth wanted to kick to kingdom come. Emmylou basked in Dawg's attention like a kitten in the sun and carefully avoided meeting JoBeth's eyes.

And then Paul—thank God for Paul—was stepping up behind her and turning her gently back around to face the lane. "I think this is where I'm supposed to tell you something moving and important, like 'Let's win this one for the gipper,' or 'Don't let him jerk your chain,' but all I can think of is 'Knock the shit out of those pins, JoBeth.' That man is not seriously interested in replacing you with that blonde blow-up doll."

JoBeth nodded her head, gritted her teeth, and focused on the pins. In her mind's eye she drew a picture of Dawg and Emmylou huddled together on the headpin, his big hand on her big ass.

It was the tenth frame. If she knocked all the pins down with her first ball, she stood a good chance of breaking 200. Even a spare could get her there.

JoBeth shut out everything around her. She brought the ball down as she made her approach, and when she reached the line, she let it fly. The ball spun madly down the center of the lane and crashed into the center pin. Pins exploded off the floor, bashed into each other, and fell down. When everything went still, only the ten pin remained standing.

"Wow, JoBeth. You are looking good, girl. Go on and pick that sucker off." A glance at her teammates showed Paul practically dancing with excitement, while Dawg continued to play the ham to Emmylou's rye.

"Hey, JoBeth. You sure are on fire!" Todd Miller, the

captain of the other team, waggled his eyebrows at her, but Dawg's hand still rested on Emmylou's rump.

"Don't mess with my concentration, now, Todd. That ten pin needs to go." JoBeth kept her tone light and her smile bright, but her whole face hurt. The strain of forcing her mouth muscles upward when they wanted to turn downward and maybe even let out a whimper, was beginning to tell. She could feel the weight of tears forming and blinked her eyelids against them.

JoBeth brought the ball up to her chest, paused for a moment, and then went up on the balls of her feet. With her gaze riveted on the remaining pin, she stepped out with her right foot and swung the ball down into its backward arc. After three quick approach steps, JoBeth swung her arm forward and released the ball. There was a hush on both lanes as the ball made an initial hook to the right, skirted up the edge of the gutter, and then began to veer left. It came within a hair's breadth of the pin, and she heard a collective gasp as the pin rocked precariously in place. For what seemed like an eternity.

"Shit." JoBeth stared at the lone pin in disbelief as it stood by itself, swaying in her ball's breeze, taunting her. It just stood there, too stubborn to fall down, until, at long last, the mechanical arm dropped down and swept it out of sight.

Conversation resumed as Paul stepped up and clapped her on the shoulder. "A hundred and ninety five is nothing to sneer at, you know. Do you want me to go beat up Dawg for you?"

She'd come so close she could almost taste it. Just as she'd come so close with Dawg. "*Close,*" her father used to say, "*but no cigar.*"

She gave Paul a small smile and shook her head. "Thanks, but if I let you do that now, I won't have anything to look forward to."

JoBeth left the alley and walked over to the table.

"You almost got it, JoBeth." Emmylou's voice had lost some of its Marilyn sound, and she looked a little nervous.

Dawg met her gaze and held it. "You're bowling real well tonight."

"Thanks. You're playing a pretty good game yourself."

He shrugged, the motion sending his ham shoulder sliding up and down between Emmylou's slabs of rye. "You set the rules. I'm just following them."

"So I see." What was there to say, really? *Unhand that bimbo or I'll . . . what?* She'd already put a pie in the man's face. Should she humiliate herself further by staging a catfight in the middle of the bowling alley?

Telling Dawg to go out and find somebody to have fun with was one thing—watching him do it was quite another. The fact that he'd chosen Emmylou to flaunt in her face made things immeasurably worse. The slow burn that had kept her going all evening turned into cold, clammy dread. "I'm going to go to the ladies' room. I'll be back before the final game, but I think you'd better find a replacement for next week."

"I'll come with you." Emmylou bent to pick up her purse and in the process released Dawg's shoulder from her bosom. "I need to powder my nose."

They covered the distance to the ladies' room in silence, but once inside, Emmylou put a hand out to stop JoBeth. "Are you finished with Dawg, JoBeth?"

She forced herself to look Emmylou straight in the eye.

She saw the sparkle there, took in the becoming flush on the blonde's cheeks—all of it put there by the man JoBeth wanted to marry. The thought of Emmylou, or any other woman, taking her place was not something she would allow herself to dwell on.

JoBeth squared her shoulders. She shook the other woman's hand off her arm and reached down deep for some attitude. "He's not exactly table scraps, Emmylou. I'm not going to wrap him up and send him home with you, if that's what you're asking."

"You know what I mean. I'm asking if you're through with him. Is the man fair game?"

JoBeth closed her eyes for just a moment, totally aghast at what she was about to say. If she had the first idea how to stop this thing she'd started, or knew any way to step back off the ledge she'd stepped out on, she'd do it. But she was already looking down at the traffic below, and the time had come to take the final leap.

"He's not mine to hand over, Emmylou. Dawg Rollins has a mind and will of his own—neither of which I seem to understand as well as I thought I did. If you want a run at him, have at it. I believe I've already given it my best shot."

13

This is *Liv Live*. It's Thursday morning, my fourth day in captivity, and I'm still kicking. Best of all, we're doing awesome in food donations." Olivia turned up the volume on the wild-applause sound effect and stood to make a half bow to the Web camera. "Way to go, ladies."

Taking her seat, Olivia lowered her voice and attempted to set the tone for the remainder of the show. "It's been an interesting morning so far, lots of phone calls coming in, but I think we've spent just about enough time on Matt Ransom. Let's move on, shall we? I'm here to talk about you—your thoughts, your problems. Go ahead and give me a call."

Olivia checked the monitor for the identity of her next caller. "Hi, Michelle."

"Hello, Dr. Moore."

"What's on your mind?"

"Well, actually, I'm a bit concerned about Matthew Ransom."

"But, Michelle, don't you think—"

"I think he needs one of my cards."

Olivia sighed. "Because?"

"Because I understand that he was knocked senseless."

"I think you mean unconscious. He was already sense-less when he got here." Diane came up with a burst of canned laughter and Olivia added the "ba-da-bing." "He was only out for a minute or so. I'm sure he's fine."

"Sometimes people appear to be fine, but actually are not. There can be delayed reactions and long-term effects. I'd advise that he be examined thoroughly. X rays would probably be a good idea, too."

"And I suppose you'd be conducting that examination yourself?"

"Well, no. But we have people who do. I'm with Brant, Merriweather and Hodgson. We're personal injury attorneys."

"Ookay . . ." Olivia dumped the call without a moment's hesitation. "Thanks so much for your concern. I'll be sure to pass it on."

She managed to keep the "when hell freezes over" part under her breath and contented herself with typing a scathing message to Diane, who was supposed to be screening her calls. Then she picked up the next line.

"You're on the air, Amanda. What can I do for you?"

"Sorry, but I just have to ask about Matt Ransom, too, Dr. O. When I logged on Tuesday, he appeared to be lying on the floor having a near-death experience."

"That's what happens when you put your face in front of someone's foot." Olivia had to stifle a smile at the memory.

"Is he all right? Does he seem strange?"

"No more than usual." Olivia went through the motions of a mimed drum riff, but didn't bother to go for the sound effects. God, she was tired of talking about Matt.

"Well, I'm a nurse, and I can tell you that any blow to the face or head is cause for concern."

"I wouldn't worry about Matt Ransom. He's every bit as annoying as he was before—which makes me think we can rule out permanent brain damage."

"Well, I'm on duty all day today at St. Joe's if he needs anything."

"Gee, Amanda, are you offering aid to the enemy? There are stiff penalties for that."

"Like eating gourmet meals and watching soap operas?"

"Well, I—"

"Or being kissed by Atlanta's Bachelor of the Year? That must have been really rough."

"Now hold on."

"In case you haven't noticed, Dr. O, you're not doing time with Hannibal Lecter in there. Half the nurses on my shift would pay good money to take your place."

"And I'd give a fortune to let them." Olivia let the call go and eyed the list of women waiting to go on the air. Most of them seemed intent on discussing Matt Ransom in some way or another. Nobody seemed to have a problem she wanted to discuss. Except herself . . . and that would require discussing the very person she didn't want to talk about.

Olivia allowed a few long moments of silence while she dumped all but the one call that listed something other than Matt as the topic. According to her computer screen, there was a woman named Rebecca waiting to discuss . . . horse racing?

Olivia peered at the monitor, trying to understand what the words Diane had typed in could possibly have to do with anything, but "jockey," "short," and "bet" didn't exactly clarify the caller's problem.

She had a horrible suspicion that Matt Ransom was starting to rub off on her. She'd been entirely too flip, and too quick to dump deserving people who wanted her opinion—even if it was about her current roommate and this ridiculous promotion.

"Okay, I've got Rebecca waiting on the line. If you have a problem you'd like to discuss, or food you'd like to pledge, start dialing now. We're almost out of time."

Olivia settled back in her chair and folded her hands on the table in front of her. She was ready for something she could sink her teeth into. Some sort of meaty relationship problem that would turn the tide of conversation and get everybody's juices flowing.

"Hello, Rebecca. You're on the air."

A twenty-something female voice came on the air. "Hi, Dr. O. How are you this morning?"

"Better now, thanks. I'm ready to get down to work. Tell me what's on your mind."

"Well, I'm not quite sure how to ask this question."

Olivia glanced down once more at the words Diane had used to preview Rebecca's call. "Is it about your boyfriend the jockey?"

"My boyfriend the what?"

"Isn't your boyfriend a jockey?"

"I beg your pardon?"

"My producer indicated that you had a question about a jockey. Do you work with horses, too?"

There was a brief silence. Then Rebecca began to giggle. At first her laughter was restrained and ladylike, but it quickly developed into whoops of rolling-on-the-floor hilarity. When she finally quieted down enough to speak, Olivia could still hear the mirth lacing her voice.

"I don't know where the horse-racing thing came from, Dr. Moore. Honest. I don't even have a boyfriend."

A sinking feeling settled in the pit of Olivia's stomach. Like an attorney who'd asked a witness a question without first knowing the answer, she'd made assumptions about her caller that were about to rise up and bite her right on the ...

"My question is about underwear. You know, boxers versus briefs? I bet my friend you'd know what kind of underwear Matt Ransom wears. He's such an incredible hunk."

Olivia closed her eyes in weary resignation. She was a mental health professional. She'd spent years earning her Ph.D., treating clients, building a name for herself. And she had been reduced to fielding questions about what Matt Ransom wore to cover his bottom.

"Go ahead and tell us, Dr. O, which is it? My friend Melody bet me he wears silk boxers. But he looks like a jockey kind of guy to me."

Matt found Olivia sitting on the couch, clutching the remote, pretending not to watch *General Hospital*. She had a large green psychology tome on her lap and a yellow pad perched on one knee, but her gaze was fixed on the television screen.

He dropped down on the couch beside her.

Clearly caught by surprise, she moved to click off the remote, but he reached out a hand to stop her. "I doubt there's a rule in the psychologist's handbook against enjoying soap operas. You're obviously interested, so why are you hiding behind all this?"

He drew the book off her lap, placed the yellow pad on top of it, and laid both on the coffee table.

"Who will take me seriously if I spend half my day fielding calls about your choice of underwear and the other half panting over soap operas?"

"You're trapped in a tiny apartment in the middle of promotion hell with no one but me for company. No one's going to take you seriously anyway. Why not relax and enjoy yourself?"

"You always have an answer, don't you? I don't want to enjoy myself, and I have no desire to be more relaxed. I like being the way I am. It allows me to get things done, to accomplish my goals, to maintain a certain level of self-respect. You may be able to blow off the whole focus group thing, but my listeners have certain expectations."

She'd turned to face him when she started her tirade, but by her last word he noticed her trying to check out the television from the corner of her eye. He put both hands on either side of her head and turned it so that she faced the screen. "Admit it. You're hooked and you want to know what's going to happen next."

"I am *not* addicted to this silly program. I barely understand what's going on."

"Right. Whatever you say." He settled back into the cushions, plopped his feet on the cocktail table, and slid an arm across the back of the sofa. "So, what did I miss?"

"You never give up, do you?" Olivia's laugh was rueful. "All right, someone that everybody is looking for is lying in bed naked while someone whose name I missed takes care of him. His wife just found his bloodstained briefcase at another woman's grave, but I don't really understand what that means. The only thing I know for sure is that she"—Olivia pointed toward the woman leaning over the naked man's bedside—"is not what she seems."

"They never are. That's the fun of it. It'll take you a while to sort everybody out. Luckily the plot develops very slowly. Look, see that guy? He's a fugitive."

"A fugitive? As in, from justice?"

"Yeah." The scene changed. "And that guy's an alcoholic, but he's trying to win custody of his son."

"Wow."

"Yeah. It gets a little convoluted sometimes."

A commercial came on, and Matt waited expectantly for the channel to change. Nothing happened. "Don't you want to see what else is on?"

"Hmmm?"

"You've got the remote. Aren't you going to check out the other channels? You might be able to catch a little bit of *Guiding Light* on CBS. Or we could watch the last couple innings of the Braves game. I think they're playing the Mets today."

"It'll just be a couple of minutes until *General Hospital*'s back on. Why jump all over the place?"

They sat for two and a half minutes while a Wisk commercial segued into one for Stayfree Maxi Pads. When the Meow Mix jingle began to play, he couldn't take it any longer. "Are you doing this intentionally?"

"Doing what?"

"Torturing me."

"Torturing you? All I'm doing is sitting here, waiting."

"Exactly. This is because of the Victoria's Secret lingerie, isn't it?"

Olivia shook her head.

"Because I ate that veal marsala in front of you?"

"Of course not."

"The Xena, Warrior Princess, thing?"

"Don't you think you're overreacting just a little bit?"

"Is it because I bet Ben you'd go ballistic the first time I left the toilet seat up?"

"You bet money on that?"

He put his hand out. "Hand over the remote or I'll be forced to show your listeners exactly what kind of underwear I have on today."

She stared at him as if he'd sprouted a second head.

"Look, just give me the remote and I'll show you how to handle it properly."

"You're going to teach me how to use a remote?"

"We'll have to hope it turns out better than the boxing thing. You've never used a remote competitively, have you?"

"This is absolutely ridiculous."

"Hand it over."

After a slight hesitation, she complied.

"Okay, first of all, a remote is meant to be used. What's the point of all these channels if you can't see what's on at any given moment?"

"Okay."

"Okay. So you want to hold it loosely in your dominant hand. Mine happens to be my right, but it works both ways. You just let it rest in your palm so that you can use your thumb to punch in your selections."

"And . . . ?"

"Then you do a run-through of all your options, take a quick peek, and move on." He began to demonstrate.

"But . . . wait. I can't tell what those programs are. How do you know whether you want to see something or not when you fly by so fast?"

"Superior male reasoning power. And intellect."

"Oh, really?"

"Absolutely. For example . . ." He flicked to a new channel, offering his rationale as he went. "Okay. This is obviously a commerical. My first glimpse tells me it's a feminine hygiene product. Unless I haven't had a date for three years, I'm gone."

"But what about—"

· "Ditto for panty hose, toilet bowl cleaners, and Hallmark cards."

"What do you stop for?"

Matt skidded to a halt on the Braves game. "Good question. I give a full two seconds to all sporting events." He watched Greg Maddux strike out Mike Piazza and then flicked past several other channels before continuing. "I'll wait up to five seconds if Maddux is pitching, assuming I haven't already decided to watch the whole game."

"What's the longest you stop?"

"Well, this is an art, not a science, so I could be a little bit off. But my longest stop is generally ten to fifteen seconds, max."

"And those kinds of stops are reserved for . . ."

"Babes. Scantily clad women. Women I *wish* were scantily clad."

He landed back on *General Hospital,* and they watched two teenagers share a kiss. Then he began to work his way through the possibilities one more time. "Do you get the idea?"

"Oh, I've got it all right. We're talking Attention Deficit

Disorder television. Whip right by, gather general impressions, and move on to the next thing. Sort of like your strategy for dealing with the opposite sex."

"You don't pull a whole lot of punches, do you?" He stopped on *General Hospital* long enough to watch the conclusion of the kiss and see the beginning of the closing credits before flying through the channels once more.

"No, I don't pull punches, and I can't say I'm particularly interested in your approach to television. I don't watch much, but when I do I actually like to watch what I'm watching."

Matt smiled. "Some people just don't have a light enough touch. I guess you're either born with it or you're not."

"Some people are not only born with it, they're full of it."

"All right. But don't say I didn't try to educate you." Matt laughed and handed her the remote. "I have to go over a few things for tonight, and then I'm going to see what kind of meal I can put together. You ready to wash dishes for your supper?"

"And analyze you to boot. Just let me know when you want me to set the table."

Ten minutes later, when he looked up from his work, she'd put the remote down on the coffee table. But now, instead of hiding behind her books and notes, she was stretched out on the sofa avidly watching *Oprah*. And if the deep belly laugh she'd just let loose was any indication, she seemed to be enjoying herself.

It appeared that the lovely Dr. Moore was far more open to new experiences than Matt had suspected. Which might make it time for lesson number two.

14

Olivia changed her clothes before dinner. She also freshened her makeup, fluffed her hair, and dabbed perfume on every available scrap of skin—blatant acts of primping that both amused and horrified her. Unfortunately, amusement and horror weren't the only contradictory responses fighting for dominance within her.

She felt oddly relaxed but totally on edge. She was warm and liquid one moment and paralyzed by uncertainty the next. Extreme sensations bombarded her at every turn and left her feeling decidedly . . . not herself.

Dr. Olivia Moore lived her life in moderation. She kept her boat on an even keel. On those rare occasions when life made her boat heel to one side or another—her affair with Matt and her divorce from James being the most glaring examples—she found a way to right it, or at least pretended that she had.

Being trapped with Matt Ransom was like being sucked into the eye of a hurricane . . . and staying there. Indefinitely. While her sails flapped madly in the wind.

She had been right to be afraid of this promotion. She

had too many unresolved feelings for Matt to come through this week unscathed. She should have kept her boat moored at the dock and refused to be pushed out to sea.

Olivia took a deep breath, opened the bedroom door, and stepped out. She found Matt chopping tomatoes in the kitchen and noticed that he, too, had spruced up for dinner. His hair was still wet from the shower, and his Levis, though well worn, were neatly pressed.

At her approach, Matt glanced up and smiled—a lazy flash of white teeth framed by dark skin. "You're just in time."

The sound of his voice sent her pulse jumping—not a welcome reaction for a woman who craved calm waters. When he bent back over the cutting board, she took advantage of the opportunity to observe him. Her gaze traveled over the thick dark hair shot through with gray, down the slanted cheekbones to the squared-off jaw. His shoulders were broad, his forearms muscled, and the hands that wielded the paring knife, strong and sure.

Matt Ransom was a pleasure to look at. But watching him dissect the hapless tomato, Olivia admitted that his movie star looks were only a small part of his appeal.

She was drawn by his simple air of confidence and the keen intellect that fueled his wicked sense of humor. He made her laugh and sputter with indignation. And while he often infuriated her, he never bored her.

"Are you going to stand there gawking, or are you going to get over here and set the table?" He added the chopped tomato to the ingredients in a large wooden bowl and drizzled oil and vinegar over the top.

Olivia inhaled the rich scents emanating from the pot on the stove. "Are we having spaghetti?"

"We are. Do you like Italian?"

"I've never met a region in Italy I didn't like."

"Smart woman." He walked around the counter to fill two glasses with a deep red wine, and Olivia's heart did an embarrassing flip-flop.

Pretending a nonchalance she didn't feel, Olivia moved toward the silverware drawer. Trying to create distance where none existed, she hugged the counter, only to discover that opening the drawer put her directly in Matt's path.

" 'Scuse me." Matt reached around her to check the sauce simmering on the stove.

Olivia sucked in her breath as his front brushed across her rear. "God, I feel like a sardine."

"No, you don't." A glimmer of humor stole into his eyes and a dimple flashed at the corner of his mouth. He put both hands up in apology as they slid out of each other's way, but he didn't look particularly sorry. "Can you hand me a dish?"

Olivia passed one of the two he'd set out and watched him place a heaping mound of spaghetti with meat sauce in the center. When he reached for the garlic bread wrapped in foil, his finger trailed across the still-hot burner. "Damn."

"Are you all right?"

"I'm fine." With quick, efficient movements, he turned off the stove and stuck the singed finger in his mouth.

"Can I rub some butter on it?"

The look of surprise that flashed across his face made her want to laugh.

"Your finger, Matt. Can I grease it for you?"

"Oh." His face fell. "My finger's fine."

"You say that now, but tomorrow morning I'll be hearing from attorneys and nurses. Let me take a look."

"My *finger's* perfectly okay." He didn't appear to be in pain, but his voice sounded a bit strained.

Intrigued enough by his reaction to stop worrying about her own, she followed him to the refrigerator. There he retrieved a block of Parmesan cheese and backed out, coming to a stop only when his rear end pressed up against her crotch.

They both froze.

It would have been comical if her heart hadn't been beating so hard. Matt turned around to face her—which didn't slow her heartbeat one iota—and then he reached over her to set the Parmesan on the counter, casually caging her between his forearms in the process.

Trapped against the wall of his chest, she became a part of every breath he took. And when he dropped his hands to cup her buttocks and pull her tighter against him, she could feel the hammer of his heartbeat against hers.

Her nerve endings jangled as he whispered in her ear. "My finger's fine, but other parts of me could use some attention."

Olivia licked her lips, but her mouth was too dry to swallow. Something hard and insistent had sprung up between them. "You don't say."

Matt nuzzled at her neck and brought his lips up to nibble on the lobe of her ear. "I'm in love with the butter idea, Livvy. Why don't we put dinner on hold and adjourn to my room for some first aid?"

Olivia swallowed.

"We can sit down at the table, eat our spaghetti, and maintain this charade. Or we can skip dinner and get right down to dessert."

His look left no doubt who would be consuming whom.

Desire coursed through her as she stared up into Matt's eyes and tried to comprehend his effect on her. She could have been locked in a room half this size with her ex-husband and have no difficulty avoiding intimacy. Being on the same planet with Matt demanded it.

And what of Matt? Was this his standard reaction to an available member of the opposite sex? Or a convenient means of embarrassing her in front of her audience? How far would he go to do away with her as a competitor?

When Olivia finally found her voice, she kept her words even and her tone light. It cost her, but she did it. "I wouldn't miss your spaghetti for anything."

Turning away from him, she picked up their dinner plates. "Why don't you bring the salads? And the rest of the wine, too. I think I need a drink."

Without a word, Matt followed her to the table. It took him a moment or two to seat himself, but once settled he raised his glass and clinked the rim of it against hers. "To calmer heads prevailing."

She tilted her head in acknowledgment and swept away a tiny shard of disappointment. Then she took a bite of her spaghetti and chewed as calmly as she could, trying to enjoy the perfect blending of flavors on her tongue.

Only when she had herself completely under control

did she allow herself to make eye contact. "Tell me how you started cooking, Matt."

For a moment she thought he was going to refuse to follow her lead, but finally his lips quirked up at the corner and he said, "Desperation. Hunger. The usual things that drive a person into a kitchen. Sometimes a man just has to learn to fend for himself."

"I'd hardly call this fending."

"Thanks."

"Was your mother a good cook?"

Matt's smile disappeared and his body stiffened. "She was at one time."

She could tell he didn't want to pursue the subject, but in her line of work that usually signaled the ideal time to forge ahead. "But . . ."

"But when I was thirteen, we had a family crisis and she stopped."

"Cooking?"

"Everything."

She saw Matt's flash of regret at the honesty of his answer. He picked up his fork and started on his meal while she watched him from across the table. Funny that she had considered herself in love with him, yet knew so little about him.

"What kind of crisis made her stop cooking?"

He stopped eating, and she knew that if there'd been anywhere for him to go, he would have found an excuse to leave. He set his fork on the edge of his plate and looked at her. "We had a death in the family."

His eyes warned her not to trespass further.

"Who died, Matt?"

"I don't need your two hundred bucks' worth tonight,

Olivia. Why don't you just do the dishes when we're finished, and leave my past alone?"

"Not until you tell me who died."

He sat back in his chair and folded his arms across his chest. It didn't take a trained psychologist to read the body language. But she was glad she had the background all the same.

"Who died, Matt?"

He reached out and picked up his wineglass. After several long sips he set it back down and looked her in the eye. "My brother. Adam."

"Was he older than you or younger?"

"He was my twin."

"Oh, Matt." She felt a brief stab of pity for the boy who had lost so much at such an early age, but she forced herself to resume the conversation, carefully keeping the emotion out of her voice. "Tell me what happened."

Matt ran a hand through his hair in a sign of irritation she was coming to recognize.

"It happened so long ago, Olivia. I don't see any point in talking about it now."

She wondered if he had ever seen the point and hoped that some adult had known enough to make him share the hurt when the wounds were fresh. "There doesn't need to be a point. Why don't you just tell me what happened?"

His voice dropped lower and she leaned forward to hear what came next. "We were all swimming in the lake near our house, and he hit his head on a boulder."

He seemed to expect her to say something, but she just sat quietly and waited for him to continue.

"None of us realized what had happened until it was too late. I thought he was just horsing around."

"And your parents . . ."

"Blamed themselves. Fell apart. I don't know, but they couldn't seem to whip up any real enthusiasm for the two of us who were still alive."

"And how did that make you feel?"

He stopped as if thinking about the answer for the first time, and she shuddered to think of the thirteen-year-old boy bottling up all that hurt and confusion. "Lonely. Guilty. Scared. And totally pissed off."

"And what did you do?"

He shrugged again. "What does anybody do? I went on. It felt like shit, but I went on. And when my sister and I got tired of ordering pizza every night, we learned how to cook."

"You became a gourmet cook at thirteen?"

He snorted his amusement. "Hardly. I had an aunt who bought my sister and me kids' cookbooks one year for Christmas. We learned how to make meatloaf and mashed potatoes—got really good at pigs in a blanket— that kind of thing. We used to take turns cooking dinner."

"You didn't cook like this when we knew each other in Chicago. Where did you learn all the fancy stuff?"

"Television."

"Ah, you didn't mention that during my remote lesson. So you also stop for . . ."

"Julia Child, when she had a regular show. Mario Batali, Paul Prudhomme, Emeril, Justin Wilson before he died, pretty much anyone standing in a kitchen who looks like they know what they're doing."

"You're full of surprises, aren't you?"

"Oh, I'm a real man of mystery, all right." He sat back in his chair and studied her closely, so she studied him in return. His smile seemed a little freer, and his eyes were no longer so cautious.

He stood and carried the dishes to the sink and piled the pots and pans on the counter next to it. "I appreciate your interest in my past and all, Olivia. But the next time I want to root around in the Ransom family closet, I'll let you know."

He came back to the table, pulled out her chair, and escorted her into the kitchen. "In the meantime, you might want to get started on these dishes. I've got a show to get ready for."

From his seat in the WTLK control room, Charles Crankower watched Olivia Moore wash dishes. She looked almost as good from the back as she did from the front, and it was kind of interesting to watch the intensity with which she applied herself to cleaning those pots and pans.

His gaze swung to Matt Ransom, who was also watching the doctor, though he was pretending not to. After observing Ransom's progress over the last few days, Charles had to admit the guy hadn't overestimated his ability with women.

Dr. Moore might not be eating out of her roommate's hand, but she was eating at the same table and seemed to be enjoying it. It was their body language and the way they kept studying each other while pretending not to that had finally sent Charles to Human Resources for a peek at Matt's and Olivia's résumés. There he had discovered an interesting tidbit that didn't appear on either of the talk show hosts' publicity bios: Olivia Moore had done an internship at the same station in Chicago where Matt Ransom did afternoon drive. And despite all the recent on-air bickering and one-upmanship, neither of them had ever mentioned it.

Charles wasn't certain yet just how to use this information to his or the station's advantage, but he recognized the significance of the omission. If their time together in Chicago hadn't meant anything to either of them, the whole world would already have known about it.

He'd caught their kiss on the couch and the way they kept rubbing up against each other in the kitchen. As he settled in to watch the evening unfold, Charles tried to imagine what, other than sex, two such opposite personalities might have shared. He crossed his long legs in an effort to get comfortable in the too-small chair and reminded himself that good things were supposed to come to those who waited.

Matt leaned way back in his chair and cleared a spot for his feet on the edge of the audio console. He missed his basketball net back at the studio and the freedom to move around without an audience studying his every move. And though he didn't plan to come out and say so anytime soon, he'd give huge sums of money for five minutes outside the too-tiny apartment.

His dinner with Olivia lingered in his mind, as did the

unprecedented conversation about Adam and his death. It wasn't a topic he shared, and he wasn't thrilled at how easily she'd pried the details out of him. Or how much better he'd felt immediately afterward. She had a way of slipping past his defenses that was nothing short of alarming.

Dawg Rollins hung on the line wanting to talk, yet again, about his failed relationship and his inability to move on. Matt shook his head in disgust. Moving on was his specialty. In fact, he could pack up and hit the emotional road faster than most men could finish a burger and fries. As in most endeavors, practice made perfect.

"Hey, Matt."

"Hey, Dawg. How's it going?"

"Okay, I guess. Except I have a question for you."

"Then I probably have an answer. But remember, I am not your high school guidance counselor *or* Dear Abby. I'm only prepared to talk about guy stuff."

Dawg's voice, already gruff, took on a puzzled tone. "Okay, then. What do *you* do when a woman comes on to you and you're not interested, Ransom?"

"Gee." Matt scratched his head and forced himself to think. "I can't remember that ever happening. Is she unattractive?"

"Nope."

"A ball buster?"

"No."

"Have bad breath?"

"Uh-uh."

"Rude to your friends?"

" 'Fraid not."

"Wanting to change you?"

"Hell, no. She looks at me like I'm God's gift to the universe."

Matt blinked. "And the problem is . . ."

"I don't know. She just doesn't do anything for me, ya know?"

"Not really." The memory of the first six months after he drove Olivia away rapped at the back of Matt's brain, but he refused to let it in. "Are you still mooning after the one who wants to get married?"

"I'm not *mooning* after JoBeth. I just miss her, that's all."

"Well, I'll tell you what, Dawg. You're just going to have to get over it. There's an old song that kind of covers this topic, called 'Love the One You're With.' Ever heard of it?"

"Not really."

"Well, that's my philosophy. If you can't be with the one you love—and you apparently can't unless you're willing to get married—then love the one you're with."

"But—"

"You're wasting time dwelling on what was, man. It's time to move on to what can be. Believe me, women are pretty much alike and not worth all this grief you're putting yourself through."

"And you've never come up against a woman who made you rethink your philosophy?"

Once again he quashed the image of Olivia so young and eager to share all of herself, opening to him completely. "No, I haven't," he lied. "But I am ready to move on to a more suitably masculine topic. Like the horrible end of the Braves' latest winning streak, or how to tell if you're about to get downsized."

"Okay," said Dawg. "I'll let you get on with things. But don't be so sure this'll never happen to you, Ransom. It seems like sometimes love just sort of tiptoes up and bushwhacks you from behind. And then nothing is ever the same again."

15

On Friday morning Olivia faced an uncontestable truth: Being thirty sucked. It was her birthday and although she'd only been awake for five and a half minutes, the added year was already taking its toll.

Too old and too tired to get out of bed, Olivia stretched her sheep-clad arms up above her head, kicked the rumpled bedsheets out of the way, and contemplated the ceiling. It was made of the popcorned plaster common in condos and apartments, and it had absolutely nothing going for it. She felt a strange sort of kinship with the pimply slab of concrete and an awful sort of lethargy that she wished she could indulge.

In the bathroom, Olivia searched through her cosmetics bag until she came up with an ancient sample tube of anti-wrinkle cream. After smearing it liberally around her eyes, she faced herself in the mirror and attempted a smile. She still had all her teeth, but the longer she looked, the more pronounced the signs of her advanced age became.

Shimmying out of her pajamas, Olivia squeezed her eyes shut to avoid discovering any suddenly sagging body parts or newly bulging varicose veins, and stepped under the stream of hot water, keeping her back to the mirror while she lathered and rinsed.

Clean, but still thirty, she slipped into her clothes and headed out to the kitchen for the cup of coffee that she prayed would help put things back into perspective. Within minutes, she'd parked herself in front of the computer, coffee mug in hand. Diane's birthday wishes awaited her on the computer screen.

Thanks, Olivia typed, unable to summon a more profound or lengthy response.

Diane gave her the vote count. Once again, donations and votes were relatively even. Olivia sensed it would take something major to obtain a real lead, but she refused to think about the consultant and his endless questions. Being thirty was bad enough.

The spaghetti looked pretty good last night, Diane typed. *I'm putting on pounds just watching you and Matt eat.*

Olivia replied, *When I get out of here we'll try hypnosis. But I'm too old to think about food today.*

Diane's next missive read, *You're only as old as you feel.*

Olivia sipped at her coffee. *Then I must have turned a hundred and two.*

You don't sound so good. Should I wake up Matt? Olivia could almost hear Diane's concern in the words she typed.

NO! Olivia typed. *I'm planning to check out retirement communities as soon as I get off the air. Until then, I'd prefer to do my show in peace.*

Okay.

You haven't told anyone it's my thirtieth birthday, have you?

There was the computer equivalent of dead silence while Olivia waited for the reassuring words to appear.

Diane, she typed. *Tell me you haven't said anything to . . .*

The doorbell and the phone rang simultaneously. With only ten minutes until air, Olivia picked up the cordless phone, brought the receiver to her ear, and moved toward the front door.

"Olivia, it's Charles."

She braced herself.

"Crankower," he said, as if there were another. "I just wanted you to know that I—"

"Hold on, Charles. There's someone at the door. I assume I'm allowed to open it?"

"Yes, yes. Of course."

Olivia turned the key in the dead bolt and pulled open the front door, an act that made her feel immeasurably better. Until she saw what awaited her.

The deliveryman looked like a bit player from *The Sopranos.* His wiry arms cradled a bulging floral arrangement, and a cloud of black balloons floated above his head.

"Got a delivery for one Dr. Olive Moore."

"That's Olivia."

"Whatever. Can I bring this stuff in?"

"I guess so." She stepped back to let him in and had an alarming thought. "You haven't been paid to take off your clothes or anything, have you?"

He looked at her as if she were deranged. "Look, lady, I just want to put this stuff down. You want me to take my clothes off, you'll have to call my supervisor."

Olivia lifted the phone to her ear. "Charles, what's going on here?"

"It's your thirtieth birthday, Olivia. The station wants to help you celebrate it."

The deliveryman continued to eye her as if she were exactly the sort of woman who might force him to perform an unauthorized striptease and then call his office to complain. "I've got a few more things down near the elevator. Can you hold the door?"

At her nod, he slid carefully around her and walked down the hall, leaving her with the phone and less than five minutes to air. She contemplated the hallway longingly.

"Charles. This is ridiculous. I don't want . . ."

The delivery guy came back with more flowers, a cane with a rearview mirror and horn attached, and two cardboard boxes with Matt's name on them. He eyed her as she stood in the doorway. "I got some other stuff to do in here. You wanna close the door?"

Olivia let the door slam behind her. "Charles. I need to go on the air. You have to put a stop to this right now."

"Sorry, Olivia, can't do it. Everything's already in motion. Just wanted to wish you a happy birthday."

"Charles, I am not willing to—"

"There's lots of interest in the story of you turning thirty, so we'll be feeding a ton of video off the Webcam today."

"Now, there's some good news. Charles, I—"

"Gotta go, Olivia. Have a great day."

She spent her last minutes before air watching the deliveryman decorate the apartment. He crisscrossed the room hanging black crepe paper and anchoring bunches of black balloons to chair backs while she watched with growing dismay.

When he started taping an "Over the Hill" banner to the wall, she wanted to go back to her room and crawl under the covers. Instead, she fielded her first call.

"This is *Liv Live*. In case there's anyone who hasn't figured it out, today is my thirtieth birthday. Hi, Wanda. You're on the air."

"Happy birthday, Dr. O. Hope it's a great one."

Wanda sounded about twelve, which was probably why she still thought birthdays were something to cheer about. Olivia tried not to hold it against her, but caught herself listening with only half an ear as she watched the deliveryman/decorator pack up and depart.

So far, the one bright spot was Matt Ransom's absence. And though her gaze strayed to his closed bedroom door more times than she cared to count, she told herself she was relieved when he didn't put in an appearance.

Drawing the conversation with Wanda to a close, Olivia moved on. "JoBeth. Has your Dawg learned to heel yet?"

"No, Dr. O. In fact, the last time I saw him, another woman had her paws all over him."

"How'd that go?"

"I told her she was welcome to the hound, and left. But I felt like rubbing both their noses in some serious—"

"Yeah," Olivia interrupted. "I know just what you mean."

"Really, Dr. O?"

"Really. I know it's hard, JoBeth, but you're doing all the right things. You've taken control of your life, and you're prepared to move on if you have to. But, you know, I heard your Dawg on the air with Matt last night, and I'm starting to wonder if you might not be able to teach him some new tricks."

"I don't know, Dr. Olivia. It doesn't look like he's going to roll over and play dead anytime soon. And I sure don't intend to sit up and beg."

Olivia smiled her first real smile of the day. Evidently even old people could still see the humor in things. "Well, JoBeth, if we continue the obedience metaphor, we could say that the rolled-up newspaper made an impression. Now you have to decide whether to give him something to wag his tail about or get out the choke collar."

"Oh."

"You know, a kind of Milk-Bones-versus-the-electronic-fence decision. You've got lots of options, JoBeth, you just need to take the time to sort through them."

"Uh, okay, Dr. O, thanks. And happy birthday, you hear?"

"Thanks, JoBeth. Keep me posted. Who knows, maybe that Dawg can find his way back home."

She segued into a commercial break with, "Don't forget to call in your food pledges. This is *Liv Live*, reminding you to live your life . . . *live*."

Olivia shut off her microphone and stretched her arms over her head to work the kinks out. She stood and strolled over to the kitchen, then turned and walked back to stare out the balcony doors. Outside, a woman and young girl walked hand in hand toward the playground in the tiny park across the road. White dogwoods flowered along the sidewalk, and pale yellow roses twined through the arched park gate. Olivia longed to be out there with them, her own hair stirring in the gentle spring breeze.

She was thirty, and she was locked in a very small apartment with Matt Ransom. Somehow both truths loomed ominously over her, unavoidable and inescapable. Turning, she headed back to the audio console and took her seat just before the commercial break ended.

"This is *Liv Live*, the thirtieth-birthday edition. We've heard from JoBeth, who's still trying to work things out with her Dawg, and I'm up for another challenge. Give me a call and tell me what's on your mind. I'll talk about anything as long as I don't have to think about how old I am."

Glancing down at the computer screen, Olivia read the words "dinner," "birthday," and "sorry." With no time to get more information, Olivia took the call. Despite the written warnings, Matt's voice took her by surprise.

"Happy birthday, Livvy."

Her gaze swung to his bedroom door, but it remained closed. Olivia sat back in her chair, folded her arms across her chest, and instructed herself to remain calm. "Hello, Matt. How *good* of you to call."

"My pleasure."

"Okay." She kept her voice even and professional, unwilling to let anyone know how completely he rattled her. "Why don't you go ahead and tell me what's on your mind."

"Why, you are, of course."

Olivia blinked.

"Getting older can be tough, especially for a woman."

"And you're calling to . . . console me?"

"I'm calling because I have a birthday present for you, and I figure you're more likely to accept it with your listeners listening in."

"And what kind of gift are we talking about?"

"A birthday dinner. In honor of your being so old and all."

"What an attractive offer. Any chance we'd be dining out?"

"Nope."

"Then I don't think I'm interested."

He chuckled with maddening good humor. "See, this is where calling in to your show really pays off."

"Oh, yeah?"

"Yeah. Because I know you won't want your listeners to think you're afraid to have a birthday meal with me."

"We've been alone for four days now and shared several meals together. Why should I be afraid *today*?"

She could practically hear his shrug. "Because you're older now, more mature? Possibly more . . . desperate?" He paused and she could picture his dimple cutting a groove into his cheek. "And you've never had my duck à la Ransom. It drives women wild."

"You're driving me wild *now*, Matt. With annoyance. But I'm not afraid of you. And I'm not *that* old."

"Good. It's a date, then. We'll have drinks earlier and dinner at eight. I assume you don't need directions."

16

___

Dawg Rollins pushed open the door of the Magnolia Diner and stepped inside. At 5:00 P.M., the place bulged with early birds wolfing down enough fried food to clog the arteries of every man, woman, and child in Georgia. Standing in the entrance, he breathed in the familiar smells of down-home cooking and scanned the restaurant for JoBeth.

"Hey, Dawg." Noreen Pitts, who'd been waitressing longer than he'd been alive, tucked a pencil behind her ear and a stray gray curl back into its bun. "Counter or booth?"

"Put me back in JoBeth's section, Noreen."

"I don't know, Dawg. Ina made chocolate meringue pie for dessert tonight. That's almost impossible to get out of your clothes."

"I'm willing to risk it. Just give me that booth in the corner there, okay?"

He moved forward with determination, dragging the small gray-haired woman along in his wake until they reached the booth he'd requested. When she didn't move, he lifted a menu out of her hands, sat down on the seat, and slid his rear end across the red vinyl bench.

"Thanks, Noreen. I appreciate it."

"I hope you feel that way when JoBeth gets finished with you." She shook her head. "I don't know what's gotten into that girl, but she sure has taken to speaking her mind."

"Hasn't she though?"

JoBeth had never been what you'd call a shrinking violet, but she'd never been the kind of woman to throw a pie in a man's face, either. Even when her parents' illnesses and demands had dragged down on her, she'd been upbeat, always trying to look on the bright side of things.

He took a minute to read over the menu, though he'd eaten at the Magnolia a thousand times. When he looked up, JoBeth stood in front of his table with her order pad out and her professional smile in place. Her normally warm gray eyes looked a bit on the frosty side.

"What can I get for you?"

"All I really want is some conversation, JoBeth."

"You can't tie up a table talking." She nodded over her shoulder toward the entrance, where several customers milled around. "People are lined up waiting to get seated."

"I just wanted to tell you about the thing with Emmylou. You see I was only trying to—"

"It's no concern of mine who you spend your time with or why. Order or give up the table, Dawg."

"All right, then. I'll start with a glass of sweet tea."

"And?" Her pencil still poised above her pad, JoBeth waited expectantly.

"You told me I had to order, so I ordered. Is there a minimum?" He sent her an innocent look.

She tucked the pencil back behind her ear and reached for his menu, but he refused to give it up.

"I think I'll hold on to this. I'm going to be here awhile and I may want to order something else."

"Fine." She turned and strode the few steps to the nearest station, grabbed up a pitcher, and returned to pour him the tea.

Dawg watched her pour the amber-colored liquid. "You know, now that I think of it, maybe I will have a little something to eat. What do you have on special today?"

JoBeth's lips pressed together in an impossibly thin line, and Dawg wondered how she'd squeeze the words out from between them. "We have fried chicken, country fried steak, and liver and onions. They all come with mashed potatoes and gravy plus your choice of two vegetables."

JoBeth slipped her pencil back out from behind her ear and held it poised above her pad. "What'll it be?"

"I guess I'll have a small house salad to start. Oh, and some corn bread. I may order a meal a little later."

"Fine." JoBeth turned on her heel and left. He watched her work her tables, taking full advantage of the chance to observe her in action. She was small and compact with lots of interesting curves that he'd spent long hours exploring. He watched her flash her sassy smile at the elderly McCauleys and heard her laughter float back across the diner as she took someone else's order. She had so much life and enthusiasm—but evidently no desire to share either with him at the moment.

Dawg took a long sip of his tea and reflected that his whole life had turned damned empty since she'd moved out. There wasn't a thing he could think of that felt the same.

JoBeth placed his salad in front of him and slid the basket of corn bread onto the middle of the table. A bowl of butter pats clattered next to it. In a minute she'd be gone.

"Nicky and the other boys all asked me to say hello to you," he got out in a rush.

"Oh." She'd already turned to leave, but stopped at the mention of the inner-city baseball team he coached. "Did you have practice?"

"Yeah. We had the batting cage for an hour and then we played a practice game against Ron Parker's team yesterday afternoon."

"How'd that turn out?"

"They creamed us. Stomped us into the dirt."

JoBeth smiled. The fact that she so obviously didn't want to made it that much sweeter. "Did Jamal get a hit?"

"Almost. I just can't convince the kid to swing unless the pitch is exactly where he wants it."

She smiled again and her eyes warmed by several degrees. "Bet he's sorry his coach played for the Falcons instead of the Braves. Did you take that knee pad I bought you so you could get down into his strike zone?"

Dawg congratulated himself on finding the one topic guaranteed to snag JoBeth's interest. As unofficial team mom and number one fan, JoBeth had rarely missed a Fuller Park Tornadoes game.

"The boy has about a one-foot strike zone. He's like you, JoBeth, small and scrappy. I like that in a woman."

"Hmmph. You didn't seem to have a problem with big and blonde the other night." The thawing process screeched to a halt and JoBeth whirled to leave.

Dawg's knees might have been shot, but there was nothing wrong with his reflexes. His hand snaked out to wrap around her wrist and twirl her back to face him. "You know I was only trying to make you jealous."

She cocked her head and waited for him to continue.

"Of course, I know you didn't fall for it. You did leave both of us alive."

JoBeth tapped a foot in a sign of impatience, but he knew he had her full attention.

"Aw hell, JoBeth. I'm not interested in Emmylou or anyone else. You do know that, don't you?"

"Hmmph," was all she said, but he could tell she was pleased. She snatched her hand away and headed for a nearby table, but her movements were noticeably looser and her shoulders didn't seem so stiff.

He reached for a warm piece of corn bread, broke it open, and drenched it with butter. As he munched on his salad, he propped the menu in front of him and began to study the possibilities. It was a good thing he hadn't eaten much today. If he was going to hold on to his table until closing time, he had a hell of a lot of food ahead of him.

Matt moved around the kitchen preparing for the birthday feast while Olivia lounged on the sofa. She'd grumped around for a good hour or so after her show, but finally joined him for a triple-header of *All My Children*, *One Life to Live*, and *General Hospital*, thereby giving ABC a nonrecorded ratings boost of significant proportions.

"I like Oprah."

"Hmm?" Matt looked up from the duck breast medallions he was preparing, to find Olivia contemplating him from the couch.

"I used to make fun of daytime television. I never really had the time for it, and most of the talk show hosts are really just there to entertain, you know?"

"Which bothers you."

She ignored his dig and continued rhapsodizing. "But she has heart. You can tell she really wants to help people and change their lives for the better."

"Like you."

She looked surprised at the compliment, as if he could have been observing her all this time and not been aware that she was genuinely motivated to help.

"Well . . . yes."

"I'm sure there're openings in Oprah's fan club. Maybe you should consider joining."

"Be serious."

"No, I won't. You're serious enough for the both of us. Besides, it's your birthday. You're required to have fun."

Matt pulled the white asparagus out of the refrigerator and began rinsing them. "If you could do anything you chose today, what would it be?"

He saw her gaze stray to the front door.

"Other than leave."

"Well, that certainly narrows the possibilities."

He leered at her, and waggled his eyebrows for good measure. "There are lots of things we could do here."

"Right. And how many of them don't involve taking our clothes off?"

"Oh. Well. If you're going to be picky."

Olivia speared him with a look and then turned her attention back to Oprah. Watching her, Matt was pleased to see evidence of the success of his relaxation campaign. Where before she would have been sitting upright, her back barely touching the back of the sofa, she now lounged on the couch with the remote in her hand. Though she didn't yet use it enough to satisfy him, she no longer treated it like a foreign object. And that wasn't the only change he'd initiated.

He'd influenced her dress code, too. At the beginning of the week, she'd been painfully starched and perfectly turned out. Today, her blonde hair was slicked back into a ponytail, and the feet that poked out under the faded jeans were bare—except for the shocking-pink toenails. Her T-shirt proclaimed, "Liv Lives Live on WTLK," and fit tight enough to outline her shapely breasts very nicely.

Matt ran his eyes along the luscious curves, remembering the heft and feel of them in his hands, until his body began to react to the images.

He worked in silence for a while, intrigued by Oprah's interview with a father who stayed home with quadruplets while his wife went out to work—a premise that zapped his erection in a matter of seconds. As he listened, he caught himself wondering whether quadruplets shared the same kind of bond that twins did, or if it somehow lessened when divided among a greater number of siblings.

His own connection with his twin, Adam, had been so strong that the severing of it had crippled him for years. Even now the hollow spot deep at his center remained, and he expended considerable energy protecting the vulnerable core.

Only Olivia refused to leave his memories and guilt undisturbed, and the more she prodded and pushed, the greater the possibility that she'd discover the emptiness yawning inside him—something he'd never allowed another soul to see.

He was beginning to question whether he could tempt Olivia, put her off kilter, and take advantage of her confusion, without damaging himself. This softening he felt toward her worried him, and so did his audience's potential reaction; Olivia's wasn't the only image the consultant would put under a microscope.

Matt peeled potatoes and put them on to boil. A few minutes later, Olivia clicked off the television and wandered into the kitchen, ambling toward him at a leisurely pace he'd never seen her use before.

Matt smiled to himself. Given a few more days, he'd have her sleeping until noon and wandering around the apartment in her jammies—preferably the sheep ones that covered everything and drove him right toward the edge of sanity.

She took a seat on a barstool directly across from him. Without asking, he opened a bottle of the Veuve Cliquot he'd had delivered and poured them each a glass.

"Happy birthday, Olivia. I hope the next thirty are even better than the first."

She snorted inelegantly, but lifted her glass of champagne to clink against his. "To my advanced age. May it make me wiser in all things." She looked him in the eye. "May I learn from my mistakes . . . and know better than to repeat them."

"I think I'll just stick to 'Happy birthday.' " Matt raised the glass to his lips and took a long sip. Olivia did the same. "Do you have any plans for the rest of the afternoon?"

Her glass halted midway to her lips. "I'm considering

something really different—like hanging around and killing time."

"Why not take a nap? You're going to need your strength to consume the meal I'm putting together."

"A nap?"

"Um-hmm. With a nice long soak in the tub afterward."

"Matt, I told you I—"

"You can have the bath all to yourself. You can even leave your clothes on if you insist." He smiled. "Of course, it's a lot more relaxing and you get a whole lot cleaner naked."

She laughed then, her eyes taking on the richness of cut green velvet. His laugh joined hers as his mind formed a picture of Olivia squishing out of the bath, with bubbles dripping from her clothes. Then there was an awkward silence while he pictured her stepping out of that same tub completely naked with tiny droplets of water clinging to her. . . .

"Matt? Are you okay?"

"Oh, um, yeah. Sure." He cleared his throat and lifted the champagne to top off their glasses. "I was just thinking about some things I need to go over with Ben. I want to prep for my show before we sit down for dinner."

"Okay."

"Why don't you go ahead and take an hour's snooze, Livvy? I'll have your bath drawn and waiting for you at six-thirty so you can be nice and relaxed for your birthday dinner."

She stood and rested one hand on the back of the barstool. "You're going to *draw* my bath?"

"But of course, *ma chérie*," he replied in his best French

accent, which degenerated into a campier version of Inspector Clouseau. "It wheel be my great pleasure."

Continuing the imitation, he put his palm under Olivia's to cup her hand so that he could drop a kiss on the outside of her wrist.

"Until six-thirty, *ma petite*. At which time I will be chomping on zee bit."

17

Olivia knew deep shit when she soaked in it. It might be disguised as hot water frothing with perfume-scented bubbles, but it smelled like trouble all the same. Incredibly, she'd slept for more than the allotted hour and would probably be sleeping now if not for Matt.

He'd banged on her bedroom door until she finally forced herself out of bed to open it, and then with a finesse that spoke of too much experience, he'd led her to the bathroom and presented her with the promised bubble bath.

So here she sat, her hair piled on top of her head, soaking her naked self, nibbling on fresh strawberries and sipping a fresh glass of champagne. She'd never felt more pampered or more suspicious in her life.

Olivia swirled a hand through the water, idly watching the bubbles slide across her skin. They parted and reunited around her, while the warm water caressed her to the bone. She knew Matt was up to something, something undoubtedly fueled by her food donation and votes jump after this morning's show, but it was hard to keep up one's guard when one felt as wonderfully lethargic as she did right now.

The juice of an especially plump strawberry trickled down the corner of her mouth, and Olivia licked it off with her tongue, enjoying the sweet stickiness.

She trailed the washcloth lightly over her body, down one leg and up her belly to pass across a hardening nipple as she imagined sharing the steamy tub with Matt. Weightless, she floated in the warmth, her body tingling. Slowly, she drew the cloth over her breasts and felt an accompanying ache begin to build deep within her belly.

Closing her eyes, she sank deeper under the water, drew her knees up, and skimmed the washcloth slowly up between her thighs. The water-weighted cloth pressed against her, and she gave herself up to the sensation, imagining Matt in the tub with her. . . .

A light rap sounded at the door.

"Livvy, how are you coming?"

Olivia dropped the washcloth and sat up in the tub. "I'm good."

She imagined her audience's reaction if she were to open the bathroom door, reach an arm out, and drag Matt inside so that she could have her way with him.

"Do you want some more champagne? I could top your glass off if you'd like."

She wanted to yell, "Fill her up," and knew she wouldn't be referring to her glass. Lying here naked with Matt a mere doorknob-turn away was doing funny things to her insides. And her brain. This was not good. "Um, no thanks. I'll be out soon."

With water cascading down her body, she stood and wrapped herself in a towel.

"I'm completely shriveled," she hollered.

When he didn't respond, Olivia released the drain lever with one toe and stepped out of the tub. Opening the bathroom door, she peeked out to make sure the coast was clear, and finding the hallway empty, she tiptoed the few steps to her room.

She dressed quickly but with care—repinning her hair into a smoother French twist and applying both eyeliner and mascara along with a swipe of blush high on both cheekbones. Then she painted her lips poppy pink and stepped into a fitted black halter dress.

In the middle of reaching into her underwear drawer, her gaze swung to the nightstand, and before she could really think it out, she was pulling out the Victoria's Secret bag so that she could shimmy into the black satin thong. *Uh-oh.*

Dropping the hem of the dress back into place, she stopped to study her reflection in the mirror. Outwardly, nothing seemed different. On the outside, she looked like the calm and collected Dr. Olivia Moore; but inside, under the black satin thong, she felt sexy and wanton and someone else entirely—a dangerous dichotomy unlikely to work to her advantage.

Olivia frowned at her thirty-year-old reflection. Subdued and decorous would see her through the evening far more safely than wild and uninhibited, and if she knew what was good for her, Matt would never suspect what she wore beneath the folds of her dress.

At his first glimpse of her, Matt's eyes lit up, and he gave an appreciative whistle. "Wow. There must have been something pretty potent in those bath bubbles."

Olivia blushed as she remembered just how potent

those bubbles had been. "It felt great, Matt. I never would have thought of it on my own."

He looked surprised by the admission, but then smiled, obviously pleased. "Here, have some more champagne while I go shower and change. I seem to smell a little more like dinner than I intended." He sent her a cheeky glance and an exaggerated wink. "Wouldn't want you to get confused about what to chomp down on first."

She smiled back and tried not to enjoy the way he was looking at her. *Subdued and decorous,* she repeated to herself as the soft fabric of her dress swished against the bare flesh of her behind. Her lips twitched up at the thought. "Go. Is there something I can stir or turn while you're gone?"

"Nope. But you can put some music on if you'd like. I'll be back in a flash."

"Good. I'm starving. And I'm not sure how long I can control myself." *Wasn't that the truth?*

"Fair enough. If I'm not back before the timer goes off, the hors d'oeuvres are all yours."

Olivia sipped champagne and wandered around the room. With a small wave to the Webcam, she knelt down next to the CD player and rifled through the CDs Matt had brought with him, surprised to discover how closely his taste mirrored hers.

The black balloon bouquets and "Over the Hill" sign still drew her gaze, but with a little effort she managed to focus on the flower arrangements instead. Matt had moved one of them to the center of the kitchen table, which he'd set for two.

She spent the rest of her time pacing and trying not to picture Matt naked in the next room, rubbing soap all over his hard-muscled body. Or showering it off under the pulsing stream of hot water. Or skimming the towel over every inch of his awesome body. *Oops.*

Olivia stopped in front of the small mirror on the foyer wall and glared at her reflection. "Okay, you. Repeat after me," she commanded. "Do not touch the chef under any circumstances. Do not get any closer to him than absolutely necessary. And whatever you do, don't drink too much."

Olivia picked up her wineglass and took another long, soothing sip. Her nerves vibrated just under her skin, and the only thing that seemed to interrupt the hum was the ingestion of wine—a very temporary fix that required constant repetition and put a great big hole in her plan to keep her distance.

So far she'd maintained the maximum clearance possible given the shortage of space, but she'd caught the amused look on Matt's face enough times now to suspect he knew just how hard she was working to keep it that way. Worse, it was becoming increasingly difficult to remember just why maintaining that distance was so important.

Somewhere along the way, they'd finished the second bottle of champagne and started on the burgundy Matt had insisted would complement the upcoming meal. Smoothing the hem of her dress over her knees, she sat up straighter on her barstool and made a stab at conversation. "Is this spanakopita?"

Matt picked up one of the triangles of puffed pastry and popped it into his mouth. "Umm-hmm. The Greek deli near the station sent them over as a birthday treat for you. Actually, a lot of our advertisers are wanting in on your thirtieth birthday."

"I can't tell you what aging before a national audience does for a woman's ego."

"Just think of yourself as a fine wine, Olivia. You're becoming richer, more full-bodied."

Funny, how his voice could go all hot and sexy without any warning like that. Olivia lifted her wineglass, drained it in one long swallow, and felt the resulting warmth seep through her.

"And?" she demanded.

"And what?"

She tried to figure out why he was being so charming, but her brain didn't seem to be up to the task. The warmth infused her and began to seep outward to her limbs.

"No cracks? No jokes about my age? Just 'You're like a fine wine'?"

"Me? Make jokes about your age?" He smiled. "I happen to think the wine analogy fits. You were cute at twenty-one, Olivia, but you wear thirty very well." His gaze swept over her, and her flesh reacted as if it were his fingers that trailed across it.

Looking for a distraction, Olivia picked up the bottle of wine sitting on the counter and poured herself another glass.

Spellbound, she watched his large, capable hands arrange the duck breast medallions on the plate. His fingers were long and supple, and for a moment she allowed herself to remember the feel of them skimming over her skin, urging her on to places she'd never been before or since. She took a gulp of wine and watched him place whipped garlic potatoes and blanched white asparagus next to the duck.

"Wow," she said. "I feel like I'm in a five-star restaurant."

"Only zee best for zee birthday girl." He winked and nodded her toward the table. "If you'll bring the wine and our glasses, we can get started."

Olivia picked up the half-empty bottle in one hand and her own mysteriously empty glass in the other. She felt warm and wonderful and increasingly comfortable with the glow that enveloped her. Being thirty felt considerably less traumatic than it had that morning.

She unfolded the napkin, laid it in her lap, and scooted her chair in closer to the table. When she looked up, her wineglass was once again full, and Matt was passing a basket of rolls in her direction.

"*Bon appétit.*" His dark eyes were warm. Very warm.

Since her mouth was dry, Olivia took a small sip of wine to facilitate swallowing, and when he continued to study her, she took another.

"*Bon appétit* to you, too," she managed.

Dragging her gaze from his, Olivia turned her attention to her plate. Her knife sliced easily through the duck's butter-soft breast, and she lifted the first forkful to her mouth while Matt watched. The exquisite mingling of port wine sauce and smoky duck flooded over her tongue to tease her taste buds, and she forgot all about Matt for a moment while she lost herself in the sensation.

"Mmmm." Eyes closed, Olivia savored the perfectly blended flavors, enjoying the taste that lingered in her mouth even after she swallowed. "God, that's good."

She opened her eyes to see him light up at the compliment, and she couldn't help noticing how the candlelight added depth and shadow to the already arresting planes and angles of his face.

"Glad you like it. I've always been partial to duck, though it can be a bit tricky."

"Well, you've certainly mastered this one." She took another sip of wine and continued to meet his gaze full-on. His eyes were like two tumblers of whiskey, amber brown and ready to drown in. She felt a delicious tightening deep in her belly that had nothing to do with digestion, and she felt her hazy glow expand in size to encompass them both.

They ate in silence for a few moments, but the silence was mostly companionable, if you didn't count the depth charges going off in her stomach.

Matt lifted his wineglass and took a drink. His didn't seem to be going empty anywhere near as often as hers was, and she wondered idly if his glow was keeping pace with hers.

"So what happened with you and Joe?" he asked.

"James."

"What?"

"His name was, I mean his name is, James." She eyed her wineglass and the untouched tumbler of ice water sitting next to it, torn.

"Okay, so what happened with James?"

Olivia reached for the wine. "I've been living with you for five days now, Matt; I know you read the newspapers. Surely you know the whole sordid tale."

"I tend to read news, not gossip columns. Why don't you tell me what happened?"

She took a sip of wine and finished the last of her potato before dabbing at the corner of her mouth with her napkin. "It wasn't anything out of the ordinary. Just your usual unwelcome brush with infidelity."

She watched him watch her and was surprised to find no smirk on his face or laughter in his eyes.

"So everything was great and then, boom, out of the blue he's sleeping with someone else?"

Funny that no one had ever asked her that question before. Even she had avoided looking too closely at what had come before the unavoidable knowledge of the affair. Good old dependable unexciting James, chosen because he seemed the direct antithesis of both her father and Matt, had turned out to be so not what she had expected.

"No, I just wasn't paying attention." Because she'd been so busy burying herself in work and trying not to admit that supposedly safe and solid added up to dull and boring. "I'm a therapist. I help other people find answers, but I seem stupendously unable to do the same for myself."

She took another swig of wine and told herself that the warmth in Matt's eyes was also wine induced. Still, she felt something stir between them. "It would appear I'm somehow not enough for the men in my life."

"Ah, Livvy. You're more than enough for any man. You've just had the misfortune to attract selfish oafs who can't leave you alone even when they know they should."

"Hmmph." A lethargy invaded her limbs and she couldn't seem to tear her gaze from his face. It was a fine face, good and true and strong. And at the moment it was completely focused on her. "My mother hasn't been enough for my father for almost thirty years now, which makes me think it might be hereditary."

She blinked and looked at her wineglass, aghast at the truths slipping out of her mouth, and unable to comprehend how her glass could be empty again. She reached for the bottle, intent on maintaining the warm, hazy glow that had wrapped so snugly around them, but Matt put a hand on top of hers.

"I can't believe I'm saying this, Olivia, but maybe you should take it a little easier on the wine."

She tingled at his touch. "You think I've had too much to drink?"

"I know you've had more than you're used to."

"Never felt more in control in my life," she said. She tried to wink at him, but her facial features no longer seemed to work independently. "You should consider going into counseling. You're not bad to talk to."

"Now I know you've had too much." His smile caused her heart to perform a funny sort of flip-flop. Her limbs felt too heavy for her body, and she could hear a loud whooshing in her ears, which seemed to be the blood rushing through her brain.

"Except for JoBeth's boyfriend. You're making a real mess of that."

"Am I now?" He didn't seem at all upset by her criticism. In fact, his voice felt as warm and wonderful as a caress.

Olivia picked up her empty wineglass and tilted it around, searching for something to drink. She eyed the little that was left in the bottle with disappointment. "Are you going to drink that last bit?"

She squinted her eyes to try to get rid of the extra Matt

swaying in her line of vision, as the roaring in her ears grew louder. Lifting her napkin to dab daintily at her lips, she somehow jammed it into the side of her nose, then stared at the napkin in confusion as it drifted out of her fingers and fluttered to the floor.

"Oops." That definitely couldn't be her giggling, because she detested women who giggled. Enunciating very carefully in an effort to maintain some semblance of dignity, she said, "Can you excuse me for just a minute? I seem to have dropped something."

Then her bones melted beneath her skin, and without warning, she slid off her chair and landed in a heap at Matt Ransom's feet.

18

Matt watched her disappear, and for a minute or two he sat and chewed, assuming she'd surface when she found her napkin. By the time he finished his last bite of potato, it occurred to him that she might be injured or unable to get up.

Since his back was already to the Webcam, he slid his chair back and lowered himself to the floor, out of camera range, where he found Olivia sitting beneath the table, her napkin in her lap.

"You okay?"

"Absolutely." She waved the napkin airily at him but made no move to get up.

"Olivia?"

"Umm-hmm?"

"We're sitting on the floor under a table."

She nodded solemnly, her eyes wide.

"You realize this is not usual after-dinner behavior?"

" 'S'okay. I don't feel usual." Her smile was crooked and went straight to his heart.

As he took in the surprising sensation, she got on all fours and crawled over to sit beside him. She sat so close he could feel the shallowness of her breathing and read the intention in her wine-clouded green eyes even before she tilted her lips up toward his.

She kissed him, and his entire body hardened. Without thought he reached out and pulled her closer.

Looping her arms around his neck, she crawled into his lap, where she pressed her breasts against his chest.

"God, Livvy."

She took his hand in hers and guided it up under her dress, where he discovered just how little separated him from the place he most wanted to be.

He groaned. "Tell me you're not wearing the thong."

"Sorry," she breathed in his ear, though it was clear she wasn't. "Didn't mean for you to know."

He ran his hands over the smoothly rounded buttocks, down the silky thighs, and back up to cup the triangle between her legs. With his thumb he manipulated the sliver of satin until she moaned and the strip of material grew damp.

Hot and hard, Matt went up on his knees to bring their bodies closer together and banged his head against the kitchen table—knocking some sense into his lust-filled brain.

"Olivia." With his lips welded to hers, his voice was muffled, and he had to open his mouth wider to try again. At which point she slipped her tongue through the opening to search for his.

"This is not a good idea." He must have hit his head harder than he'd realized, because that seemed to be his voice sounding the note of reason.

Olivia didn't bother to respond verbally, but her nonverbal responses couldn't have been clearer. Her thumb traced the curve of his ear, while her tongue found and parried with his. Her breasts splayed across his chest, their hardened nipples pressing intimately against him, until all he could think of was pushing her onto her back and driving himself inside her. Under the table. In the middle of the kitchen. With an Internet audience wondering where in the hell they'd gone.

Matt halted the kiss. He bracketed her face in his hands and turned it up to his. She was all of the things he'd been angling for all week: dazed, confused, and totally hot for him. So why did he feel so reluctant to take advantage of the opportunity?

He stared down into the trusting green eyes and groaned inwardly. "Olivia, we need to stop this right now."

"But I want you," she mumbled, somehow managing to sound more sad than surprised. "Always wanted you."

He saw her eyes lose their focus and watched her head tilt sideways. Then she yawned, tucked her head up against his chest like a kitten seeking comfort, and went completely limp in his arms.

Some of the starch went out of him then, too. The pounding of his heart slowed, the heat that possessed him cooled, and the throbbing in his loins dulled to a mild ache. He stroked her hair and dropped a kiss onto the silken top of her head. As she snuggled more tightly against his chest, he gathered her in close.

Then he did the only thing he could think of on the spur of the moment: He dragged her out from under the table and slapped her gently on both cheeks while mouthing, "Olivia, are you all right?" for the benefit of the Internet audience. Then he slung her over his shoulder like a sack of potatoes and carted her off to her bedroom, where he managed to rouse her long enough to pour some water and two Tylenol down her throat before tucking her into bed.

JoBeth stopped beside Dawg's table. Reaching into the pocket of her apron, she asked, "What'll it be? I've got Zantac, Pepcid AC, or the old standby." She dropped a packet of Alka-Seltzer onto the tabletop.

"Can I take all of them?"

"Don't see why not. You've had everything else on the menu."

Dawg put a fist to his mouth and belched discreetly. "That I have, darlin'. And I have to admit I'm a mite full."

"Dawg Rollins, you were ready to explode two hours ago. I've never seen a man pack away that much food in one sitting."

"That's what desperation'll do for you. Thank God you're off the clock. I don't think I could have held that table for another minute."

"Well, Ina's bound to wonder what's going on, but I doubt she'll complain about a ticket this big. I've got a doggie bag packed for you to take home." She grinned evilly as she pressed the brown paper sack into his hands. "In case you get hungry in the middle of the night or something."

Dawg groaned. "It *is* the middle of the night, and even if it weren't, I don't plan to eat ever again."

They walked together out into the empty parking lot, and JoBeth looked around in confusion. Her car sat under the streetlamp where she always parked when she worked nights, and the cook's battered pickup sat a few spaces from it, but there was no sign of Dawg's bright red Jeep.

She eyed him suspiciously. "You don't look like a man who thinks his ride has been stolen. What's going on?"

"Had a friend drop me."

"Oh, really?"

"Now don't get that angry tone going, JoBeth. I knew I wasn't leaving the diner without you, and I didn't see any reason to juggle cars."

"You are entirely too sure of yourself, Dawg. If you think you can *eat* your way back into my good graces, you are sadly mistaken."

"All I'm hoping for is a chance to talk, JoBeth. I spent more than six hours eating; don't you think I've earned the right to be heard?"

JoBeth took out the keys to her twelve-year-old Cadillac. "Fine. I'll drive while you talk. But don't even be thinking romance."

"Get real, woman. I've been eating for six hours, I don't have a romantic inkling in my body."

He held the driver's door open for her like he always did, and JoBeth brushed by him to take her seat. Outwardly she remained cool, but her insides felt all warm and gooey. The man had eaten a refrigeratorful of food just to be near her; in her book it didn't get much more romantic than that.

The Cadillac caught on the second try, and JoBeth gave it a little extra gas before putting it into gear.

"Don't forget to take the car in to Joe for servicing. He told me he thought he could take care of that starter for you."

"I won't forget, Dawg."

She drove through the parking lot to Magnolia, where she took a left and merged into traffic. Even at this time of night, people in Atlanta seemed to be on the run. She flipped the radio on to WTLK, and for a startling moment Matt Ransom's voice filled the car. She grimaced, and when Dawg didn't comment, she turned the radio off. The last thing she wanted to hear right now was whatever stupid thing Ransom might have to say.

She drummed her fingers on the steering wheel. "So. What did you wait so many hours to tell me, Dawg? It's late, and I'm ready to call it a night."

"I thought it might be time to talk about marriage."

JoBeth's heart slammed into her chest. Was this the conversation she'd been waiting for all this time? She smoothed her hair behind her ears and licked her suddenly dry lips.

"You know, the concept of it and all."

JoBeth exhaled the breath she'd been holding and felt her shoulders slump. That didn't sound like the beginning of any marriage proposal she'd ever heard of.

"I've never talked too much about my marriage to Suzy. I don't even like to think about it. But you need to understand why I feel the way I do."

Dawg kept his eyes on the road in front of them. When she looked over at him, all she could see was the strong beak of a nose with its extra bump, and the careful set of his lips.

"I was just out of college when I got married. I'd made a name for myself at the University of Georgia, and all I could see ahead was a life of football and more millions than a man can count. With a woman who loved me by my side."

JoBeth heard the hurt in his voice and wondered which loss bothered him more, the woman or the career.

"It all started out great. You know I ended up here in Atlanta with the Falcons. Had a big church wedding. Suzy found us a house and decorated it, gave parties, met up with me on the road. She loved being the wife of a professional football player."

"And that bothered you?"

"Hell, no. I loved it, too. But you see, I thought she loved me for *me*, that the NFL career was just kind of icing on the cake, you know?"

JoBeth sat silent, her eyes on the road before her, her attention focused completely on Dawg.

"Then I got my knee stomped on during that game in Miami. I knew it was over even before they carried me off the field." He shook his head at the memory. "My professional career lasted one year and one week—must be one of the shortest in NFL history. And my marriage didn't even make it two months more than that."

"She couldn't adjust to your change of career?"

"Adjust?" His voice rang with disgust. "She never even tried to adjust. She married a professional athlete, and I wasn't one anymore. She hung around just long enough for the doctors to confirm I'd never play again, then she hitched her star to another player's wagon."

JoBeth reached a hand out to squeeze Dawg's. She wanted to pull him against her breast and stroke his poor head until he felt better, but she managed to resist.

"I swore then that I wouldn't make the same mistake twice. I've told you that I love you, JoBeth. I've told you more times than I've ever told any woman. You have to know that it's true."

"You have. And I'm not accusing you of lying. But it's just not enough anymore."

She pulled up in front of Dawg's house and put the car in park, letting the engine idle in the early morning darkness. She'd thought she'd spend the rest of her days in this house with Dawg, imagined raising their children there together. She fought back the moisture pressing against her eyelids and drew a long, shaky breath.

When he reached out to take her face in his large capable hands, she tilted her head to rub against one callused palm, reveling in its gentle strength. She'd miss everything about him: his quiet steadfastness, his fierce protectiveness, the way his body completed hers. She was her best self when she was with him, but she wouldn't settle for scraps any longer.

"I love you, too, Dawg. But I can't waste any more time or breath trying to convince you that I'm worth marrying. If you can't tell the difference between me and Suzy, then that's your loss."

She tilted her face out of his grasp and turned to look out the windshield, unable to stare into the blue of his eyes a second longer.

He reached out a hand to turn her face back toward his, and she forced herself to shrug it off.

"All right, then, let's just start fresh," he said. "Let me take you out tomorrow afternoon. We can go shoot some pool and have a pizza at Mario's afterward, just like we did on our first date. All I'm asking for is time."

JoBeth turned to face him then, forcing herself to look him square in the eye, steeling herself against the turbulence that she saw. She summoned all her resources to keep her voice steady, though she couldn't totally eliminate the quiver of regret. "I'm not available tomorrow, Dawg. I've accepted a date with someone else, and I think it would be best if we said our goodbyes now."

She watched the emotions flit across his face: the surprise followed by outrage and, ultimately, by an almost comical look of disbelief. "You're going out with someone else?"

"Yes, I am."

"Another guy? You're going out with another guy?"

"Yes, I believe I already said that."

"Well, if that doesn't beat all." He drew his hand back and ran it through his close-cropped blond hair. "Here I am dredging my guts up to try to make you understand where I'm coming from, and you're going out with someone else."

His eyes narrowed. "This is a payback for Emmylou, isn't it?"

"No. It's not a payback. It's a date. Period. If we're not going to be together, then we need to look for people better suited to what we want."

"Right." He opened the car door and slid out, leaning back in through the open window after he slammed the Cadillac door shut. "I guess that's it then. You go your way and I'll go mine."

It all sounded so logical and correct. So why did she feel so crummy? And why did the expression on Dawg's face make her want to climb out of the car and wrap her arms around his great hulk of a body?

He stood there for what felt like forever and ended up being nowhere near long enough. Then he tapped his fist on the hood of the car and offered her a crooked smile. "You'd best go on then, JoBeth. 'Cause if you stay here a minute longer, I'm going to carry you up to the house and have my way with you. You know that, don't you?"

She closed her eyes and tried to swallow back the feelings his words dredged up in her. She couldn't think of anything she wanted more than to feel his big hands move over her in that surprisingly gentle way he had. She craved the completion that came when he eased himself deep inside her and made her whole. She longed to give in and feel all those things one more time. But even as she had the thought, she knew that if she allowed him to lay so much as a finger on her, she'd never find the strength to leave.

She slipped the transmission into drive, blinked back a fresh crop of tears, and whispered, "You take care of yourself now, Dawg. You hear?"

And then she pressed her foot to the accelerator and drove right out of Dawg Rollins's life.

19

No," Matt said for the hundredth time. "Olivia just did a little too much celebrating. I'm sure she'll be fine by morning."

Amazing how preoccupied his listeners were with Olivia's well-being. Virtually every one of his callers had inquired after her health or begged for intimate details. They'd all either seen or heard about the proper Dr. Moore "unbending" on her milestone birthday; but while her dignity might have suffered slightly, her reputation was still intact. And it was his own damn fault.

Only he had witnessed the determination with which she crawled into his lap and her all-too-successful efforts to rouse him. And then when he'd had the chance to turn the camera on her and squash her once and for all, what had he done? Covered for her, that's what. He'd acted like she was ill and carted her off to bed, going so far as to come right back out of her room so there'd be no speculation. What the hell was wrong with him?

For four long hours, he bantered with callers while he fought off images of Olivia in the black satin thong.

Finally it was time to sign off and he was able to turn the controls over to Ben.

Still on headphones, he started to pack up his things.

"Great show, Matt," said Ben. "I haven't been able to get anything out of T.J. or the consultant about what the research is saying, but I'm sure this show will put us back on top with the popular vote."

"Thanks, Ben. Everybody was definitely fired up tonight."

"Yeah." Ben cleared his throat. "Speaking of 'fired up,' do you really think Dr. O is okay?"

"I'm sure she'll be her old bushy-tailed self by morning." Matt started to remove his headphones.

"But nobody's heard a peep out of her since you . . . since nine-thirty. Aren't you going to check on her?"

Actually, Matt was planning to do exactly that, though he doubted Olivia would appreciate anyone knowing it. "Didn't anyone ever tell you you're too young to be such a worrywart?"

"I think one or two people may have mentioned it." Ben's voice turned conspiratorial. "Do you want me to adjust the camera so you can check without everybody knowing?"

"How would you do that?" Matt asked.

"Well, the camera's remote is here in the control room. Crankower monitors it a lot of the time, and all of the producers are supposed to keep an eye out during their shifts. All you've got is the power cable."

Hmmm. The power cable. The old on, off. Matt stroked his chin and thought about the possibilities. "Thanks for the offer, man, but I'm sure Olivia's fine. I'm going to unwind a little bit, and then I'll probably just call it a night."

Matt shot his most innocent look up at the camera lens as he took off his headphones. Then, to throw off anyone who might be watching, he puttered around for a while.

He blew out the candles still flickering on the table and poked around the kitchen long enough to bore to tears anyone watching. Then he stretched out on the couch and read for another thirty minutes, almost putting himself to sleep in the process.

At 3:00 A.M., when he figured anyone still watching would be too glassy-eyed to notice, Matt ambled over to the entertainment armoire. Careful not to look down, he used his foot to gently work the power cable away from the wall.

When he had a sizable loop around his shoe, he turned away from the armoire, stepped forward, and pulled the cord out of its socket.

For appearances, he stumbled slightly and made a point of not looking over his shoulder to watch the monitor go dark. It seemed important to be able to claim ignorance later, though why he felt compelled to protect Olivia's reputation was a question he refused to ponder.

Unwatched for the first time in five days, Matt walked purposely toward Olivia's room. Once through the doorway, he moved to the bed for a closer look and immediately wished he hadn't.

Olivia lay on her side, her dress rucked up around her waist. His gaze followed the tempting trail from delicate ankle, up lightly muscled calf, across sculpted thigh to the smooth white swell of a nicely rounded buttock.

One bare forearm disappeared upward beneath the pillow on which her head rested, while the other hung limp across her waist. Her breasts strained against the clingy black material of her halter top, filling it to overflowing.

Olivia moaned in her sleep and rolled onto her back, throwing both arms out wide and opening her eyes. Matt sucked in his breath and sank down on the edge of the bed.

Even heavy with sleep, Olivia's green eyes carried an awareness of him that hiked his pulse up another notch. As he settled down beside her, the confusion that had clouded them gave way to alarm.

"What are you doing here?"

"I wanted to make sure you were all right."

"Good grief, Matt ..." She went up on her elbows and turned her head toward the bedroom door.

"It's okay." He reached out to smooth the dress back down to her knees. "The Webcam suffered a mysterious accident. No one saw me come in here. And no one will see me leave."

She collapsed back down onto the bed, and he could almost hear her trying to kick her brain back into action.

His own brain and all of his senses were full of Olivia. She was the magnet that never failed to draw him, and as he stared down into the green depths of her eyes, he realized there was no way in hell he was leaving this room without making her aware of at least one elemental truth.

"I don't know what it is, but you do something completely ..." He tried to find the right word and failed. ". . . visceral to me. And I know I do the same to you."

Olivia went still.

"I want to make love to you. Right now. Right here."

He reached out to caress the corner of her mouth with his thumb. "I'm tired of being this close to you and not having you."

He bent down and brushed his lips over hers. "And I think you want to make love to me for the same reason. Not because you've had too much to drink and can't help yourself, or because you're thirty. But because you want to."

She regarded him silently.

"It's your call, Livvy. I want you, but what happens next is completely up to you."

Olivia slipped off the last bonds of sleep and wine to stare up into Matt's assessing brown eyes. Her brain had cleared enough to comprehend what he was saying, and she could feel her blood beginning to boil. Not because he assumed she wanted him—he was, unfortunately, completely right about that—but because he was trying to make her admit it.

She sat up, bringing her face in line with his. "You're going to force me to decide?"

She put her hands on his shoulders. "What's wrong with you? Have you forgotten how to get a woman drunk and take advantage of her? I've been responsible my entire life. I have always done the right thing, the well-considered, logical thing. And now, after thirty years of toeing the line, I'm going to be denied this one perfectly good opportunity to hide behind alcohol and be swept away by . . . by . . . blinding passion?"

She shook him. "How dare you?"

Matt laughed. "Are you telling me you'd prefer drunken groping under a kitchen table to getting the attention you deserve?"

Olivia jumped off the bed and turned her back on him to pace the narrow confines of the room. "You are so dense!"

She paced for a few seconds while she worked up a good head of steam. She'd dreamed about this man for most of her adult life. For five days she'd been actively fantasizing about this very possibility, and what did he say to her? *I'm tired of waiting, so let's hop in the sack!*

He wasn't even allowing her time to worry about whether reality could compare with the memories she'd hoarded. Or how in the world she would find the strength to deny herself the thing she wanted most.

He stood in the middle of the room, next to the bed. "Come here, Miss 'I Am Woman Hear Me Roar.' "

She made a military pivot and marched back to face him.

"Your time is up," Matt said.

When she just stood there glaring at him, he pulled his shirt up over his head and dropped it on the floor.

"Oh." Her gaze fell to the broad shoulders, the wide expanse of chest, the arrow of dark hair beckoning downward. As she watched him unbuckle his belt, she realized that the pounding in her veins was no longer a result of anger.

"What'll it be, Olivia?" He smiled a lazy, sensuous smile that turned her bones to butter. "You still want to bite my head off?"

Boy, did she ever! And she wanted to do a whole lot of other stuff, too.

She took a step closer. "My listeners *are* wondering whether you're a brief or boxer kind of guy."

"Well then." He cocked his head and moved his hands

away from the waistband of his pants. "Let's conduct a little audience research."

Olivia Moore did something then that she'd never done before in her life. Tired of thinking, tired of doing the right thing, tired of denying herself what she wanted most—she just reached up in her brain and like a metaphoric hand on a light switch, she flipped the damn thing off.

Then she reached for the snap of his pants.

20

Matt and Olivia lay spoonlike, their naked bodies tucked into each other, their breathing and heartbeats eerily in sync. With her backside wedged against his front, and the top of her head jammed up into his chin, Matt could feel the rise and fall of her chest beneath his arm as she burrowed deeper against him.

He let his fingers skim over the warm silk of her breasts and breathed in the scent of lovemaking that still clung to her skin.

Olivia moaned and pressed her fanny tighter against him, and Matt pressed a sleepy kiss to the hollow of her shoulder.

It had taken turning thirty and an impressive amount of alcohol to unleash the passion beneath the controlled facade, but once she let go there was no one like her.

Matt swept the tips of his fingers up one bare arm and back down to rest on the curve of her hip.

She'd tried to use wine to drown the chemistry between them; then she'd tried to use the wine to allow it—and ended up under the kitchen table.

He smiled slowly over the annoyance in her eyes when

he'd forced her to admit she wanted him. But once she'd given in to it, they'd made love for hours, their bodies reconnecting like parts of some not-quite-forgotten whole. Even now, they fit perfectly together, two spoons lined up snugly in the drawer. It was amazing how entirely right it felt to wake with Olivia in his arms.

Matt's eyes flew open at that alien and alarming thought. A heartbeat later a cell phone rang shrilly beside the bed.

His mind still on Olivia, he flipped open the phone. " 'Lo."

"Matt?" Diane Lowe's shocked whisper carried the impact of a pail of cold water. "Why are you answering Olivia's cell phone? Is she all right? What happened to the Webcam?"

"Whoa." Matt sat up in bed, trying to gather his wits. "Hold on a minute. I'll be right with you."

He covered the mouthpiece of the phone with one hand and used the other for an exploratory nudge of Olivia's shoulder. She yawned and rolled over onto her back with her eyes squinched shut.

Matt uncovered the mouthpiece and brought the phone back up to his ear. "Olivia's a little under the weather right now. I'm sure she'll be fine in a little while."

"She doesn't have a little while, Matt. She goes on the air in fifteen minutes. Let me speak to her."

Shit. Matt looked down at Olivia. Her blonde hair swirled over the pillow in total disarray, and her body had spread across the space he'd just vacated. He wanted to drop a kiss on her left breast and then work his way down to the heart-shaped freckle on the inside of her right thigh.

Instead, he reached a hand out and shook her a little harder. Her naked body did some really wonderful things, but her eyes remained shut. "Too tired," Olivia muttered. "Have to sleep."

"She, um, can't come to the phone right now, Di."

"What have you done to her, Matt? Is she all right?"

"She'll be fine. Why don't you just—"

"Oh, no you don't," Diane hissed. "You're not going to get away with this."

"There's nothing to get away with. I told you she's just not feeling—"

"Fine."

He could hear the panic in Diane's voice now, but really didn't think Olivia would appreciate his describing exactly what kind of condition she was in.

"You talk to Charles, then. He's right here cackling in my ear."

Matt sighed. He looked down at the sleeping woman beside him, taking in the satisfied smile on her lips—the smile he'd put there and kept there throughout the wee hours of the morning.

"Yeah, Charles. What's the problem?"

"Problem? No problem." Charles's gleeful tone brought home the possible repercussions of the situation more forcefully than Diane's panic had.

Matt almost laughed. Here he was in the exact position he'd worked toward most of the week, and all he could think of was protecting Olivia . . . and keeping that smile on her lips. He heard Crankower's weasely voice on the other end of the line and knew he couldn't throw her to the wolves.

"Why don't you just plug that Webcam back in, Matt,

and then wake the woman in bed beside you," the weasel chortled. "I should have trusted you'd have some scheme up your sleeve."

Matt cradled the phone against his shoulder and tried to rouse Olivia, but she rolled over onto her side and drew her legs up beneath her. His gaze swept down the elegant curve of her naked back.

"Sorry to disappoint you, Crankower. There is no scheme. Just too much to drink and maybe a touch of"—this one was going to hurt—"food poisoning."

Matt walked around the bed and crouched down to peer into Olivia's face. She wore a dreamy expression, and she looked so peaceful he couldn't bring himself to haul her out of bed.

"So is she planning to do her show or what?"

"I'm not sure, Charles." Matt picked her dress up off the floor and tossed it on the bed. "I'll go into her room and see what she's decided. Hold on, okay?"

Feeling slightly foolish, he went over to her door and slammed it. With a groan, Olivia flipped over on her other side and pulled the covers up over her head. He stomped loudly across the bedroom floor for effect, then quietly tried to shake Olivia awake once more.

"Come on, Liv," he whispered. "You can do it. Just get up so you can do your show."

He could hear Olivia's muffled voice through the bedding.

"Can't." She balled up tighter. "I'm so tired."

Matt sat down on the side of the bed next to the mound of covers that was Olivia. "Charles? She's not feeling well." He ran a hand through his hair. "So, uh, we've decided to switch shows today."

"You what?"

"Yeah. We thought it would be a good gimmick, you know, to give our listeners a dose of a different perspective."

"You're going to do *Liv Live*?"

"Yep. I just over-slept, that's all. I'm not used to getting up this early."

"You're joking, right?"

"What, you don't think I can keep a bunch of women entertained?" Matt made a point of sounding offended.

Charles laughed aloud. Matt could almost see him rubbing his hands together in anticipation of the rating points. Of course, just whose points they'd be was an interesting question.

"Oh, no, Matt. If anyone can keep a group of women happy, it's you. Just do me a favor, will you?"

"Sure, Charles."

"Don't forget to plug the Webcam back in. I don't want to miss a minute of this."

"Good morning, everybody. Welcome to *Liv Live*, or maybe we should call it *Matt Live*. Actually, I'm more like semi-alive this morning. You're going to have to bear with me. The good doctor and I have decided to switch shows for the day. You can catch her tonight at ten doing her version of *Guy Talk*."

Matt punched up the theme song, left it up full as he marshaled his thoughts, and took the music back down.

"This is all a little new to me. But I'm here and ready to, uh," he cleared his throat, "discuss your problems."

He looked down at the computer screen to check the list of waiting callers, but there were none.

"All right. No wimping out now." He drummed his fingers on the table, but nothing happened. Not a name. Not a blip on the screen. He didn't know if it was Diane's doing or if there just weren't any women out there who wanted to speak to him.

"Right. Okay. So I don't have the doctor's credentials, but I do have something better." He paused while he tried to figure out what he had that Olivia didn't. All he could come up with was a penis.

"I'm a guy. I can tell you what men really think. And what they want." He paused again for emphasis. "I'm here to answer your questions. Truthfully. Completely. Anything you want to know about the man in your life and how he thinks, I can tell you. Start dialing."

Matt punched up the commercial break and went to put on a much-needed pot of coffee. When he got back to his seat, the monitor was full of waiting callers.

"Okay, that's better. Let's start with caller number one. Rita M., you're on the line."

Rita sounded nervous and very Southern. "I'd really feel a lot more comfortable talking to Dr. Moore about this."

"Well, you can call back tonight between ten and two, or you can go ahead and give me a shot. How bad can it be?"

"Okay." There was a brief pause and then, "I went out with someone for the first time last week. And it was great and all. He made me feel really special."

"And the problem?"

"Well . . . he said he'd call, but he hasn't."

It didn't sound all that pressing to Matt, but it was, as they said, her dime. "All right, let's take a look at this. How many days has it been since your date?"

"Five. It's been five days, but I'm thinking maybe my answering machine is on the blink."

"Nope. Sorry, but if he were planning to call you, he would have done it by now."

"How do you know that?"

"Because I'm a guy. And because there's a sort of unwritten time limit in the guy handbook. If a male over the age of fifteen hasn't called within two or three days after a first date, he isn't going to."

"But he said he was going to call."

Matt shrugged. "I hate to be the one to break this to you, Rita, but 'I'll call you' is kind of like 'Have a nice day.' Nobody really cares whether you have a nice day or not. It's just an expression."

"But is there a chance he'll call?"

"After five days?" Matt shook his head. "No way in hell."

Matt moved on to the next call. "Okay, who's up next?" He cracked his knuckles and settled back in his chair, folding his hands behind his head. "This is Ransom. You're on the air, Marty."

"Hi, Matt." The caller responded with the upbeat cadence of a former cheerleader. "How are you this morning?"

"Just fine, darlin'. What's on your mind?"

"Well, it's my boyfriend's friends."

"Yeah?"

"Yeah. They keep dragging him to bars and strip joints."

"And he's complaining about this?"

"Well, not exactly." Some of the perkiness went out of her voice.

"And he'd rather be . . . where? The symphony?"

"Well . . ."

"The opening of a new gallery?"

"Well, I don't—"

"Dinner at your parents'?"

There was a protracted silence.

"Marty, sweetheart, wake up and smell the coffee. Unless your boyfriend has been bound and gagged, chances are he's a willing participant."

"But—"

"Men like strip clubs. That's why they exist. You know, naked women shaking their ta-ta's in your face? Guys love that stuff."

"But they go every week. He stuffs money in their . . . well, I *hope* he's only putting it in their garters."

"Marty, it's relaxation, an innocent taste of the unknown, a chance to unwind. A guy always appreciates a woman who understands that."

"When will Dr. O be back?"

"Tonight, sweetheart. But believe me, I know what I'm talking about. Dr. O may not recognize the value of strip clubs in male bonding, but I do. Give the guy a break."

Pleased, Matt waited out another batch of commercials—confirmation of *Liv Live*'s popularity—and walked over to the kitchenette to pour himself a cup of coffee.

He couldn't detect sound or movement from Olivia's room, which meant she must still be asleep. He had no doubt she'd have been out of bed and dressed in a heartbeat if she could hear him doing her show. Truth was, he was starting to enjoy himself. Hell, you didn't even have to stop and think about this stuff, you just told everybody the way things were and moved on to the next caller. He was practically performing a public service.

Matt took his coffee back to the control panel and sat down to wait out the end of the last commercial.

As woman after woman called to complain about the behavior of husband, boyfriend, or lover, he began to wonder how men and women ever managed to connect at all. Women obviously didn't see things the way men did, and in his humble opinion, women wasted an inordinate amount of time worrying about how their relationships were going.

Other than trying to let women down easy, he'd never really stopped to think about what they might be feeling. And he'd certainly never fallen for any of their protestations of love for him. All he'd ever wanted was to have a good time.

His next caller was JoBeth, Dawg's girlfriend, and he could tell from her tight little hello that she was not a happy camper. "I just want you to know that I don't appreciate any of the advice you've given Dawg."

"Me? Up until today I've been very careful *not* to give advice. I just told him to stop sniveling and get on with his life."

"You made him feel like there was no reason to make a commitment."

"Hey, I just call 'em like I see 'em. It was not my intention to get in the middle of your life."

"Well, you're there. Smack dab in the center of it."

Matt ran a hand through his hair and rubbed the back

of his neck. He wouldn't have minded Olivia poking her head out about now.

"You told him to be a man and hang tough, Matt, whatever that means. Dawg Rollins loves me and I love him. And now we don't live in the same house, and in an hour I'm going to be eating barbecue with an old boyfriend." JoBeth's voice broke.

"Jeez, JoBeth. Don't cry."

"I'm not crying. I hate crying." She blew her nose. "It's just that everything's such a mess."

Her misery traveled through the phone line and all but smacked him in the face. Had he ever really thought about what his comments to Dawg might mean to this woman? No, of course not. He'd been flip, half-assed, and unwilling to be bothered with their personal problems. Now, dangling on the hook as he was, he forced himself to think about his response.

"Look, you just have to make the best of this situation. Dawg doesn't want to get married and you do. It's right to go out and try to get what you want."

"But, but, that's what Dr. O said."

"Well then, as strange as it feels to say so, Dr. O must be right."

There was a long pause.

"You okay, JoBeth?"

"Yeah." She gave a small sniff and an embarrassed little laugh. "Sorry to get so heavy on you. I just . . . I guess it's time to go get ready for my date."

Matt sank down in his chair and eyed the computer screen warily. *Diane,* he typed as calmly as he could, *I need another caller. Just make sure she isn't going to cry.*

21

___

Kevin Middleton was considerably shorter than JoBeth remembered. When he rose from his side of the picnic-style table in the back room of the Smokehouse Barbecue, she couldn't help noticing that he barely topped her five foot four inches. The hand he extended in greeting was also small, and JoBeth had the disturbing thought that she could probably outwrestle him if she had a mind to. She covered the thought with a quick smile.

"Hi, Kevin. It's good to see you."

"Same here, JoBeth. You sure are looking fine."

"Thanks." JoBeth slid onto the bench across from him and opened the menu the waitress handed her. She scanned the items briefly and then looked over the top of her menu at the man her parents had chosen for a son-in-law.

"I was sure sorry to hear about your folks. I always meant to get by and see them, but it just didn't seem . . ." His voice trailed off and JoBeth knew then that he hadn't forgotten the awkward end of their relationship, the long, dragged-out months during which Kevin and her parents lobbied for marriage while she stalled without understanding why.

Would she sit across a table from Dawg someday while he tried to recall what he'd seen in her? She pushed the thought firmly from her mind.

"They talked about you up until the very end," she said. Now there was your classic understatement. Through three years with Dawg they had never missed an opportunity to chastise her for what she'd thrown away. "They always thought you were the best thing that ever happened to me."

"Shows how purely intelligent they were."

She looked up quickly in surprise and was relieved to see a smile on his face.

"They were fine people." Kevin lifted the glass of sweet tea he'd ordered and held it out toward her like a salute. "I'm sorry for your loss."

They stared at each other for a long moment, taking each other's measure. JoBeth saw a medium-sized man of medium coloring with unremarkable brown eyes. There was nothing flashy about him, but she noticed he'd put himself together with care. The manicured fingernails and carefully pressed oxford shirt proclaimed him a man aware of the picture he presented, as did the freshly barbered hair, each strand perfectly in place.

Watching him converse with the waitress, JoBeth gave him points for the way he handled himself. He was friendly without passing over the line into flirtation, just as Dawg had always been. And when he placed his order, it was clear he knew his mind.

Kevin took a sip of his sweetened tea and then turned his attention back to her. He seemed less tentative than

he'd been when she'd first joined him, and JoBeth reminded herself that this lunch had to be awkward for
him, too.

"I haven't been to the Smokehouse in ages. Do Hank
and SandySue still own it?" she asked.

"They do. And I still handle all their accounting. They
opened a second location in Snellville, and there's talk
about franchising."

"You said this business would take off, and I guess you
were right." She was starting to remember a lot more
than that. There'd been lots of Thursday night dinners at
the Smokehouse as guests of Kevin's grateful client.
Sunday afternoons after church had been spent at her
parents'. "I'm thinking about going back to school to finish my business degree."

"Why, that's great, JoBeth. You always did have a good
head on your shoulders." He smiled and his features
sharpened. "Except, of course, when you dumped me."

JoBeth could feel the blush spread across her cheeks.
Both he and her parents had expected her to become Mrs.
Kevin Middleton; even she had assumed it would happen
one day.

"I never dumped you. I just wasn't ready to get married
back then." Lord, she sounded like Dawg. "I don't think I
understood how much that probably hurt you at the
time, and I'm sorry for that."

When their combo plates arrived, they ate quietly for a
while. In his own precise way, Kevin managed to put
away almost as much as Dawg, though he didn't seem to
expect to finish what she left on her plate, like Dawg did.

They made small talk as they ate, and while she didn't
feel any major fireworks in Kevin's company, she re-

minded herself that she'd had plenty of that with Dawg, and it had gotten her exactly nowhere.

Studying Kevin over what remained of her chopped pork, JoBeth thought about how funny life could be. The man across from her didn't make her heart race or her palms sweat, but she could tell by the way he was checking her out when he thought she wasn't looking, that he was still interested. And not just in her mind, either.

An hour into their "date" they split a slice of mud pie and nursed cups of coffee. She still wasn't dazzled, but had to admit that Kevin Middleton was a nice, solid man who would make someone a nice, solid husband. As it turned out, their minds appeared to be running along similar lines.

"You know, I wasn't sure what to think when you called me. I've been busy, I've been dating. Life's been pretty good," Kevin said.

JoBeth took the last bite of mud pie, chewing it carefully, taking her time with it while she tried to figure out where the conversation was headed.

She'd just put her hand over her coffee cup to discourage the last round of refills, when Kevin finally got to the point.

"But I've never found anyone I could imagine settling down with like I could imagine it with you."

JoBeth's gaze flew to his face.

"I'm thinking this whole thing could be fate's way of giving us another shot at a life together."

JoBeth tried to open her mouth to say something. She knew she should protest, speak up, do something. But Kevin Middleton had already taken the snap, and while she sat there openmouthed, he took the conversational ball and drop-kicked it right through her goalposts.

"We don't need to call the caterers right now or anything, JoBeth. But I think we should spend some time getting to know each other again."

He beamed at her, delighted, the dapper young accountant pinning down a workable plan for the future. "Why don't we spend tomorrow up at my lake house? I could invite a few neighbors over for supper."

His voice became an intimate whisper that did *not* make her heart go pitter-patter. "Or we can be completely antisocial and spend the day alone."

Charles Crankower sat in the WTLK control room watching Matt Ransom construct a turkey sandwich.

On Saturdays, WTLK, like most radio stations, ran at considerably less than its usual warp speed. Sales and administrative staffs were off, and other than promotional appearances and special events, only those responsible for putting programming on the air reported to work.

Here in the main control room, a lone engineer monitored the syndicated program that currently played on the air, but Charles's attention remained riveted to the Webcam's view of Matt and Olivia's current quarters.

Idly, he zoomed the camera in to the kitchen, giving up a big chunk of the living room in order to study Matt's movements more clearly.

He watched Ransom spread designer mustard on the insides of two slices of bread, then add a dash of mayonnaise, which turned the condiment into a muted shade of gold. He piled several deli slices of turkey on one piece of bread, added two slices of what looked like Swiss cheese, and topped it all with a whopping slice of tomato and a large leaf of lettuce.

After adding chips to the plate, Matt positioned a pickle spear on the other side, then opened a beer. Without bothering to put the ingredients away, he slid the plate and bottle across the counter and walked around to sit on a barstool.

Charles studied his subject through the camera lens and grinned to himself. Matt Ransom sported a look and posture any male over the age of twelve would recognize. In stark contrast to the tension that had practically ricocheted off him before last night, his movements now were loose and comfortable, and he had a loopy smile on his face.

Matt had definitely gotten laid, and based on the way he appeared to be humming under his breath, it had probably happened more than once.

Charles thought about that one for a minute, allowing himself to imagine Matt Ransom and the straitlaced Dr. O going at it. He felt almost giddy. The promotional opportunity of a lifetime was knocking on his door, and all he had to do was invite it in.

Exposing a sexual relationship between Matt and Olivia would be bad news for the doctor's reputation and career, but the amount of attention it would generate for the station was unlimited.

At first, people would tune in for the lurid excitement of it all. Then they'd be tuning in to find out why a respected therapist with a decidedly feminist attitude would put out for Atlanta's Bachelor of the Year. The fact that they'd known each other before and kept that information secret just made the whole thing juicier.

Charles watched Matt turn his back on the camera as he took his seat at the counter. He looked like he was settling in for a while, so Charles used the remote to zoom and pan the camera, changing the angle and scope at random, curious to discover what else the camera might reveal.

Interestingly enough, it was possible to make a sideways move to the right, tilt the lens down, and pick up a new sliver of room close to the French doors. Charles had assumed that area was out of range because the lens had to point the other way to pick up the largest slice of the room. He suspected the occupants of the cage no doubt thought of this as a safe spot, but the camera had an eyeball lens and could theoretically do a 360 if necessary.

Charles filed the information away for future use and zoomed back in to see if he could get close enough to identify the magazine Matt was reading.

Ransom's producer entered the control room just as Charles gave up on the tight shot. They eyed each other with suspicion.

"I hear you're going to be running the show for Dr. Moore tonight."

"Yep," Ben replied.

"Were you surprised when Matt did Dr. O's show?"

"Well, sort of." Ben looked like he might say something else, but apparently thought better of it.

"Any idea what she's going to do?" Charles asked.

"No. Matt says she's still a little under the weather. I think she's just going to field calls like he did."

"Come on, Ben. You and I both know the only weather that woman's been under is Hurricane Matt."

He heard the producer's reluctant bark of laughter. But then the kid bit his lip and looked away.

"The only thing I don't understand is why your boss is protecting her. He could have left that Webcam on and walked away with the whole enchilada."

"Maybe he's just got a little more class than you give him credit for."

"Oh, what? Matt Ransom doesn't kiss and tell? Puhlease! We're talking career here and beaucoup bucks. Matt is one of the most ambitious, competitive on-air talents I know. None of this makes any sense."

"Maybe he figures he can beat her fair and square. I've got the tally here, and after Matt's show last night and his guest stint this morning, the doctor's lead is down to almost nothing. She'd have to stand on her head naked tonight to pull ahead again."

Charles zoomed in on the doctor's closed bedroom door, trying to picture Dr. O resorting to such a thing. "Well, who knows. If she slept with Matt, standing on her head might not be such a stretch after all. Of course, the website votes don't mean squat compared to the consultant's report."

They didn't yet have the final report, but Charles knew the numbers had been phenomenal from day one of the remote. The press snapped up every morsel he fed them, and even the consultant had been walking around the station with a smile on his face.

The company was happy, T.J. was happy, and Charles knew that made him look good. But being a hero would be even better—and could keep the national office out of his hair for years to come.

It didn't matter whether Matt or Olivia won the ratings war, at least not to him. The station was a big winner no matter whom the audience preferred. But if he could engineer something totally unexpected, something bigger than the skirmishes Matt and Olivia had waged so far, his career would be made. And that, of course, was job number one.

Charles looked at the sliver of room again and tried to imagine how he could use it. He panned left to the furniture grouping and back again to the balcony, but nothing popped out at him and shouted, "Do this!" He stared at the screen a little longer and then moved the camera back to its wide-angle shot.

Charles told himself not to despair. He had a day and a half to come up with something he could use to his advantage, and his first move would be to take over the camera operation and monitoring full-time. Then, like a spider contemplating two juicy flies, he'd be ready when one of them stumbled into his web.

22

Thirty was too old for hangovers. Olivia buried her face in her pillow and drew her legs up into the fetal position. Reaching down to pull the sheet up over her head, she encountered bare skin and stopped in surprise. Keeping her eyes shut, she felt around for her pajamas and discovered she wasn't wearing them. Or anything else. *Shit*. Her thirtieth birthday came flooding back to her in graphic detail, and she cringed. Thirty should be too old for stupidity, too. But apparently it was not.

Fortunately, she appeared to be alone. Neither snores nor body warmth emanated from the other side of the bed, which meant Matt was definitely gone.

Head pounding, Olivia pried her eyes open and made a valiant attempt to bring the room into focus. She noted the closed door, the black dress lying in a heap on the bed (*shit*, again), and finally the clock beside the bed.

She squinted at the Roman numerals in an attempt to make some sense of them, certain there was no way they could be right. "Shit." She blinked and tried again, but the little and big hands continued to point to the four and the twelve.

Olivia rolled over on her back and turned her face carefully toward the window, where bright sunlight pushed its way past the drapes. If it was four o'clock in the afternoon, "shit" didn't begin to cover it.

Trying not to panic, Olivia got a grip on the cell phone next to the bed and hit speed dial. Her mouth was as dry as the Sahara, and her head pounded like the concrete beneath a jackhammer, but before she went in search of aspirin and the biggest glass of water she could find, she had to know the worst.

"Diane?"

"Mmmph." There was a gulp followed by the sound of cellophane being crumpled—all the earmarks of Diane's old standby, the Oreo Diet.

"Olivia. Is that you?"

"It's me."

"What happened? Are you okay?"

"I'm okay. But I think I need to ask the questions here." She grabbed her throbbing head with her free hand and braced herself. "Why didn't you wake me this morning?"

"I tried to."

"But?"

"But Matt answered your phone and he wouldn't let me speak to you."

The surge of disappointment was immediate. Obviously, he'd seen his chance and grabbed it. When had she started expecting something more from Matt Ransom?

"What happened to my show?"

"Why—"

"I can't believe I let this happen. It's the end of the remote, isn't it? Oh, God. I left a great big hole in the schedule. T.J. must be totally pissed off."

"Olivia?"

"I mean, how unprofessional can you get? I should have had my head examined before I agreed to be locked up in here with—"

"Dr. O?"

"What!" Olivia snapped.

"There wasn't a hole."

"What are you talking about?"

"Matt did your show."

"It's not nice to tease a woman teetering on the edge of a nervous breakdown, Diane. What are you saying?"

"Well, Matt said you were sick, maybe with food poisoning, and that you'd decided to switch shows for the day as a publicity gimmick."

"Matt did *Liv Live*?" Olivia's throbbing head tried to take it in. "You're telling me Matt Ransom went on the air and did my show?"

"Um-hm."

"They must have eaten him alive."

Diane laughed. "Don't tell him I said so, but in his own totally offensive way he was really pretty good."

"He gave advice? To women?"

"Yeah. He offered the male point of view and then decimated everyone with the horrible, though probably accurate, way men actually think."

Olivia smiled to herself at the picture. "You're kidding."

"No. I'm not."

"So I'm not totally disgraced and on my way out?"

"Well, everyone knows you had too much to drink. And the Webcam did get mysteriously disconnected in the middle of the night. But there's no proof of anything, and for some reason that no one can fathom, Ransom's not talking."

Incredible. Olivia closed her phone and propped herself up against the pillows, tucking the sheet up under her chin. The Matt Ransom she'd known in Chicago would have brought the camera right into the bedroom with them if it would bolster his career, but for some reason he'd refrained from exposing her. Literally.

The throbbing in her head dulled, probably because there wasn't enough room in there for both hangover and confusion. A memory of their lovemaking tried to elbow its way in, but she tossed it out, not willing to crowd her poor brain further.

Dressing hurriedly, Olivia considered the contradictions between the man she knew and the behavior he'd exhibited, but she couldn't come close to reconciling the two. Either Matt Ransom had turned over some wonderful new leaf, or he had something even more awful than professional embarrassment up his sleeve.

She found him in the living room lying on the couch with his eyes closed. The last inning of a baseball game played out on the TV, but Matt was in no position to notice.

Olivia went into the kitchen, found two Extra Strength Tylenol, and washed them down with an industrial-sized glass of water.

Her thirst quenched, she clicked off the television and took a seat on the second couch. For several minutes she watched him sleep and listened to him breathe while she attempted to sort through her contradictory feelings.

In sleep, Matt Ransom looked like a lot of things he

wasn't—namely sweet, vulnerable, and easy to handle. In fact, if it weren't for the shadowy stubble covering his face, he might have been a little boy tuckered out after a strenuous day of play. Except for all the really incredible stuff that started just below his neck.

Olivia let her gaze travel down the length of his lightly muscled torso, hesitating for just a moment at the waistband of his jeans before traveling on to the part of him with which she had become intimately reacquainted.

This was no child. And if he was tired, it was because he'd stayed up all night making love to her. Being with Matt turned her into someone she barely recognized. She wanted to hate him for it, but just thinking about last night brought a satisfied smile to her lips.

No, anger wasn't going to cut it. There was no blame to be cast. He hadn't pressed alcohol on her, he hadn't taken anything she hadn't been embarrassingly anxious to give, and this morning, when he'd had the chance to expose her to her listeners, he hadn't. Matt Ransom just kept popping out of the box she kept trying to stuff him into.

Yanking her gaze back up to his face, she found his eyes open.

"Well, good morning, sleepyhead," he said.

"I wish it *were* morning."

He gave her a smile that made her want to curl up next to him on the couch. She combated the weakness by reminding herself that doing one teensy-weensy honorable thing didn't make a man trustworthy.

"Really? I don't know how you face all that angst first thing in the morning. If you ask me, those women are way too—"

"Matt," she interrupted. "I'm trying to say thank you."

"Oh, it was nothing. I enjoyed myself too, Livvy." He waggled his eyebrows at her.

"We're talking about you filling in for me. Diane told me what you did."

"Oh . . . your show. Well, I enjoyed that, too, in a way, but it wasn't anywhere near as great as—"

"Matt," she warned.

"Why, Liv, you're blushing." His eyes danced. "You're very cute when you blush."

"I'm not in the mood for jokes or compliments, Matt. I haven't figured out what you're up to yet, but I won't let my guard down like that again." She felt the heat climb to her cheeks again and dropped her gaze.

"Ahhh." Matt stretched his arms out and then folded them to pillow the back of his head. "Would you care to be more specific?"

"Last night was a one-time thing. It won't happen again." She watched his face carefully, looking for some sign of the regret she felt, but his smile never faltered.

"I assume you're not referring to the meal."

"You know perfectly well what I'm referring to."

"Well, why don't you go ahead and spell that out, too. We guys can be incredibly dense sometimes."

She cleared her throat. "I'm sorry I came on to you, um, under the kitchen table."

He nodded sagely, but the dimple in his cheek nearly split his face in two.

"I shouldn't have done that," she continued. "And we shouldn't have had sex. It was inappropriate and counterproductive, and it muddies the water between us."

Matt crossed one ankle over the other and settled deeper into the couch. "Ahh, Livvy. There you go again, making this more complicated than it needs to be. The water's perfectly clear."

"I beg your pardon?"

He shrugged. "We had sex. It was great, really great. But it's no big deal."

Olivia stiffened.

"It's just sex, Livvy. There's no reason to beat yourself up over it."

She stood, drawing herself up to her full height.

"Silly me. I forgot it's just a physical thing for you." She looked down at him, her eyes carefully blank, determined to match his careless tone. She'd cut out her tongue before she admitted how deep his lack of interest cut. "I guess we're both in agreement then. We have three shows left between now and Monday morning. It's time to take the gloves off and come out swinging."

23

Olivia did more than come out swinging; she came out kicking butt. If Matt had thought Olivia would shy away from him or the audience after he'd saved her glorious rear end, he was dead wrong. And if he thought she was upset by his attitude about their night together, well, he had that wrong, too.

He'd actually been relieved when she pronounced their encounter a one-time thing. As a master of disengagement, he'd been quick to use the opportunity to piss her off and push her away. Somehow the woman had gotten too close and become much too important. Again.

He could have told her it wasn't the sex that muddied the water. It was the totally unfamiliar and completely unacceptable urge he kept feeling to protect her that was screwing everything up. And of course she wasn't behaving even remotely like he'd anticipated. He'd expected some sort of reaction—tears, recriminations, something. Instead, she'd been prancing around the living room all night, flaunting herself in front of him and the Internet audience as if she had nothing on her mind but winning rating points and votes.

At nine forty-five they both went on headphone with *his* producer to discuss her coming stint as host of *Guy Talk*.

She was coolly professional, not at all like the naked woman who'd come apart in his arms the night before. Focused and competent, Olivia appeared ready for four hours of live radio with potentially hostile callers, while he sat on the couch fantasizing about her like some teenage boy with a thing for the teacher.

"Hello, everyone. Welcome to *Guy Talk*. I'm Dr. Olivia Moore, and I'm here to field your calls and take your pledges. The number is 1-555-GUY-TALK. Call me."

She punched up Matt's theme song, and once it was established, she lowered the volume until only the tune remained audible. "Okay, guys. You can put away the baseball scores and forget about your automobiles. I'm here to help, and I'm ready to talk to anyone who's prepared to share their feelings."

Matt held back a laugh. Like his listeners had any interest in baring their innermost thoughts to a total stranger. Sheesh. He settled in, certain they would either refuse to call in or, better yet, call and make mincemeat out of her. Each option held its own special appeal.

"Ah, good," he heard Olivia say. "I see we've got callers lined up waiting to go on the air."

Okay, so he'd go with the mincemeat. He bit back another grin as she took on her first caller.

"Hi, Marvin," Olivia said. "Tell me what's on your mind."

"Well, it's my wife."

"Yes?"

"She wants me to give up golf and I can't do that, not even for her. I won't."

Matt thought Marvin sounded a bit hysterical, and no wonder, the poor slob had married a woman intent on sucking the last kernel of enjoyment out of him.

"Has she asked you to give it up?"

"Well, not yet, but I know it's coming. She says it takes up too much of my time."

"How much time do you spend playing golf?"

"Not so much."

"How much, Marvin? Once a week, twice?"

"Well, let's see. I have a regular foursome on Saturdays. I usually play another nine Sunday. On Tuesdays, I may go out and hit on the driving range after work. And, well, of course on Wednesdays I take off from work to play, but everybody does that."

"And this doesn't seem excessive to you?"

"No, why?"

"Okay. Let's look at this in another way. Do you ever ask your wife to join you on any of these occasions?"

"Well, she used to play on Sundays with me, and sometimes we'd go to the driving range together on Tuesdays, but she's kind of lost interest."

"Because?"

"Because we have one-year-old triplets?"

Matt saw Olivia's eyes narrow and began to suspect it wasn't Dr. O who was going to get minced.

"You have three one-year-old babies in your home?"

"Yeah. Two boys and a girl. Very cute. My wife's doing a wonderful job with them."

"And you're wondering why your wife resents all the time you spend playing golf?"

"Well . . ."

Matt could almost see the guy squirming in his chair.

"Marvin. Grow up. Get with the program. You're lucky you haven't been murdered in your sleep or had your golf balls cut off."

Matt grinned. Olivia looked like an avenging angel ready to swoop down and give old Marvin a head butt with her halo.

"Marvin. Your wife and children deserve more of you than what you're squeezing in between golf games."

"I've already traded the Porsche for a Suburban, and I've cut my golf trips down to two a year. A guy's gotta have some fun."

"Marvin. Do you hear what I'm saying to you?"

"Well, I . . ."

"Marvin. Fix it. Do better. Please. Or the next show you'll be appearing on will be *Divorce Court*."

And then she dumped the call. Impressed despite himself, Matt nonetheless wanted to rub his hands together in glee. After hearing Olivia maul Marvin that way, 90 percent of the waiting calls had probably hung up. He'd just sit here and watch her shoot off her own foot with all that feminist business. Guys didn't want to hear that kind of stuff.

"Well, look at those phone lines light up," Olivia crowed. "Hang on, fellas," she said as she prepared to punch up a commercial. "I want to talk to each and every one of you."

Olivia turned to Matt. "Gee, this is kind of fun. Maybe I've been preaching to the wrong half of the relationship all this time." She stood and stretched, drawing his gaze up her long torso, over the wonderful breasts, and up her long, sinewy arms. She threatened everything he cared about: his show, his equilibrium, and, at the moment, his ego, and still he couldn't take his eyes off her.

She brought a Diet Coke back to the audio board with her and sipped it thoughtfully, totally tuning him out as she prepared to take her next call. It galled him that she could do that, when all he could think about was her. And it irritated him even more that *his* audience seemed to be falling all over themselves to talk to her. Traitors.

The next caller was young Jason of Fantasy Island fame. Matt perked up.

"Hi, Dr. O." Jason's voice broke on the "O," turning it into a painful symphony of sounds.

"Hi, Jason. Are you sure you're allowed to be up this late?"

"Sure." His voice broke in the middle of the word, and Matt bit back a laugh. Olivia hastily disguised hers behind a cough.

"So, what are you calling about, Jason? No more raft fantasies, I hope."

"No'm." Jason evidently had a parent somewhere who believed in manners. "I'm real sorry about that. My mom says it's this puberty thing. I . . . well, I'm always imagining everyone naked."

"Gee." Olivia's tone was dry. "That is rough. Now, what can I do for you?"

"Well, actually." He cleared his throat, and his voice broke, yet again. "That *is* my problem."

"I'm sorry?"

"Every time I see a good-looking woman—even older ones like you—I . . ."

Olivia blinked, and once again Matt managed not to laugh.

"I get, um, well, you know. Sometimes I can barely walk. And I spend a lot of time hiding behind things until I can get the picture out of my mind, you know?"

"Well, Jason, I think that—"

"I mean, I even imagine my Sunday school teacher without her clothes on. Religion class is getting really rough."

Unable to stop himself, Matt laughed out loud as memories of his own adolescent fantasies came rushing back to him. One of the steamiest had starred Victoria Ramsfeld, the local librarian.

Olivia shot him a murderous look but kept her tone calm as she addressed her caller. "Jason, I think that—"

"And I was wondering, too." The boy's voice dropped to a whisper. "Is it true that you can go blind from too much . . ."

Olivia opened her mouth to answer, while Matt's memory slipped backward again. He and Adam had been twelve when they discovered the joint marvels of *Playboy* magazine and their own anatomies. If that old wives' tale had been true, he would have required a seeing-eye dog by the age of fifteen.

"How old did you say you were?" Olivia asked.

There was a telling pause while Jason evidently tried to figure out how many years to pad.

"Seventeen. I'm seventeen."

"Right," she said. "Well then . . ." Olivia tried once again to reassure her caller that his vision was safe, but suddenly Jason's already urgent tone turned frantic.

"Sorry, I have to go." And then, with all the anguish of adolescence, he wailed, "I think my mother's coming."

Olivia laughed. "Hang in there, Jason. I promise you what you're experiencing is extremely normal. Everything will, uh, ultimately calm down."

Still smiling, Olivia took the next call. And the next. And the one after that.

Matt's own smile over her deft handling of the boy began to fade as he listened to his callers lap Olivia up like cream. They called in unprecedented numbers, pledged huge quantities of food, and then waited their turn to spill their guts, thanking her for her sage advice when she was done.

The very same men who had screamed for her blood when her advice interfered with their love lives now couldn't wait to beg her advice. They were Benedict Arnolds the whole bunch of them, thought Matt. Put a pretty woman with a Ph.D. in front of them, and they fell all over themselves to share their most intimate secrets.

Or else they called to hit on her. Like Beau from Beaufort, South Carolina, who spent a nauseating amount of time explaining just how easy it would be to pop into the Mercedes and head on down to Atlanta. And who apparently had nothing more pressing to share than his lust for Olivia Moore.

"So, Dr. O." Beau's voice was Southern and smooth. "From what I can see on my monitor, you are looking lovely tonight. Are you feeling better?"

"Why, I'm just fine," Olivia drawled back, her voice like honey. "I think you could say I've recovered fully from what ailed me." She shot Matt a "take that" kind of look. "Is there something you want to discuss with me?"

"Well, I'd rather talk over drinks and dinner."

"All right, already." Matt jumped up from the couch. "What is this, *The Dating Game?*"

Olivia ignored him. "Did you have a question, Beau? Or are you just trying to make my heart go pitter-pat?"

"I'd like to know if there's something going on between you and Ransom. Because if there isn't, I'd like to ask you out."

"Olivia?" Matt strode over toward the control board, covering the floor in two angry strides. "Do you really think this is appropriate on-air behavior?"

Olivia spoke into the microphone, but her gaze stayed on Matt. "There is nothing *important* going on between my colleague and myself. But I don't date listeners any more than I would date patients. That would be inappropriate behavior."

"Well, damn," said Beau as Olivia dumped his call. Her obvious lack of interest in the man cheered Matt considerably.

And so it went until well after midnight, Matt's irritation growing with each fawning caller, his hackles rising with every flirtation and sexual innuendo. For a man who believed he didn't have a jealous bone in his body, it was downright disconcerting.

At 1:45 A.M. Dawg called in. Olivia had been drinking coffee since midnight, but Matt could see the fatigue setting in. He had the strangest urge to lift her in his arms and tuck her into bed. It took him a full minute to pull himself out of that fantasy and into the conversation with her last caller of the night.

"Okay, Dawg. You're on the air. I've been waiting to hear what's happening with you and JoBeth."

"Oh, lots of things are happening, and none of them are good."

"Why do you say that?"

"JoBeth went out with her old boyfriend today—the one her parents thought walked on water."

"And why does that bother you? When she told you she needed a commitment, you told her no. What's the problem?"

"I love her, Dr. O. I told her that. I was very clear."

"And?"

"And I even told her why I don't want to get married. I mean, after my wife walked out on me when my life and my career were in the toilet, I said never again."

"Do you think JoBeth is like your ex-wife?"

"No."

"Can you see her treating you that way? Walking out, leaving you to fend for yourself?"

"Hell, no. She nursed her parents, both of them, for almost two years, and I've never met a meaner, less appreciative couple."

"Dawg, don't you see? You've tarred JoBeth with your ex-wife's brush. Your fear of being hurt again is causing you to lose the woman you love. Are you going to let that happen?"

Matt listened to the urgency in Olivia's voice as she tried to make Dawg grasp her point. For the first time, Matt realized her words could apply just as easily to him. Dawg had at least had a wife. He'd never let anyone in after Adam died. Not even Olivia had been allowed, though she'd made the biggest dent in his heart.

He glanced over and noted the surprised look on

Olivia's face and wondered if her advice to Dawg held special meaning for her, too. The unwelcome bout of introspection left him feeling decidedly grumpy. And like a bear with his paw stuck in an unfamiliar honey jar, he couldn't quite figure out how to shake it off.

24

Olivia hadn't seen the vote tally yet, but she'd been in the business long enough to know her Saturday night stint as the host of *Guy Talk* had been a resounding success. Matt's listeners had been incredibly responsive, and there'd been a ton of them. She only hoped her own audience hadn't deserted her after her birthday slide under the table and the alleged bout of food poisoning that followed.

Olivia yawned. Finishing one show at 2:00 A.M. and starting another at 9:00 A.M. wasn't something she'd want to do on a regular basis. She could understand why Matt was not a morning person.

Her stomach growled. She'd forfeited breakfast in favor of sleep, and she definitely needed some fuel. This morning's show had been her last of the survivor series—thank you, God—and it had gone well enough. The topic, temptation and how and when to avoid it, had seemed particularly appropriate to a Sunday morning crowd. And she'd needed to hear the message herself.

She was sitting at the counter waiting for a fresh pot of coffee when Matt appeared. Once again he had on considerably fewer clothes than she deemed acceptable or wise, and she bristled at his total disregard for her wishes. With effort, she kept her gaze averted from his bare chest and somehow managed not to swivel on her barstool to catch the back view as he passed her on his way to the refrigerator.

"Morning." He sounded surprisingly cheerful for someone who had to be trailing badly in both votes and donations.

With only twenty-four hours left in captivity, Olivia decided she could afford to be magnanimous. "Good morning. Sleep well?"

"I did."

Her gaze dipped down below his neck and got stuck in his chest hairs. Gravity being what it was, it took a massive act of will to keep her gaze from straying to the waistband of those dratted gym shorts. Or past what lay under them to the muscled thighs below.

Better to focus on Matt's annoying habits rather than his physical attributes. Luckily there were plenty to choose from. Like the way he was leaning against the open refrigerator door with the carton of orange juice raised to his lips.

"You just waking up?" she asked.

He lowered the carton, shook it to see if there was anything left, and took one final swallow before putting the empty carton back in the fridge. "Nope. I've been up since nine. Didn't want to miss your show." He smiled. "I didn't realize you were planning to give a sermon."

"A sermon?"

"Well, you did cover quite a lot of biblical ground— temptation, the wages of sin. I just kept waiting for the prerecorded amen's. Who was the sermon for, sweet-heart—your poor listeners or yourself?"

"Why, you sanctimonious . . ."

"Hey. I'm not the one who spent three hours harping on the pitfalls of purely physical relationships. But I am probably the only listener who had any idea what you were ranting about."

"Oh, really?"

"Really." Matt advanced to the counter.

On the bright side, she no longer felt even remotely tempted to look at Matt Ransom's chest.

"I think you can't stand being out of control for a second, Olivia. You are horrified that you can't control how your body reacts to mine. And it galls you that you want more of what we had the other night."

Olivia gasped in outrage. "Is that right?"

"That's right. I don't need a Ph.D. to recognize lust when I see it. You're just upset that it's me you want. I'm not exactly thrilled about the fact that my body seems so intent on yours either, but you don't see me wasting a show beating myself up about it."

"No, you're not wasting shows, never that. But you sure are wasting your life."

One of Matt's eyebrows shot up, but Olivia ignored the warning. Something perverse in her wanted him just as angry as she was. Getting up off her stool, she marched around the counter so she could confront him without anything blunting her anger. She could feel it bubbling up through her bloodstream, and for once she didn't smash it back down. If he felt free to bash her over the head with his version of the truth, then she would do the same.

"Maybe if you stopped swaggering around sleeping

with every woman you meet, you could actually explore what it is that keeps you from sharing yourself with anyone. For an allegedly outgoing guy, you are one of the most secretive people I've ever met."

She pointed a finger at his chest, and in her anger practically drilled a hole with it. "Getting to know you feels a lot like extracting teeth. Without Novocain. You call me buttoned down, but you are completely zipped up, and you aren't even trying to let anyone in. Pretty soon people will just stop bothering. And then you can have what you want—lots of unimportant sex with women who don't really care about you."

They stood there toe to toe, neither moving. Olivia's finger felt welded to Matt's chest, and both of them were breathing heavily. In a romance novel, the sexual energy surging between them would have forced them into each other's arms and ultimately led to declarations of undying love. But romance novels weren't set in front of Webcams and didn't feature diehard fans eagerly waiting for the hero and heroine to tear each other apart.

Matt found his voice first. "Well done, Olivia. Wouldn't want our last afternoon in captivity to be as ho-hum as your last show. I'll write you a check for your on-the-spot analysis."

Olivia took a step back. "Don't bother." She looked up into the brown eyes that moments before had sizzled with heat and now revealed absolutely nothing. "Let's just consider it a parting gift. Someday you might actually use it."

JoBeth sipped her wine and looked longingly around her. Kevin's vacation place, a two-bedroom stilt house on a mountain overlooking North Georgia's Lake Burton, nearly took her breath away. Both bedrooms were masters, separated by a central great room with floor-to-ceiling windows overlooking the view. The house, which Kevin walked her through with obvious pride, had two fireplaces, a wraparound deck, and a screened dining porch off the fully equipped kitchen.

JoBeth loved the house, its location, and its incredible view. She especially liked rocking on the deck and looking down the mountainside at the now placid lake below. It was only Kevin she wasn't so sure about.

"What are you thinking, JoBug?"

He'd already started calling her by the nickname she'd once found appealing. And she had the traitorous thought that if he'd just stop talking, everything would be fine.

"Oh, I'm just swept up by the view, Kevin. It's incredible out here. So still and beautiful."

"It is, isn't it?" He rocked in silence for a moment and then said, "I bought this property while we were still together."

"You never told me that."

"I know. I meant it to be a wedding present." His tone grew wistful. "I had this crazy idea of us camping out up here for our honeymoon." He gave an embarrassed laugh and looked away.

"Oh, Kevin. I'm so sorry."

"Well, it all worked out okay. I've enjoyed the house. But I always wondered what you'd think of it." He turned back to her, waiting for her response.

"Why, it's fabulous. I can't think of a thing I'd change." She only wished she could get as excited about him as she was about the stacked-stone fireplaces and the two-person Jacuzzi. She rocked a little harder as she puzzled it out.

Kevin smiled, and JoBeth reminded herself what a good catch he was. Kevin Middleton was attractive and nice, and he'd certainly done very well for himself. Apparently "catching" him would not be a difficult task, since he didn't appear to be running at all.

She could tell from the way his doelike brown eyes regarded her when he thought she wasn't looking that he still cared about her, and she tried to dredge up some answering feeling of her own. But all she could think was how much Dawg would enjoy fishing on the lake. And how fine it would be to sit and rock with him on a summer evening while the fireflies sparked around them.

"It's getting late, Kevin. I have to go."

She stood and walked to the railing for a last look at the view. Kevin joined her and she fell back a step, realizing that the last thing she wanted to do right now was kiss this man, when Dawg was so much on her mind.

Ignoring her body language, Kevin stepped closer and put a hand out to caress her cheek. "You never stopped being important to me, JoBug, and I plan to be important to you again. In fact, I'm going to make sure of it."

Charles Crankower sat in the control room while Matt and Ben talked on headphone. Within twenty-four hours they'd have the consultant's report, and in another few weeks the book would be out with the final ratings breakdown. Right now, the only existing measurement of talent popularity was the weeklong printout of votes and food donations Charles held in his hand. There'd been the expected upward swings after noticeably strong shows, but in the end the statistical difference between the two hosts didn't amount to much.

In Charles's experience "too close to call" wasn't anywhere near as promotable as a landslide victory and somebody eating crow. Matt Ransom knew these facts as well as he did. He had one more show and almost twelve hours left to put Olivia out of the running, but for some reason the man seemed to have lost his edge.

Charles reached a hand out to tap Ben on the shoulder. "Let me borrow your headphones, will you?"

Matt's producer eyed him as suspiciously as ever, but passed them over without protest.

Charles fit the headphones onto his head and spoke into the tiny microphone. "Hey, Matt. Hope you're getting ready to pull out all the stops. I know you don't want to lose out to the doctor at this stage."

"What do you want me to do, Crankower, set myself on fire? I don't have to see the numbers to know the station has no room for complaints."

"Well, I just don't want to see you blow this opportunity for a decisive victory. If Olivia were compromised in some way . . ."

Charles saw Ben's head whip around. Turning away from the producer, he lowered his voice. "The sexual thing between you is already obvious to anyone who's paying attention. Maybe it's time to let our listeners know what happened between you two in Chicago."

There was a long silence and then, "Forget it, Charles. I'm not interested in your bag of dirty tricks. The show

I've got planned will be more than enough to keep me on the air."

"Goodness, you've gone all noble on us."

Ransom actually growled at him, which Charles found very interesting. "Give me Ben, Crankower. And keep your sticky fingers out of my pie."

Charles returned the headphones and fiddled with the Webcam a little longer. Every once in a while Matt looked up and glowered through the lens at him like some jungle animal protecting his lair, which Charles found intriguing as hell. Could the luscious Dr. O mean more to Matt than a convenient piece of ass? Now there was an idea with incredible potential.

25

At 10 P.M. Olivia put on her sheep pajamas and crawled into bed. She felt a bone-deep weariness that had little to do with lack of sleep and too much to do with the words she and Matt had hurled at each other earlier.

They'd spent the afternoon in full-combat readiness, both ready to strike if another offensive was launched. Dinner had been a painful affair with none of the easy camaraderie she'd come to look forward to. It was hard to believe the Matt Ransom she faced today was the same one who had taken her to the moon and back just a day ago.

Turning on the radio, she wondered what topic he'd pull out of his hat for his last show. She knew he'd never go out without attempting to eradicate her lead, but she wasn't seriously worried. After the votes she'd pulled in Saturday night, it would take a real doozy to do any more than just even the score. She'd worry about the consultant and the upcoming ratings book when she had to. Right now, all she wanted was out of this remote and this place. And out of Matt's way.

Matt's theme music came up full, and Olivia turned off

the bedside light and settled in to listen. It didn't take long for her weariness to be replaced, once again, by a white-hot anger.

"Okay, guys," Matt said. "This is it, the last show of the last day of captivity, which means the last chance to vote for Yours Truly. We've taken in a ton of money and food, thanks to you. We'll have the totals to announce tomorrow morning during our release. Ahh, what a glorious word. Release."

She heard another tune sneak in under his voice, but she couldn't quite recognize the music.

"In fact, release is an important aspect of our topic tonight. So is freedom."

Now she could make out the song. It was "The Wedding March," cranked up full in all its simple glory. It took no imagination at all to picture women in white dresses floating down church aisles toward their adoring grooms.

"Tonight we're going to hear about some great escapes." The music didn't just stop then, it screeched to a halt as if someone had dragged the needle of a record player across it.

"That's right, gentlemen. Tonight we're going to hear first-person testimonials from men who almost succumbed but"—another dramatic pause and a drum roll—"managed to extricate themselves at the last possible moment and at great personal peril."

Male applause and cheers came up full. Olivia sat up in bed and crossed her arms over her chest. She could feel her teeth clench.

Matt came on as glib as ever. Olivia could practically hear him chortling, and she felt an overwhelming urge to go out there and drag him away from the microphone, stuff him in a footlocker, and drop him off a very tall bridge.

"All right, gentlemen. Say hello to Barry, who found a unique way out of the ties that bind. Barry, tell us your story."

"Well, I was sitting at the rehearsal dinner the night before the wedding."

"Okay . . ."

"And I'm eating the shrimp cocktail, and I look up and notice that not a single one of the men at the tables around us is talking. These are all the guys who've married into my fiancée's family, and they're just nodding their heads and saying, 'Yes, dear, No, dear.' "

"Scary." Matt said.

"Scary? I tell you, all of a sudden I couldn't breathe."

"So what did you do?"

"Well, I had to think fast, you know. I mean, you can't just pull the woman aside and say, 'I'm sorry but I don't want to turn out like all the other poor stiffs who married into your family.' "

"No, that probably wouldn't go over well."

"So, I'm sitting there nodding my head like the rest of them, you know, just sort of blending in. And I'm thinking, okay, what can I do to get *her* to call this off."

"Very good, Barry."

Olivia could tell Matt was eating up every horrible word. All she could think of was the poor woman who was about to see her dreams blow up in her face.

"So I asked her younger sister to dance."

"And this is grounds for calling off a wedding?"

"Not at first. But pretty soon I dance her onto the edge

of the dance floor, right between our table and my future in-laws."

"Yeah?"

"And I start kissing her, really kissing her, you know?"

Matt laughed, and Olivia heard gasps of horror play up full.

Encouraged, Barry continued. "And then, just to be sure there's no mistake what's going on, I grind my pelvis against her—a real Elvis number."

"Jesus, Barry. What happened then?"

"Well, I can tell she's getting ready to huff off the floor, and I'm afraid no one sees what's happening, so I put my hand down the front of her dress."

Matt remained silent.

"Then the sister screams, the place gets real quiet, and my fiancée storms over and throws the ring in my face." Barry sounded genuinely happy.

"Did everybody just stand around and watch, or what?"

"Not exactly."

"What do you mean?"

"Well, I heard it turned into a real slugfest, but I wasn't there for that part of it."

"You just left?"

"No, not exactly."

"So where were you?"

"In the ambulance on my way to the hospital."

"Gee, Barry," said Matt. "This isn't sounding like the cleanest escape I ever heard of."

"Well, her father did beat me to a bloody pulp."

"Aw, Barry . . ."

"But you know, even now after the plastic surgery and

the physical therapy, I remember all those silent men yearning to be free, and I count myself a lucky man."

"There you have it, gentlemen, escapee number one." Applause sound effects played, and chants of "Woo, woo, woo" came over the radio. "Our next caller managed to make his escape *without* bloodshed, but his story, too, has some, uh, real ups and downs. We'll hear from our next runaway groom in just a minute."

Olivia spent the commercial break pacing. Matt had chosen a surefire winner for his final show. His audience was no doubt falling over itself laughing, just as Matt intended. But Olivia couldn't stop thinking about Barry's fiancée's public humiliation, her rehearsal dinner a shambles, her family's money sunk in a wedding day that would never be. Who knew what horrible tale groom number two would have to tell.

If she needed more proof of Matt's feelings about commitment and the likelihood of his ever sharing a life with someone, she had it. He had no respect for women in general or for her in particular. To him, everything was one big joke. What she wouldn't give to shake some sense into him.

"Okay, everybody, our next caller is Michael. And his story is a little different than the last one we heard, though the end result is the same. Michael, you're on the air."

"Hi, Matt."

"Michael. Did your escape land you in the hospital?"

"Actually, it landed me in Missouri."

There was a pause, and Matt laughed. "We're all ears."

"Well, Meredith and I took skydiving lessons together. We'd been talking about maybe getting married one day, and the next thing I know, we're planning to get married during a jump."

"That's one way to keep the guest list small."

"Yeah, it was going to be just the two of us. A friend who's a notary was going to marry us on the way down."

"You're not going to tell me someone's chute didn't open?"

"No, everyone walked away from that jump. Well, actually, I flew away."

"What does that mean?"

"Well, as soon as the plane started climbing, I started having doubts, you know?"

"About jumping?"

"No, about getting married."

"Uh-oh."

"Yeah, that's what I thought. So I'm starting to panic a little, you know. We're approaching jumping altitude, and the plane's starting to level off, and I don't think I can go through with it. Only there's no time to discuss it. We're really close to our jump site, and Meredith and the notary are already moving over to the open doorway."

"So what did you do?"

"Well, it was too loud in the plane to talk, and shouting that I don't want to get married seemed, I don't know, it's just not something you yell at somebody, you know?

"So we leveled off at twelve thousand feet, and Meredith unhooked her lead line, flashed me this big smile, and jumped. Our friend, the notary, went right after her. And I'm standing there, you know, like my feet are nailed to the floor of the plane or something."

"Jeez, man. You just let her float away?"

"It was kind of surreal. I saw their chutes open—hers

had a red heart painted on it for the wedding—and I saw them both look up, but it was too late. I paid the pilot to drop me at a small rural airport in the next state, and I just laid low for a while."

"Wow."

"Yeah. It was a narrow escape."

"Did you ever see Meredith again?"

"Not really. She wouldn't talk to me after that. I heard a while later that she married our diving instructor. He evidently made it out of the plane with no problem."

Matt laughed. "You see, guys, it's never too late. Right up until the moment you say 'I do,' you can decide you don't. Don't forget to call and make your pledges to the food bank. This is *Guy Talk* . . . where a guy can be a guy."

And so it went, each story worse than the last. One caller had jumped ship, literally, diving headfirst off the cruise ship booked for his wedding. Another fled back down the aisle of the church with his fiancée and the flower girl clinging to the tails of his morning coat.

Olivia's slow burn began to build. She forced herself to listen to every word, took in every annoying barb and chuckle, all of it a slap in the face to every woman who had ever expected anything from the man she loved.

She wondered if he really thought all women were just grasping, needy beings trying to trap a man into taking that walk to the altar. She wanted to go out there and yank him out of his chair and show him just how full of shit he was.

When he finally signed off, still chortling over his callers' great escapes, she sprang out of bed and began to pace. She paced for a good twenty minutes, trying to blow off enough steam to ignore the affront to herself and womankind. She knew she should just go back to bed, but the more she replayed the show in her mind, the angrier she became.

When her need to tell him off became too much for her, she threw open her door and stormed into the living room.

"How dare you?" she demanded.

"I beg your pardon?"

Olivia marched up to where he stood in the center of the living room. "What is wrong with you? Have you no concern for anyone else? No sensitivity for other people's feelings?"

"Olivia, you're wearing sheep pajamas, and you're shouting like a fishwife. How do you think that's going to look to our audience?"

Beside herself with fury, she could hardly acknowledge the merit of his warning. With a hand to his chest she pushed him backward across the room and out of camera range until his back was flush up against the French doors that led to the balcony.

In the station control room, Charles Crankower, super spider, unfurled his long body from the chair it had been folded into for the last six and a half hours. Quietly, so as not to alert Matt's producer, who was still clearing up after the show, he panned the camera to frame up the shot he'd discovered earlier. His heart leapt for joy at what came into view.

Matt stood with his back to the balcony doors. Olivia stood facing him with her back to the camera. He could see Matt's face and its look of surprise. At first their body language was completely adversarial, all rigid angles and barely leashed tension. But as he watched, Olivia moved closer, and the next thing he knew, she was kissing the hell out of Matt Ransom.

With a big thank-you to the PR gods he'd almost given up on, Charles checked to make sure the camera was recording.

He would have sold his soul for audio at that moment, but he didn't dare ask Ben to turn up the microphone for fear the producer would warn the two people framed in stark relief through the camera lens. As he settled in to watch, he reflected that it was too bad he could only see Matt's face and not Olivia's. But then he reminded himself that beggar spiders couldn't be choosers.

26

Olivia pressed herself against Matt. His physical response was swift and immediate, and for some reason this made her even angrier.

Surprising them both, she kissed him. Hard. "We're all the same to you, aren't we, Matt? Push the right button, kiss the right spot, and voilà! Matt Ransom's ready for action."

Totally on the offensive and anxious to prove her point, she rubbed her body against his. Once again, his response was immediate and unmistakable.

"So, I guess that happens for everyone, huh? Doesn't matter who it is, or what's going on. Is that right, Matt?"

Without giving him time to respond, she bracketed his face in her hands and kissed him again, using her tongue and her teeth and all of her fury.

She suckled his earlobe, ran her tongue down the side of his face, and came back to his lips. "And when I do this, it doesn't matter that it's me, Olivia? Will any pair of hands, any lips really do?"

Matt didn't answer. His erection felt like a slab of marble between them, and as she kissed him, she felt his heat rise until his skin actually became hot to the touch. His look of surprise had been replaced by sharp-featured desire that she wanted to know was only for her. "A woman is a woman is a woman, right?" she taunted. "Can you tell us apart in the dark, Matt? Do you care?"

"Jesus, Livvy." His arms snaked around her, and his hands cupped her buttocks as he pulled her closer.

Olivia was beyond reason. Somehow she would devour him as he had devoured her and use his own lust to make him admit that what was between them was more than physical. She wasn't buying his "love the one you're with" crap a moment longer.

"Do you recognize my touch, Matt? My scent, my voice?"

Focused completely on the man in front of her, Olivia brought her mouth back to his. Her fingers moved to the top button of his shirt, and when they fumbled, she gave in to her impatience and ripped the shirt open, sending buttons flying across the room.

She ran her hands over the smorgasbord of skin. They traveled up his chest to tangle in the mat of dark hair, then followed the dark arrow back toward the waistband of his jeans.

"How about my mouth, Matt? Do you think you'd recognize that?"

She bent her head to circle a nipple with her tongue, and drew the hardening bud between her teeth.

Matt's hands slipped up under her pajama top and over her bare back, skimming, exploring, heating her skin to the same temperature as his. Olivia straightened and twined her arms around his neck. Going up on tiptoe, she pressed against him, fitting herself over the hard swell of his erection.

Desire, hot and insistent, coursed through her bloodstream, in spite of her anger.

She'd just dropped her arms and lifted her fingers to the snap of Matt's jeans when his hands clamped down on her shoulders, halting all movement. Olivia's gaze flew to Matt's face. The look there told her something was horribly wrong. She tried to turn around, but his hands on her shoulders held her in place.

"Don't move," he ordered. "I have to figure out what to do."

"What's wrong?"

Matt let go of her shoulders. "Don't move," he instructed again. "And don't turn around. We seem to be on camera."

Her heart seeming to plunge into the pit of her stomach, Olivia disobeyed. Turning, she looked up and encountered the unblinking lens of the Webcam. Her gaze flew to the TV monitor beneath it, where she could see Matt still framed from head to just below his waist, with her frozen in front of him.

She felt the heat flare up to scorch her cheeks. Good God, she had just attacked Matt Ransom in front of an Internet audience. She was beyond humiliation. She was finished.

Numb, she watched Matt stride over to the entertainment center and rip the Webcam's power plug out of the wall.

"How did the camera get pointed this way?" she asked.

"I don't know."

"You don't know? How can you not know?"

"I just don't. During my show it was in its usual position. I never looked again after that." He smiled tentatively. "I was preoccupied."

"Don't you dare make jokes. My whole reputation's shot to hell in some futile attempt to force you to admit all women aren't the same."

"I think you more than made your point."

"You think this is funny! I have lost all credibility. Who will ever be able to listen to my advice without picturing me throwing myself at you?"

"It's not quite that bad, Olivia. Until you turned around, all they could see was the back of a blonde head."

"Oh, right, like there's been more than one blonde in this apartment this week."

"Well, you seemed pretty concerned that I might have you confused with someone else."

She shot him a withering glance and started to pace. "I don't believe this!" She stopped pacing to turn on him as the pieces started to fall into place. "You. You set me up."

"Olivia, be reasonable. There was no way I could know you were planning to corner me and, er, have your way with me." He didn't seem particularly concerned that he'd been caught engaging in serious foreplay on camera. But this just made him all the more macho, didn't it? And what did it make her?

A prize chump.

"All week I've been trying to figure out what you were up to. 'Relax, Olivia.' 'Don't be so uptight, Livvy.' 'What good is success if you can't enjoy it, Liv?' As if you cared one bit how I actually felt."

She did an about-face and paced in the other direction, unable to look him in the eye. What in the world had she been thinking? How had she allowed her anger and frustration to get the best of her? She was totally out of control, and it was all Matt Ransom's fault.

"You feed me a tiny bit of your real self, little dribs and drabs that make me believe you're actually reachable and capable of feeling, and what do I do? Turn myself upside down trying to find the rest. I'm the one who should have my head examined."

Matt plopped down on the sofa and put his feet up on the coffee table. "Olivia, just calm down. There's got to be a way out of this."

But she was beyond thought, beyond giving him the remotest benefit of any doubt. Another thirty seconds and a national audience could have watched her bury her face in Matt Ransom's crotch without any understanding of the reasons why. Hell, she no longer understood the reasons why. She only knew that she had come to trust him in some subliminal way and he had betrayed that trust.

Olivia whirled around to face him. "What did you do, pay someone at the station to reposition the Webcam so you could lure me into a compromising position?"

"Lure you? Do you hear what you're saying, Olivia? Do you think I had any way of knowing what was coming?" He shook his head and spoke calmly, which just incensed her further. "I don't think *you* knew what you were going to do before you did it! When did I have the chance to warn the mystery cameraman? Calm down and let's think this through."

"*We* are not thinking anything, Matt. There is no *we* here."

Then she tuned him out, completely. Like she should have done the day the door clicked shut behind them.

Charles Crankower danced a little jig in the empty WTLK control room. The Webcam had been disconnected, but it couldn't have mattered less. He had exactly what he needed, exactly what he'd wanted but hadn't dared hope for.

Jubilant, he picked up his cell phone and started placing calls. The last number he dialed was the Operation Manager's home number. T.J. Lawrence picked up on the second ring.

"Crankower, do you have any idea what time it is?"

Charles smiled to himself. "I do, boss. It's 3:30 A.M. and our ship has come in."

"Crankower, if this is some kind of prank . . ."

"No, T.J., it's nothing like that. It's the remote. There's been an unexpected development."

He heard T.J.'s tone turn serious. "Are Matt and Olivia okay?"

"Oh, they're fine, though I suspect they may be duking it out in earnest right now."

In a rush he told the OM exactly what had happened, careful to make it sound like the camera movement had been unintentional, just a changing of the audience view to keep things visually interesting. T.J. had always had a soft spot for Olivia, and Charles doubted T.J. would want to know to what lengths he'd gone to set her up.

"Jeez," T.J. said. "I can't believe this."

"Yeah, me either," said Charles, when what he really wanted to say was, *I can't believe my good fortune.* "You'd better come down here and see the video, T.J., so you'll be prepared for the press when we go over to release Olivia and Matt from the apartment."

"The press already knows?"

"Yeah, somebody must have been monitoring the website," Charles lied, glad he'd had the foresight to call his contacts from his cell phone before T.J. could forbid it.

"All right, but just how explicit is this video, Crankower? Are we going to be running into trouble over that?"

"No. I'll call Legal if you want me to, but I don't think it's going to be an issue. There's no actual exposure even though it's pretty clear what's happening."

Charles heard the rustling of sheets and pictured T.J. trying to slip out of bed without disturbing his wife. "Olivia must be totally freaked out," said T.J. "Call Diane and Ben in to the station, will you? I'll call the apartment from my car."

"Okay, boss. I've already called the security company to send some people to meet us at the apartment. One thing we can stop worrying about is getting coverage for the end of the promotion. If I'm not mistaken, it's going to be a mob scene."

27

T.J., Crankower, and two burly security guards met Olivia and Matt in the apartment at 8:00 A.M. on Monday morning. T.J. brought the morning paper with its grainy reprint of the Webcam freeze-frame under the headline "Sexy Shrink Succumbs to Guy Talk," and clucked around them nervously trying to prepare everyone for the insanity waiting outside the building.

In contrast, Charles practically floated above the floor in what looked like ecstatic anticipation, while one of the guards gave Olivia an obvious once-over and the other sent Matt a man-to-man wink that made Matt want to deck them both.

Walking out the front door of the apartment held none of the satisfaction he'd anticipated, and a glance at Olivia's face as they walked down the long carpeted hallway to the elevator told him she was too caught up in her own misery to appreciate their newfound freedom.

They stopped in the lobby for a last pep talk from T.J., which amounted to encouraging Olivia to ignore the seamier questions and begging Matt not to hurt anyone.

"Let's just focus on our listeners' contributions to the food bank and try to steer clear of the rest, shall we?"

They all nodded as though this might be possible, then T.J., Charles, and the security duo pushed through the doors and were swallowed by the clamoring crowd.

Matt wanted to offer aid, but Olivia had shrugged off every attempt to discuss the situation since the phone call from T.J. at 3:30 that morning. Shortly afterward, she'd gone to her room, where he'd heard her pacing and muttering until 6 A.M., when she'd slipped into the bathroom to shower and dress.

Now they stood side by side waiting to go out and face the media, and the expression on her face made him want to offer her . . . what?

"You know, no one actually saw anything, Olivia. For all they know I was feeling faint and you were giving me mouth-to-mouth."

"Right." Her voice was bitter. "And I ripped your shirt open so you could breathe better."

"Look, Olivia, we're both single, consenting adults. What happened is a little embarrassing, but the Clinton presidency survived worse."

"I've got a news flash for you, Matt. This may be just one more amusing peccadillo to your listeners—they expect this sort of behavior from you. But I'm a therapist. My listeners need to be able to respect and trust me. This is not okay."

"I'm sorry, Liv. If you want to deny everything, I'll back you up."

"I don't need you to back me up. And I don't need you to lie for me. In fact, I don't want anything from you."

Olivia turned away from him and pushed through the front door. Matt followed closely behind.

He had less than a second to register the beauty of the day before the shouting started.

"Are the two of you involved?"

"What was going on in there at night?"

"Which one of you pulled the plug on the Webcam?"

"How was she, Matt?"

Matt felt Olivia tense beside him, and he couldn't blame her; the crush of reporters resembled nothing so much as a pack of baying dogs. They kept barking their questions, even though they remained unanswered, and all of their questions centered on identifying what they'd caught a glimpse of before the cord was pulled.

Charles stepped forward and raised a hand for silence. A sea of video cameras pointed his way, and microphones were thrust up in the air. Back behind the crowd, two reporters did their stand-ups for a live report.

Matt was surprised by the presence of the wire services and cable news networks. It must have been a slow news day, or perhaps the story of a therapist giving in to her baser instincts was an even bigger story than he'd imagined. Or maybe someone had tipped them off.

When the crowd fell silent, Charles dispensed the good news—an unprecedented amount raised for the Third Harvest Food Bank, audience participation at an all-time high. But as he spoke, all eyes stayed on Matt and Olivia, and those eyes were full of speculation as each reporter tried to imagine what had taken place in the locked apartment.

Beside him, Olivia began to tremble. Instinctively, he stepped closer to lend his body as support. He wanted to put an arm around her shoulder and drag her away from the mob, or at least speak up in their defense, but every glib response that sprang to his mind died on his lips because he couldn't come up with one that wouldn't damage Olivia in some way. His concern for her overrode his normal instincts for self-preservation so completely that he hardly recognized himself.

Charles finished his lengthy recap of the promotion's success and stepped back next to T.J. Shouts rang out again, and the mob surged closer. The limo waiting at the curb might as well have been miles rather than yards away, since they'd have to push through the assembled reporters to reach it.

Olivia stepped forward, and Matt watched her square her shoulders and clear her throat. He braced himself for whatever was to come.

"There is no way to satisfactorily explain what went on in this apartment, and I'm not going to try." There were groans of protest and more shouted questions, but Olivia stood firm. "I'll just say that I'm glad the week produced such great results for the food bank, I'm thrilled our listeners responded in such a generous way." She flashed a wry smile. "And being locked up for a week with Matt Ransom is enough to drive any woman to desperation."

She turned to him, the tenseness of her body belying the smile on her face and the casual tone of her words. Then she waited, without a word, for him to cut her off at the knees.

Matt felt a swift burst of pride at her bravery. Because he wanted to, and because he knew she wouldn't flinch away from him in front of an audience, he stepped up and slung one arm across her shoulders. Then he gave her an exaggerated wink. She tensed but managed to stay put, her smile firmly in place as he said, "Well, if you can cop an insanity plea, I guess I can, too." He turned his gaze to the waiting reporters, taking in their sharp-faced curiosity. "All I have to say is . . . ditto."

Dissatisfied, the mob screamed for more. A young reporter with gelled hair and a feral grin pushed to the front. Matt recognized him as a stringer for *Atlanta Leisure* magazine. "Is it true you two had a relationship eight years ago in Chicago?" he asked.

Olivia whirled around to face Matt.

Without waiting for a response, the reporter flung out another question. "Did you really bet your staff you'd have Dr. Moore flat on her back before the week was out?"

Matt watched the outrage suffuse Olivia's face. He lowered his voice and said, "It's not the way it sounds, Olivia."

The outrage turned to disgust. For a long moment she stared at him as if he were a form of plankton, and then she shook off his arm and plunged forward down the apartment steps.

Like offensive guards protecting their quarterback, the burly duo sprang into action. One of them caught up with Olivia while the other fell in at Matt's side. Together, they cleared a path through the crowd to the getaway car. Matt could hear the whir of camera motor drives and frantic footsteps following them down the sidewalk, while the same questions echoed in the morning air.

Matt slid onto the bench seat after Olivia. Crankower and T.J. dove into the facing seat, the door slammed behind them, and the car pulled away from the curb.

For the life of him, Matt couldn't think of a thing to say.

Unable to argue his innocence and unwilling to dissect his original intentions in front of Charles and T.J., he remained silent as the driver worked his way through morning traffic. Olivia kept her back to him, staring intently out her window at the rapidly disappearing park across the way. Turning to look out his own window, Matt watched the apartment building grow small and fall out of sight and wondered who'd been feeding the *Atlanta Leisure* reporter inside information.

Charles broke the silence. "Did you see the feature reporters from Fox and NBC? The networks are going to be lined up begging for interviews. Maybe we should start with *Good Morning America*."

Matt and Olivia continued to stare out their respective windows. Olivia held her body away from his, and when they rounded a curve she was careful not to allow herself to touch him. He could feel the hurt and anger rolling off her in waves.

"All right. I guess a nice, friendly 'No comment' could be considered appropriate in a situation like this," T.J. said.

Olivia continued to stare out her window, ignoring all of them.

"Er, whatever the situation *is*," T.J. amended.

T.J. and Charles waited expectantly, but Matt and Olivia remained silent. "Okay, then," T.J. continued. "If you don't feel like sharing yet, I guess I need to formulate a strategy to deal with the fallout. We won't do *Liv Live* or *Guy Talk* today. We'll let the audience simmer down first. They'll tune in in droves tomorrow."

He turned to the promotions man beside him. "Charles, get Diane and Ben on the phone and tell them to pull 'best of' programs to air today. We'll drop Olivia and Matt off at their homes, let them get some rest, and we'll all meet back at the station this afternoon."

The limo turned into Olivia's neighborhood and took a left onto her street. They sat, with the engine idling outside of Olivia's house. Only T.J. had anything to say. "In light of the, um, rather spectacular ending of the promotion, I've asked the consultant to conduct a final focus group and an additional call-out to gauge audience reaction. I'll have his report and Detroit's reaction by the time we meet."

The first person Olivia ran into at the station was Matt. Refusing to greet him, she stood and waited for the elevator in silence. They rode up with three co-workers who could barely contain their curiosity. The two men slapped Matt heartily on the back, and she suspected if she hadn't been present they would have congratulated him as well. The woman in the car just looked on pityingly, before averting her gaze. It was chillingly reminiscent of the kind of reaction she'd gotten when word of James's cheating had gotten around, and too much like the glances she'd given her own mother when she'd played the doormat for Olivia's father.

She and Matt traversed the endless hallway to T.J.'s office under continued scrutiny. Conversations died and movement ceased as each person they passed took time out from gossiping to study the objects of their speculation.

Was it her imagination, or did Matt seem to walk taller with each step as she shrank ever lower in embarrassment? She fanned the flames of her anger and told herself it didn't matter. Already she was trying to formulate the words she would say during tomorrow's show to square things with her audience. Assuming she still had one when this meeting was over.

Outside T.J.'s office, Matt took her arm and pulled her around to face him. Onlookers fell silent as they strained to listen.

"I didn't set you up, Olivia. I was just as surprised as you were when I looked up and saw that we were on camera."

Olivia jerked her arm out of Matt's grasp. "Right. Well then, that solves everything, doesn't it? And your whole campaign to help me relax had no motive other than improving my quality of life? Come on, Matt. This is me, Olivia, remember?"

"Oh, I remember all right. Maybe better than you do. And I'll admit that I did think throwing you a bit off balance might be helpful. But that was only at first, before . . ."

Olivia's thoughts turned back to the meals he'd cooked for her, the soap operas he'd introduced her to, the spirit of fun he'd brought to their captivity—all of it a calculated effort to put him in the winner's circle.

"Before you decided to get me—how did that reporter put it—flat on my back?"

"Olivia, I didn't—"

"And I suppose it wasn't you who told everybody about Chicago? Did you tell them how you had me flat on my back there, too, until you decided you were finished with me?"

"Olivia, believe me, I didn't—"

"I'd have to be a fool to believe anything you said to me now. And all appearances to the contrary, I'm not a fool." She turned her back on him and stormed into T.J.'s office.

T.J., Charles, Ben, and Diane were already waiting. Olivia sat next to her producer, while Matt took a seat next to Ben, the battle lines clearly drawn. No one spoke as T.J. flipped through the folder on his lap. "So," he inquired casually, "did either of you rest?"

"It's kind of hard to do that with the press camped out on your lawn," Matt drawled. "And then I made the mistake of checking my voice mail." He turned to Olivia. "I heard from *People* and *Soap Opera Digest* and a couple of sleazy tabloids I've never even heard of. And they all want us to come clean and tell all."

Olivia's gaze dripped scorn as it met his.

"Don't worry, I'm only a little tempted," Matt deadpanned.

"Yes, well, I don't think we need anyone telling all at this point," T.J. interrupted. "I thought you both did a good job of *not* telling all this morning. Why don't we just let everybody keep wondering until Charles works out a promotional plan."

Olivia tried to imagine her listeners putting up with that. Her heart sank every time she thought about her audience's reaction to the whole ugly mess.

The intense media scrutiny just made it worse. Even if their numbers ended up statistically too close to call, Olivia knew she'd become a liability. She was a dispenser of advice who couldn't control her own actions, a radio therapist who didn't know how to deal with men.

Diane and Ben fidgeted in their seats, and Olivia envied their energy. She felt too tired and heavy to move, though her brain continued to function at warp speed. Matt looked calm and unconcerned, though she knew him well enough now to know it was just a pose. Crankower appeared even more starched than usual.

T.J. closed the folder and began. "Bottom line," he said, "this promotion has been a huge success."

Charles preened like a peacock. He stood and took a brief bow before T.J. continued. "Matt and Olivia are already getting national attention. Plus, we know the numbers are going to be great, which means new advertisers will be tripping over themselves to sign on the dotted line."

Olivia leaned forward in her chair. "But what about the research? There's no way my listeners are okay with what happened between . . . well, what happened."

"No, they're not. Your credibility has suffered, and your core audience is furious," T.J. said. "They haven't tuned out, yet, but they feel betrayed and angry. Sixty percent of your P1's don't approve of your behavior."

Olivia clenched her fists. She was dying to stand and pace. "And you consider this a success?"

"Yes." T.J.'s smile was blinding. "You've more than offset any potential loss with new listeners. You picked up P1's who already consider WTLK their station of preference but hadn't listened to you before, and 95 percent of P2's responded favorably to *Liv Live*. It won't take much to turn them into a P1 audience."

Matt asked, "What about *Guy Talk*?"

"You've come out of this smelling like a rose. Your P1's are totally with you, and 85 percent of P2's like you."

"So, what does this mean in terms of who stays on the air?" Ben wanted to know.

T.J. leaned forward, his forearms on his knees. "That's the best part. I just got off the phone with Detroit." He smoothed a hand over his head. "In view of the research, the anticipated numbers, and the expansion of both your audience demographics, Olivia and Matt both win. The company has decided it can afford Gravy Train *and* Alpo."

"What?" Matt, Ben, and Diane sounded like a Greek chorus.

"Matt's Gravy Train, I'm Alpo," Olivia bit out. "But you're wrong, T.J." She looked directly at Matt. "Regardless of what the numbers say, if I've lost the trust and respect of my audience, I've lost. Period."

Feeling every bit as betrayed and angry as her core audience, Olivia slung her purse over her shoulder and stood. "That would make you the winner and reigning champ, Matt. Congratulations. You worked hard for it."

T.J. stood, too. "You're missing the larger picture here, Olivia," he said. "You and Matt are no longer just local celebrities. Detroit's convinced your audience will stick with you. They want to put *Liv Live* and *Guy Talk* on the rest of the company-owned stations; that's nineteen more markets apiece."

Olivia stared T.J. in the eye. "You're the one who doesn't get it. Those P1's and P2's aren't just numbers to me. They're people with issues and problems, and I've let them down. Now I have to figure out how to make them understand something I don't even understand myself." She shook her head in disgust. "I'm not interested in hearing what Detroit wants right now. My agent will be in touch when I am."

"Olivia, please," T.J. called out, but Olivia marched

across the room and out of the office without a backward glance.

For a tense moment no one spoke, and then the recriminations started.

Diane glowered at Matt. "Everything would have been fine if you'd fought fair."

"Me?"

"We all heard you bragging about how you'd have her flat on her back. I never thought you'd be able to do it. I should have warned her." Diane wrung her hands.

Matt shook his head. "That was just talk. I'm not the one who told us our shows were at risk and locked us in a peanut-sized apartment for a week." He stood and crossed over to tower over Charles and T.J. as realization dawned. "This was bullshit all along, wasn't it? You just used the budget thing to get us in there."

Only Charles was stupid enough not to look shocked at the accusation.

"And then you turned on a camera and let us perform." Matt's anger grew, and he focused all of it on Charles. "Ben told me you were always fooling with that camera, Crankower. I should have paid more attention. You were just waiting for your chance, weren't you? I assume you're the one who told the press about Chicago?"

"It's not a state secret. It's right there in your résumés." The Promotion Director sounded smug.

"Now, gentlemen." T.J.'s tone was conciliatory, but Charles didn't seem to perceive the danger.

"You are a piece of shit, Crankower."

"I wouldn't be so self-righteous, Ransom," Charles sneered. "We just got you into the apartment. What happened there was your own doing."

The feel of his fist connecting with Charles's chin afforded some satisfaction, and it did stop the words. Unfortunately, Matt reflected, as he stepped over Charles's inert body and headed out the door, it didn't make them any less true.

28

At seven-thirty Tuesday morning, Olivia backed her car down her driveway, past the waiting group of reporters, and on to WTLK with all the enthusiasm of someone about to face a firing squad.

After watching Jay Leno poke fun at her expense, she'd spent much of the night nursing her anger at the station and its corporate parent, and the rest of it trying to understand her feelings for Matt. She'd hoped for a healing night's sleep. Instead she'd spent it tossing and turning and attempting to gain some understanding of what had happened to her.

As she alternately pounded her pillow and paced the rooms of her home, she told herself she hated Matt Ransom, that this whole mess was entirely his fault, and that what had happened between them belonged in the category of really great sex, not serious lovemaking. But a part of her wanted to believe she hadn't imagined the connection she'd felt, that there'd been something real between them—something she could understand and somehow find a way to explain to her audience.

She would have liked to whip herself into a frenzy of

indignation, but her conscience wouldn't allow it. Much as she wanted to, she couldn't deny how alive she felt when she was with him. Or how much she'd enjoyed sparring with him, eating with him, even cleaning up after him. Getting to know him over a meal had been a gift. He wasn't the same man he'd been in Chicago, even though he kept trying to act like he was. And when he'd had the chance to ruin her completely, he hadn't taken it.

Leaving her car in the underground garage, Olivia took the elevator to the station lobby. During the ride up she teased herself with fantasies of breaking through Matt's defensive armor to the rich bed of feeling she suspected lay underneath. And then she chided herself for being such an optimist, because really, what were the chances that he'd ever let her or anyone else in?

Diane met her in the control room with a smile, a hug, and a box of Krispy Kreme donuts.

"Still off the wagon, huh?" Olivia asked.

Diane shrugged. "Just think of it as the Dozen-Donuts-a-Day Diet. I figured we could both use a little pick-me-up."

Olivia helped herself to a glazed chocolate donut. "Today I'll take my comfort any way I can get it. How about you, Di? Are you ready for whatever comes?"

"I think so. I fielded some pretty hostile calls yesterday. You have a lot of listeners who aren't at all happy about what happened with Matt."

"I can't say that I blame them." Dread pooled in the pit of Olivia's stomach. "I'm not too happy about it myself."

Diane studied her. "Did you hear what happened after you left the meeting yesterday?"

Olivia bit into her donut and tried to appear disinterested.

"Matt punched Crankower and knocked him right out. He accused him of framing up that final shot and telling the press you and Matt had a thing for each other in Chicago."

"He knocked him out?"

"Oh, yeah. Charles made one last snide comment, and Matt coldcocked him. And he told T.J. off, too."

"Well, what do you know?" Olivia marveled. "Maybe Matt has a few heroic bones in his body after all." She tucked the thought away for future consideration and turned to the business at hand. "All right, Diane. Stash the donuts and let's do radio. You find me a good first caller to set the tone, and I'll take it from there, okay?"

"Okay."

Olivia tuned out the bustle around her as she sat down in front of the microphone.

In the wee hours of the morning, she'd finally decided that for this show she'd have to go with the flow; not exactly her forte, and something that would have been out of the question a week ago. She wondered if Matt would tune in as he had during the last week, and the mental picture of Crankower crumpled on the floor brought a reluctant smile to her lips.

Her theme music played itself out, but when she checked the monitor to see how many callers were waiting, the screen was blank. Her smile disappeared, and her heart plummeted as she looked through the plate glass at Diane. Her producer grimaced and shrugged in apology. Taking a deep breath, Olivia went on the air alone.

"This is the *Liv Live* Thank-God-we're-back-in-the-studio edition. And I'm waiting to hear from you. For those of you who may have forgotten, the number is 1-555-LIV-LIVE. While you're dialing, I'd like to take a minute to try to explain what happened during my week of captivity.

"The bottom line here is, I'm only human." She paused to let that sink in. "I'm a trained therapist, and I think as an uninvolved third party, I bring new insight to your problems and issues." She caught Diane's eye and shrugged as her tone turned wry. "It's not always so easy to do the same for myself."

Olivia wanted desperately to stand and pace the small space, but she was tied to the microphone and through it to her audience. As she spoke to her listeners, certain basic truths that she had avoided facing during the long, grueling week became clear. She doubted anyone was more surprised than she was at the words that came out of her mouth.

"I have feelings for Matt Ransom that are not easily defined. I first knew him when I was way too young, and it ended badly. The only feelings I could admit to before this week were hurt and anger. But there's more than that."

Olivia saw Diane take a call, and as she talked, additional phone calls came in.

"It occurs to me that I keep urging you, my listeners, to be honest and follow your hearts even when it's difficult." She laughed ruefully. "*Especially* when it's difficult."

She folded her hands on the table in front of her as she continued. "I haven't cut you one inch of slack. But when it came to myself, well, I took a lot of rope and hung myself with it. I couldn't admit that what I felt for Matt could be anything more than righteous anger and disdain. And ultimately lust."

She saw Diane go still in the control room and imagined a hush falling over the station. She wondered where Matt was and wondered, again, if he was listening.

"What you saw Sunday night was my totally misguided attempt to force Matt Ransom to own up to his feelings for me. You see, I wanted and expected him to do something I couldn't even do myself. Denial is an incredible thing. I focused on his shortcomings, his walls, his methods of coping, and I found them unsatisfactory. But I refused to take a look at my own."

All the phone lines were lit up now. Diane typed frantically on her keyboard, but Olivia couldn't stop talking. She had to come clean.

"So you see, I'm a fraud. Not because I couldn't resist Matt Ransom, but because I couldn't follow my own advice."

The truth hit her then like the proverbial ton of bricks. She was in love with Matt Ransom. Still. Always. Her mouth snapped shut as the realization sank in. All the anger, all the jealousy, all the mind-numbing sexual tension were obvious indications of the intensity of her feelings for the man, and she had managed to deny or rationalize every single reaction.

Stooping to his level, and in the most inept way possible, she had tried to force him to admit that she was more important to him than the other women who'd wandered in and out of his life.

"Matt Ransom is juvenile and completely annoying." She paused, and when she continued, she could hear the horror in her voice. "And I seem to be in love with him."

Olivia fell silent as the ramifications of what she'd said began to sink in. She was in love with Matt Ransom. She was in love with a man who treated women as conveniences, a man who had erected walls around his heart that were all but unscalable and then topped them with twists of barbed wire to discourage even the most foolhardy.

Was she really that foolhardy? Olivia scanned the list of waiting callers, hoping against hope that Matt's name would be among them. In her little fantasy world, he would hear her admission of love and, zing, he too would realize that they were destined to be together. Right. And then he'd propose to her on the air. And carry her off to Never Land to play with the other lost boys. She'd have to change her name to Wendy. And move to London.

"So." She finally noticed Diane's frantic hand signals. "So I guess I'll take a call while we all let that little bombshell sink in. Let's see . . ."

She noticed JoBeth's name on the monitor and put her on the air.

"Gee, Dr. O." JoBeth sounded almost as uncertain as Olivia felt. "I kind of hate to interrupt."

"No problem," Olivia replied. "I just, uh, needed to clear the air." *Too bad she'd used a sledgehammer to do it.* "Tell me what's happening."

"Well, I'm still trying to decide what to do," JoBeth said. "I mean, both you and Matt said that if I wanted to get married and Dawg didn't, that I should move on."

"He said that?"

"Yep." JoBeth sounded far too resigned for a woman contemplating marriage. Olivia could still remember settling for James when all she'd wanted was Matt. Today, of all days, she didn't want to see JoBeth make the same mistake.

"You know, JoBeth, when you peel everything else away, there's really only one thing that matters: Which is more important to you, being married or who you share your life with? When you know the answer to that, you'll know what to do."

"I was hoping for something a little more specific."

"I know," said Olivia. "But I think I've already given you more answers than I should have. It's time to start trusting your gut."

Of course, it was her gut that had prompted her to make such an outrageously public confession, and all she had to show for it was a hollow feeling in the pit of her stomach and a dim ache in the region of her heart. The potential for even greater humiliation loomed on the horizon.

At the signal from Diane, Olivia ended the call and waited out the scheduled commercial break.

She knew that if Matt hadn't been tuned in when she signed on, someone must have clued him in by now, but although lots of callers were waiting, not a single one of them was Matt. She thought about the baggage he carried with him, about the loss and pain he'd buried so deeply, and wished he'd let her help him through it. More than anything, she wanted him to be free to love her back in a way she could accept.

Coming out of the break, Olivia considered how she would have counseled a caller in her predicament. She'd told JoBeth and countless others to pursue their dreams and go after what they wanted.

It was her misfortune to want Matt Ransom, but want

him she did—all of him, on a permanent basis, and in every possible way. It was time to start scaling a few walls and long past time to start practicing what she preached.

In a healthy relationship both parties shared their thoughts and feelings. Expectations were to be . . . expected. She was entitled to know how Matt felt about her.

She closed her eyes and took a deep breath. Her heart hammered in her chest.

"As I mentioned earlier, I, uh, seem to be in love with Matt Ransom." She paused. "And I think the time has come to find out how Matt feels about me."

Her hands shook, but it was too late to turn back now. "If you're out there, Matt, you need to pick up a phone and give me a call. And you need to be ready to share."

Olivia did another scan of waiting callers, but Matt's name still wasn't among them. Her mouth was dry, and she felt strangely light-headed, but in her heart she knew she owed it to both of them to be clear about what she wanted.

Taking a deep breath, she issued a final challenge. "Come on, Matt. Pick up the phone and give me a call. Let's see if you have what it takes to leave Never Land behind."

29

Matt considered calling Olivia for all of five seconds. He'd been in the shower when she signed on, toweling off when she first uttered the L-word, and breaking out in a cold sweat by the time she challenged him to call.

Tucking a towel around his hips, he wiped steam off the bathroom mirror and caught a glimpse of his face. Grooves of panic sliced across his forehead, and his eyes were those of a cornered animal. His usual expression of detached amusement was nowhere to be found. Olivia had turned the tables on him so neatly, he had no idea what he felt or how to respond.

Matt covered his cheeks with shaving cream and jerked the razor downward, nicking an ear in the process. He couldn't imagine what Olivia was thinking, but if she expected him to call and "share" his innermost feelings on demand, she was living in a fantasy world screwier than the one she'd accused him of inhabiting.

He'd call her when he was good and ready and had some earthly idea of what to say. And not a moment before.

In the meantime, he'd put some miles between them. He was way overdue for a trip home to Chicago. This was an excellent opportunity to catch up with his mother and sister and spend some quality time with his nephews. The station could go find some other trained monkey to fill in for him. After the shit they'd pulled, he didn't owe them squat.

Matt added clean clothes to the duffel bag still sitting on his bedroom floor and called the station, refusing to talk to anyone but T.J. Then he backed the car out of the garage and headed toward I-75, where he pointed the nose of the Corvette north and applied his foot firmly to the accelerator.

He spent the next 422 miles trying to fathom the turn his life had taken. He still couldn't believe Crankower and T.J. had pulled off such a sordid little scheme, any more than he could come to terms with the whole mess between himself and Olivia. Once again she'd managed to scale walls he'd spent years erecting, and once again she wanted to drag him to a place he'd sworn he'd never go.

She'd made him talk about Adam, forced him to share feelings he'd kept locked away for a lifetime, and no matter how hard he tried, she refused to let him slide back to his comfort zone. Olivia Moore expected more of him than any woman ever had, and it annoyed the hell out of him that some perverse part of him wanted to give it to her.

He stopped for the night at a Holiday Inn just north of Louisville and was registered by a smiling, pink-cheeked college student who seemed younger than he'd ever been. She actually blushed when she asked him if he was traveling on his own, and he told himself it was only fatigue that stopped him from inviting her to join him for dinner.

Letting himself into his room with the key card, Matt dropped his bag on the bed. He'd made good time, first on 75, then jogging west on 24 around Chattanooga, and under other circumstances he would have driven straight through, but now that he'd put Atlanta behind him he was strangely reluctant to reach his destination. Maybe he'd take a couple of extra days before he faced his past, *not*, he hastily assured himself, that that was the reason for this trip.

While driving, he'd purposely left his cell phone in his bag in the trunk so he wouldn't be tempted to use it, but he pulled it out now to call an old friend who lived in the area. His next call would be to his sister to let her know when to expect him.

All he was looking for was a little R and R, a little time to regroup and get his head back on straight. There was no reason at all why he couldn't hang with friends and enjoy himself a little.

As far as Matt was concerned, there wasn't a damn thing wrong with Never Land as long as you still knew how to fly.

JoBeth handled the overflow lunch crowd on automatic pilot. She waited on customers and cleared tables, smiling and nodding her head at what felt like the right moments. It was a damn good thing her mouth and body could work independently of her brain, because her brain was full of the question Dr. O had raised the day before. And her gut was too busy churning to provide her with an answer.

She wanted to fall in love with Kevin Middleton. She

already loved his mountain house and the lifestyle he offered, but every time she tried to examine her feelings for him, her brain shut down and her stomach hurt.

At three o'clock she untied her apron and clocked out. All the way home she told herself she was finished with Dawg, that Kevin deserved a chance. That there didn't have to be wild heart-throbbing love for a relationship to work. But the thought of never feeling that again filled her with such sadness she wanted to cry.

By the time she got home and parked in the drive, she had calmed down enough to think rationally. She was too old to worry about true love and old enough to appreciate the importance of compromise. Two people who shared the same vision could build a life together, she told herself. She could live without excitement and passionate lovemaking if she got children and security and respect in return. And she knew she could make Kevin Middleton happy.

But not to hold Dawg in her arms again? Never to feel him settle inside her and rock her world to pieces? Could she really live without that?

JoBeth spent the rest of the afternoon cleaning house. She chased nonexistent dust bunnies out of corners, wiped baseboards that already gleamed with fresh paint, and took a toothbrush to the newly installed tile in the guest bathroom. While she worked, her head and her heart battled, her brain arguing the logic of a life with Kevin Middleton, her heart clinging stubbornly to its memories of Dawg Rollins.

By six o'clock her tiny house sparkled. Spent, JoBeth poured herself a tall glass of sweet tea and carried it out to the porch, where she sat and rocked for a time, studying the bright yellow daffodils that bordered the walkway and testing her resolve.

She would go for moderately-happy-ever-after with Kevin Middleton. She would settle for less than a love match in exchange for the family she wanted to build, and she would make it work. But not before she had one last night with Dawg.

There was nothing like rejection to put a woman in touch with her insecurities. As Olivia rediscovered in the aftermath of her confession, neither education, occupation, nor social position could prevent a woman from falling into the pit of self-doubt. Nor could they predict how long it would take her to claw her way back out.

Despite her training and the years spent counseling others, Olivia Moore, Ph.D., handled Matt's rejection in much the same way early cavewoman must have handled hers when her Neanderthal man used his club to drag another woman back to the cave. That is to say, she handled it badly.

For two point five days Olivia did *Liv Live*—which used to last only three hours and now seemed to go on forever—and then she went home and engaged in pathetically clichéd behavior. Like countless women before her, she donned her fuzziest bathrobe so that she could sit on her couch and eat large quantities of Ben & Jerry's straight from the carton, which was immediately followed by more chocolate than the law allowed. At night, suffering from insomnia and her self-induced sugar high, she paced the rooms of her home until she could have called out their dimensions in her sleep—if only she could have gotten some.

For two point five days she wallowed and paced. And paced and wallowed. Not even James's betrayal and the resulting divorce had shaken her so completely.

And then on Friday afternoon, when it was finally possible to leave town without looking like she was running away, she took a flight to Tampa and picked up a rental car for the drive over the Howard Frankland Bridge to St. Petersburg. With her hair whipping around her face and the salt-tinged air filling her lungs, she followed the familiar scent to the Gulf of Mexico where a small beach road took her toward the southernmost tip of Pass-A-Grille.

New multimillion-dollar homes dotted the sandy white beach, but there were still plenty of small funky beach cottages lazing under the swaying palms. It was in front of one of these, on the corner of a tiny street that stretched from the beach to the bay side, that Olivia parked.

The house was hers, bought with her first radio money and held on to with steely determination through the chaos of her divorce. It had a faded picket fence, a crabgrass-and-sand lawn, a sagging front porch, and gulls wheeling in the blue sky. Less than a block away, the waves kissed up to the shore.

Olivia breathed in the damp salt air and felt her heart lighten a notch. She and James had lived in a well-manicured north Tampa suburb, but this had always been her preferred retreat. It was a place for getting heart and head in line, and its magic had never failed her.

Pulling her bag and a sack of groceries from the car,

Olivia held the screen door out of the way and fit her key into the ancient lock. Minutes later every window in the house had been thrown open to the late afternoon breeze, and she and her glass of wine were outside beside a sand dune, waiting for the sun to sink into the sea.

On Saturday and Sunday she woke with the sun and crossed to the beach to begin her trek toward the northernmost tip of St. Pete Beach, where she sat at a concession stand with an egg sandwich and orange juice and people-watched until she was ready to head back down the beach again. She walked countless miles under blue skies stuffed with cotton-ball clouds, and the slap of hard-packed sand against the soles of her feet soothed her in a way indoor pacing never had.

In the afternoon she lathered on sunscreen and stretched out on a blanket to read. Or gave herself up to the enjoyment of the ever-changing light that danced across the swells, reassured to see that fiddler crabs still scurried across the wet sand, and seagulls still knew how to cage food from the less savvy tourists. All the while her mind whirled with the jumble of thoughts and feelings that had brought her here.

By Sunday evening her hurt and humiliation had been tempered by a new sense of calm. She'd been honest and ultimately true to herself and her feelings, just as she counseled her listeners to be. Matt Ransom was either uninterested or unable to do the same.

She had only one course of action open to her: to pick up the pieces and go on. She'd survived Matt Ransom eight years ago with far fewer tools and resources at her disposal than she had now. She could survive him again. She had a life and a career to pour her energies into, and if the ache in her heart hurt even more than the egg on her face, she'd make sure no one else ever knew it.

Early Monday morning as she flew back to Atlanta, the concept of survival was still very much on her mind. Women survived heartache and disappointment all the time, and daily demands that men could never fathom. An idea mushroomed as she worked her way out of Hartsfield Airport and into the flow of rush-hour traffic.

She called Diane from the car to pull some music and give her a heads-up while she contemplated what she wanted to do on the air. She'd try not to bash too hard, but she intended to have her say. This morning's show would be dedicated to all the women out there who knew how to survive ... and the men who couldn't seem to keep up with them.

30

———

JoBeth reached across Dawg to switch off the alarm clock before it rang. The move brought her breast in direct contact with his arm, and she saw him smile automatically in his sleep.

She wasn't sure why she'd set the alarm, when she'd had no intention of sleeping. At 3 A.M., when he finally drifted off after their last round of lovemaking, she'd propped herself up on one elbow to watch him breathe, not wanting to miss a single minute of her last night with Dawg.

"Mmmm." Dawg reached out one big hand and ran it slowly down the curve of her hip. His eyes remained closed, but hers were riveted on the familiar planes and angles of his face and the golden morning stubble that covered it.

Her gaze traveled down the massive chest with its curly golden-gray mat of hair. He was warm and solid and smelled of their lovemaking. Quietly she drank him in, branding this man and this moment into her memory forever.

When she couldn't ignore the clock any longer, JoBeth

eased gently out of bed, careful not to wake him, and walked to the bathroom, closing the door behind her.

It was the muted sound of the shower that penetrated Dawg's sleep-filled brain, but it was the image of JoBeth climbing in all dewy and delicious that brought him fully awake. Rolling over and stretching contentedly, he considered joining her.

Instead he lay there grinning. Lord, he felt good. Tired, even a little bit sore from all the gymnastics, but deep down good and satisfied.

He'd just hit town after a run up to the Northeast when he picked up the message from JoBeth. It had been too many days since he'd seen her, too many days in the cab of his rig with nothing to think about but their relationship. Days he'd used to hash out his feelings. For the first time, he was ready to discuss what might come next.

But for the first time in who knew how long, JoBeth had not been eager to discuss the future. In fact, she'd hardly seemed interested in *talking* at all.

Dawg settled onto his back and pillowed his head in his hands. He could hear JoBeth singing in the shower, and he grinned again as his mind played over the night they'd spent together.

She'd greeted him at her front door wearing the crotchless black teddy he'd given her for her birthday. When he'd tried to tell her what he'd been thinking about their relationship, she'd put a finger over his lips to shush him and crawled into his lap. All the blood in his body had immediately rushed to his head, and he didn't mean the one that supported his baseball cap.

She'd teased him with the crotchless lingerie until he'd been wild with wanting her. He'd dropped his pants and taken her the first time while she bent way over into the refrigerator, supposedly looking for a bottle of wine. And a second time on the living room floor after she undressed him in the candlelight.

By the time they made it to the bedroom, the only sounds he was making were groans of ecstasy. It was a night he'd remember until the day he died.

Dawg blinked and sat up in bed as he realized just how strange JoBeth's behavior had been. She'd always been a willing sexual partner, and they'd passed some great hours in bed, but he couldn't remember her ever being quite so aggressive. And why hadn't she wanted to talk?

He swung his legs over the side of the bed and stood. After a brief knock on the bathroom door, he pushed it open.

"JoBeth, why don't you come on out here and sit down so we can talk about us?"

He watched her wrap the white terry bath towel around her body and tuck one end in above her breasts.

"Can't do it, Dawg. I'm already late for work."

His eyes narrowed. "But what if I have something I want to tell you? What if I want to—"

She stepped forward and put a finger over his lips just like she had the night before. "No, Dawg. Let's not spoil what we've just had. Didn't you think it was the most awesome night?"

"Well, of course, I . . ."

She picked up a brush from the bathroom counter and ran it through her short curls. Her face glowed, and her lips looked all shiny and kissable.

"There's really nothing to talk about," she said. "I'm still floating on air from all the lovin' you gave me."

He heard the word "love" and opened his mouth to tell her what he'd been thinking, but she put her finger to his lips again and brushed by him on her way into the bedroom.

He followed her, trying to figure out just what was going on, and got there in time to watch her drop her towel and wiggle into a lacy white bra and panties.

"I really have to run. Noreen'll never be able to handle the breakfast rush without me."

She stepped into her uniform and pulled it up. Moving in front of him, she presented her back for zipping. He obliged and then put his hands on her shoulders, thinking he'd turn her around so they could talk, but she slipped out of his grasp and scurried over to the closet, where she poked around until she located her white cushioned loafers.

"But, JoBeth, I'm trying to tell you I—"

"I'm sorry to have to run off like this, Dawg. There's coffee in the cupboard and some muffins in the bread box." She smiled sweetly, but he was starting to think he'd been had. "Will you lock the door behind you when you leave? You don't need a key to do it."

"JoBeth, why don't you just call in sick? I have something I want to tell you."

"Sorry, can't do it." She went up on tiptoe, gave him a friendly peck on the cheek, and practically ran out the front door.

Dawg watched the door swing shut. In the empty living room he muttered, "I guess I won't be needin' to get down on one knee today." And wondered why he didn't feel relieved.

At 9:00 A.M. Olivia went on the air looking for a little satisfaction. "Good morning, everyone," she said. "This is *Liv Live* fresh from the beach, back in the saddle, and eager to deal with your problems. But before we start with your questions, I'd like to do something a little different."

Olivia punched up the music she'd asked Diane to put together, a compilation of female affirmations from the seventies and eighties. Helen Reddy's "I Am Woman" bled seamlessly into Gloria Gaynor's "I Will Survive" as Olivia prepped her listeners.

"My recent experiences have forced me to take an all-too-personal look into the male psyche, and I have to tell you it's not pretty in there. In my opinion women are looking for answers, while men—at least the kind of men who dwell in places like Never Land and Fantasy Island—are busy trying to duck the questions. Today's show is about coping with reality, women's reality.

"My declaration last week, and Matt Ransom's lack of response, is a prime example of how differently men and women handle their lives. I find myself wondering how many men could survive even one day as a woman."

Olivia let the question hang there for a few seconds and then continued. "So today, just for fun, and because I really need to vent, we're going to create our own version of *Survivor* . . . for men."

She winked at Diane and settled into her seat. "Here's the deal: Ten men get dropped in suburbia and have to survive a woman's life. They each have an SUV, three kids—all of whom play at least one sport and take either music or dance lessons—and little to no help from their significant other.

"Your job is to help figure out what hoops they have to jump through."

Olivia brought the instrumental track of "I Will Survive" up full and then took it under. A glance at the monitor showed callers stacked up and eager to play the game.

"Okay, I've got Miranda on the air," Olivia said. "What else do you think our contestants should have with them?"

"The family dog," Miranda chirped. "She's in heat, wearing diapers, and the kids are asking questions."

"Gee, that's really good, Miranda. Any other ideas?"

"I think they should have to shave their legs and wear makeup."

Olivia's next caller was a woman named Dawn.

"It's the middle of summer and they have to wear panty hose—the twelve-dollar-a-pair kind that run just before a big presentation. And high heels with pointy little toes."

"Been there, done that." Olivia smiled. "And why don't we go ahead and outlaw fast food while we're at it? I think our contestants should have to cook everything they serve." She smiled again as the number of waiting calls doubled. "Hi, Tina. You're on the air."

"Hi, Dr. O. I think we should make them do the laundry and clean up after a sick kid at 2 A.M. And I don't think they should be allowed to watch television until the kids are asleep and all the chores are done."

"Cool." Olivia grinned evilly. "And let's make sure none of the TVs have a remote."

Diane punched up a sound effect of gasps of horror while Olivia kept the music low underneath.

"This is your fantasy, ladies. Don't hold back," Olivia said as she took another call. "Carmen, it's your turn. Tell me what you have in store for our contestants."

"I'd like to see them sit through a PTA meeting and accurately report the results. Or build a model of Mount Vesuvius out of flour and water—the night before it's due. Better yet, let's let them convince a three-year-old to eat a spoonful of peas."

Olivia blinked. "Gee, this is getting kind of scary."

Carmen laughed. "Yeah. Real life can take a lot more out of you than the Australian Outback or the Dark Continent."

Olivia couldn't help smiling as she prepared to segue into the commercial break. "You know, if we throw in potty training and trying to get the opposite sex to admit their feelings, our contestants will be begging to get voted out."

Olivia sneaked in Sister Sledge's "We Are Family," letting it continue underneath her voice as she headed into the commercial break. "As far as I'm concerned, we have a hit TV show on our hands. Thanks for helping me vent, ladies. I think it's time to move on to your issues now. If you've got something on your mind, give me a call. I'm ready to help you live your life . . . *live*."

Matt stepped onto the front porch of the home he'd grown up in. It was a low, sprawling house built in the once popular Prairie style, and like the more impressive Victorians and Tudors that dotted the tree-lined

Northside Chicago neighborhood, it had been painstakingly maintained.

He rang the bell and soon saw his mother's figure approaching through the art glass inset in the old wooden door. He could still remember her shouts of "Don't slam it, you'll break the glass," but couldn't remember a time he or Adam had ever heeded the warning.

The door swung open, and his mother stood there. Before the smile lit her face, for just that instant before she caught herself, her gaze swung to Matt's right, where Adam had always stood. And even after twenty-three years, she seemed surprised to find him missing.

In the past he would have ignored it, made a joke, let it go, but thanks to Olivia's damned interference, he'd spent too many hours remembering, and he was too raw for that. "You've never once looked at me without wishing Adam were here."

The smile froze on her lips, and he knew she wanted to deny it, but the truth radiated from the brown eyes she'd passed on to both her sons. "No," she admitted. "I haven't."

Matt opened his mouth expecting to make a typically glib response, but came out with, "And I've been trying to live a big enough life for Adam and me. I'm not sure how much longer I can keep it up."

He wasn't sure which of them was more surprised.

"Goodness, Matthew. Whatever happened to 'hello'?" Margaret Ransom went up on tiptoe to peck his cheek.

He saw the shimmer of tears in her eyes and watched her blink them away before she turned on her heel to lead the way into the kitchen. He felt like a complete and utter shit.

"Your sister and the children are here. She and Dan just got back from Italy, and she's made us some of her new specialty. It's something, something over fettuccine."

Matt dropped his bag in the foyer and followed his mother into the heart of the house. Funny that he thought of it that way when it was he and Sandra who had forced that heart to beat. He stepped into the kitchen and sniffed appreciatively, determined to drop the introspection and get back on more familiar emotional ground. He enjoyed food and cooked for his own amusement, but his sister had channeled their childhood discovery into an increasingly successful Italian restaurant.

"What's that I smell? Pomodoro? Marinara? Something smells downright incredible."

Matt's nephews jumped up and threw themselves at him while his older sister looked on with an affectionate smile. "Downright? I think someone's been in the South too long."

He ruffled the twins' hair. "Ya'll think I have a funny accent?"

Kyle and Kenny giggled and tried to reach his head to ruffle him back.

"Hey, I'd be careful how I treated the uncle who's holding some fine seats for tomorrow night's Cubs game."

There were shrieks of joy as Matt held up the proof. "Dugout level. Seven P.M. Be there or be square."

"Matt Ransom, tomorrow night is a school night. The boys have—"

He walked to his sister and bussed her on the cheek. "Chill out, San. When you're nine and your uncle comes to town, baseball is required. You and Dan can come, too, if you behave."

He reached past her to the stove, lifted the lid of the largest pot, and studied its contents. "Here I thought you'd learned something new and exotic during your travels, but I see you're still relying on Ragú."

Sandra grabbed the lid back and pushed him out of the way. "Ha. You know better than to use that word in my presence. Now open that bottle of wine, pronto. I want to try this dish out on you."

She looked him up and down. "And then I'd like to hear what in the world is going on between you and Dr. O."

31

Just as she'd hoped, the trip to the beach had broken Olivia's cycle of wallowing and hiding. She still had trouble falling asleep, and she woke way too early, but now she made a point of putting those late-night and predawn hours to good use.

She spent time every morning on the new book she'd pitched to her editor about why women were reluctant to ask for what they wanted most. When it got light out, she did a three-mile run, took a quick shower, and downed a bowl of cereal. By seven forty-five she was on her way to work.

There she funneled her energy into her callers and their problems, squashing speculation about why Matt hadn't called and shrugging off offers of sympathy with a "win some, lose some" philosophy she wished she could actually feel.

At noon, when *Liv Live* was over, she went out for lunch with friends, or used the time to do research for her book. She accepted a speaking engagement, and was careful not to get too defensive when Matt's name came up.

She knew from experience that if she continued to

pretend that she was fine, at some point she would be. So she threw her shoulders back, held her head high, and strode through her life with all the gusto she could muster. Inside she was a quivering mass of Jell-O, but since nobody could see inside, she managed to keep the wobbliness to herself.

Though she would die before admitting it, some days she found herself in front of the television set at one o'clock, when *All My Children* came on. And still sitting there when *Oprah* ended at five.

Worse, she couldn't bypass a Braves game on TV, and her skill with the remote was improving at an alarming rate.

Diane was the only person who seemed aware of the terrible dichotomy between Olivia's outer calm and her inner turmoil, and Olivia suspected her producer's latest diet and exercise regimen had as much to do with trying to keep an eye on Olivia as it did with improving her health.

Olivia sat on her front porch step waiting for Diane to arrive for their after-dinner walk. The evening was mild, and the shouts of children playing in a nearby cul-de-sac mingled with the hum of a lawn mower two houses away. When Diane pulled up to the curb, Olivia ambled down the driveway to greet her. After a few discreet stretches, they began their walk.

At the half-mile mark Diane announced, "I swore off Twinkies this afternoon."

"That's great," Olivia replied.

"And I'm thinking about working with a personal trainer."

"That's great, too. I'm glad to see you so serious about

your new exercise program." Olivia smiled and picked up the pace. They walked for a whole minute before Diane asked, "So have you heard anything from Matt?"

Olivia stumbled over an uneven spot in the sidewalk and took her time righting herself. "No." She eyed her producer, but couldn't bring herself to ask the same question in return.

As it turned out, Diane required little to no pumping. She got a little heel-toe action going and swung her bent arms as she confided, "Ben says Matt's out of town, but he doesn't know for how long."

Olivia wanted to ask where he'd gone and whether he'd said anything about her on-air confession or the jab she'd taken at him with the "Survivor" show, but asking Diane to ask Ben to ask Matt how he felt smacked of high school machinations. The last thing she intended to do was let people know how much Matt's actions, or lack thereof, mattered.

They walked in silence for a time, and just when she'd decided there was no way she could bring up Matt's name without embarrassing herself, Diane said, "I know you told me you're not interested in the gory details, but Ben thinks Matt's in Chicago. T.J.'s the only one who's heard from him."

"Um, thanks," Olivia managed.

They completed a full circuit of the neighborhood and walked up the hill to stand in front of Olivia's mailbox. Diane bent and wrapped her hands around the backs of her knees in a very impressive stretch. Straightening, she did a few quick air punches and said, "Well, I really enjoyed our walk. Maybe we could make it a regular thing."

"Absolutely. You sure you don't want to come in for a cold drink?" Olivia asked.

"Nah. I've got a bottled water in the car, and I want to get my sit-ups in before bed."

Olivia's eyebrows shot up. "You're really serious this time, aren't you?"

Diane nodded and pulled her car keys out of her pocket. "And I'll tell you something else. Although I personally don't believe he's fit to lick your Nikes, if you think of anything else you don't want to know about Matt, I'll be glad to ask around."

Time was supposed to fly when you were having fun. But if this week was any indication, it also flew when you weren't. JoBeth knew her life must look pretty fine from the outside: She had her own home, work she enjoyed, and Kevin Middleton waging a serious campaign to "win her back." If only Dawg would stop trying to get together to discuss their relationship, she was certain she'd be on cloud nine.

It was a glorious Saturday morning, and she was spending it on a brown vinyl couch in the waiting area of Joe's Garage.

She eyed the two other patrons and then let her gaze roam around the room to the small corner table with its hours-old pot of coffee and plate of picked-over muffins. She resisted for about fifteen minutes before walking over to scope out the plate, which contained one blueberry muffin and a small mound of crumbs. Idly, she pushed buttons on the wall-mounted TV just above it. Unable to get a picture, she headed back to her seat.

For a few minutes she used her growling stomach as a diversion so she wouldn't have to think about the twist her life had taken.

Seducing Dawg had turned out to be an incredibly bad idea. Now she had more memories than she'd intended; memories that popped up at the worst possible moment, like when Kevin took off his shirt at the lake and revealed his scrawny chest, or when she tried to imagine a lifetime of waking up as Mrs. Kevin Middleton—which would require going to bed as her, too. If her regrets were only physical, it might not be so tough. But no matter how many times her head voted for Kevin, her heart cried out for Dawg.

Looking for another distraction, JoBeth dumped the contents of her purse on the scarred table in front of her and began a serious search for food. She found one cellophane-wrapped breath mint, two smashed M&Ms, and about a pound of accumulated trash, which she spent ten minutes separating into piles before tossing them into the can Joe had so thoughtfully provided.

She looked up to find both of the other customers watching her. "I hate waiting around, don't you?"

No answer.

"Either of you want that last muffin?" she asked.

One of them shrugged, and the other shook her head.

"Great." JoBeth walked over to claim her prize. Her cell phone rang, and she used her free hand to paw through her purse.

Dawg's cell phone number appeared on the phone's tiny face, and JoBeth froze. She knew if she let herself have so much as a conversation with him, she'd crumble like a potato chip. Knew that if he said he loved her one more time, she'd say she loved him, too, and apologize for starting the whole marriage conversation. And then where would she be?

She wanted a partner, a partner who would share the good and the bad, who would be a father to their children and a mate for life. She wanted all kinds of things Dawg Rollins didn't. And that was that.

All week she'd been careful not to be where he might be, and she was prepared to claim all sorts of phone and technical failures if it ever came down to it. There was no way she could give Kevin a fair shake if she kept thinking about Dawg all the time. She turned the phone off and crammed it back in her purse.

JoBeth ate the muffin without tasting it, and when she couldn't take hanging around anymore, she stepped out into the work area of the garage. She found Joe bent double over the front of her Cadillac, his head stuck beneath the raised hood.

"How're you coming?"

"Almost done. Should be able to have you out of here in just a couple minutes."

"Good." JoBeth took her checkbook out of her purse, opened the driver's door, and leaned in to set her bag on the seat. She heard the hood thunk down into place. When she came back around the car, Joe was wiping his hands on the greasy towel that hung from his belt.

"What do I owe you?"

Joe finished with the towel and looked up in surprise. "Dawg just called and said he was on his way over to take care of it."

"No, I'm paying." She flipped open her checkbook, her

heart starting to race. She needed to be on her way before Dawg arrived. "How much, Joe?"

"JoBeth, I don't want to get in the middle of anything. The man wants to pay the bill."

"Joe Larson, this is my car and my responsibility. You tell me how much I owe you right now, or I'm going to call the Better Business Bureau and report you for, for . . . refusing to take my money."

Joe laughed, a big belly laugh that made his midsection jiggle. "First I ever heard of being reported for *not* charging somebody. I got to remember that one."

"Fine. You go on ahead and write it down *after* you tell me the amount." She did not want to run into Dawg now, after a whole week of successful ducking and hiding.

Joe mumbled an amount that had to be too low. Her pen flew as she scribbled out the check, adding another twenty dollars just to show them both who they were screwing with.

Not waiting for her receipt, she jumped into the Caddy and started her up, noticing even in her hurry that the engine turned right over. Then with a last "Thanks" and a wave, she backed out, threw the car into drive, and burned rubber in her haste to escape.

Two traffic lights later, her pulse had slowed to something resembling normal. Resting her forehead on the steering wheel while she waited for the light to change, she told herself she'd done the right thing.

Right now, avoiding Dawg Rollins was a matter of self-preservation. Kevin Middleton was a fine man who would make a good husband. He'd already started talking about his vision of the life they could have together, and she suspected he was very close to popping the question. All she had to do was find a way to fall in love with him.

Dawg Rollins peered through the window at the indoor running track on the YMCA's second floor. It was a fine spring day, but he hadn't wanted to run alone where his thoughts would have nothing to settle on but JoBeth. Here, other runners were already pounding out their miles on the cushioned rubber oval, and because it was open to the workout area below, there were plenty of distractions to help the time pass quickly. Of course, given his knees and his forty-four years, the more forgiving indoor surface was nothing to be sneered at.

Fitting himself into the flow of runners, he started out easy, regulating his breathing and finding his pace. After the first two miles, he slowed and took an inside lane to get a better view of the activity below.

StairMasters, treadmills, and exercise bikes lined the mirrored walls. The center of the room had been divided into two sections, with free weights occupying the left side of the great room and strength-training equipment on the right. A Sunday afternoon crowd huffed and sweated its way through a hundred different workouts. Dawg's gaze skimmed over the group, picking out the serious lifters from the weekend warriors, enjoying the sight of the women who belonged in spandex and trying to avoid looking at those who didn't.

About mile four, he found himself focusing on an elderly couple working their way through a series of machines. The woman moved slowly, as if putting one foot in front of the other required great effort and concentration. One side of her body seemed frozen, and Dawg wondered if she'd had a stroke.

The man, whom Dawg assumed to be her husband, looked fit and comfortable, but he slowed his pace to match his wife's, and he held both of their towels, a water bottle, and a card for recording workout progress. He didn't look around, but focused all of his attention on the woman beside him.

When a machine became available, the man would adjust the weights and settings, help the woman carefully onto it, and then talk her through the exercise, penciling in the number of repetitions on the card when she finished. The woman's attention turned to each new machine, while the man's remained riveted on her. Dawg could almost feel his iron will joining and solidifying the woman's, and though he couldn't hear his words, Dawg imagined their loving tone.

Dawg's heart squeezed as he imposed himself and JoBeth into the scene. Perhaps it would be JoBeth leading him around, helping him grow strong again. Maybe they'd be lucky and never need to draw this deeply on each other's strength.

But whatever happened, he now understood that this was what it all came down to: the complete giving of oneself to another, the sharing of the good and the bad that life had to offer. This was what JoBeth had been asking for, but until recently he'd been too busy sidestepping the whole issue to actually listen to what she was saying.

Dawg slowed to a walk. He'd been such an incredible fool, it was no wonder she'd been avoiding him lately.

It was time to stop circling around the issue. He loved

JoBeth Namey, and he knew now just how much he wanted to marry her.

He left the track and went down to the locker room to shower. He needed an engagement ring. Then he needed to find JoBeth and tell her what he'd decided. He could just imagine the joy on her face when he finally popped the question.

Dawg toweled off, dressed, and walked out through the strength-training area, hoping for one last glimpse of the couple who'd finally made him understand what an oaf he'd been.

He saw them making their way toward the water cooler, their hands joined and their heads bent toward each other. Dawg stood for a minute watching them move slowly through the sweating, jabbering crowd, and then he stared at himself for a minute in the mirror. He was more than ready to make JoBeth Namey his wife. Thank goodness he'd come to his senses before it was too late.

32

Matt had been in Evanston for more than a week now, and he still wasn't sure what he was doing there. He'd visited Adam's grave, wandered old haunts, and spent time with his nephews, who seemed eerily like he and Adam had been at their age. He told himself he wasn't there for a reason, that he didn't have to put himself under a microscope like some unfortunate bug just because Olivia thought he needed dissecting. And then proceeded to do exactly that.

He spent even more time thinking about Olivia herself. She popped into his head without warning, and it took a huge amount of effort to shove her out. When he caught himself contemplating how much brighter and more endearing she was than other women he'd known, he knew something was very wrong.

He gave it his best shot, but nothing he did seemed to cure the emptiness he felt or point him in a direction that made sense. Everything that had mattered most to him—his work, his lifestyle—suddenly seemed unbearably shallow and lacking in some elemental way.

Even the bedroom of his youth offered no real

answers. Floor-to-ceiling shelves still bulged with boyhood treasures. Little League trophies sat next to the airplane models Adam had painstakingly assembled. A complete set of Hardy Boys mysteries leaned against a plexiglass cube that contained a baseball signed by the 1974 Cubs. Everything that had mattered before the age of thirteen was on these shelves.

Matt had made the transition to teenager alone in this room. But even as the sports posters he and his twin chose together gave way to Matt's budding passion for rock bands and fast cars, Adam had always been there, the missing part of him standing to his right and sharing his life.

Matt closed his eyes and remembered. He'd lost his virginity at the age of sixteen in the twin bed he now sat on. He'd been nervous as hell, afraid his parents would come home early and catch him and MaryAnn Hightower doing the deed, but sex had been the first thing that knocked Adam out of his brain. He'd been seeking that oblivion ever since.

A knock sounded on the door, and Matt welcomed the interruption. "Come in."

"Hi." His sister stood in the threshold. "Thought you might like to come to the restaurant for lunch today."

"Love to. Mom said something about a walk down to the lake, but we've talked about doing that every day since I got here, and it still hasn't happened. I'm not counting on it."

Sandra walked over and sat next to him. "She's never been able to go back there."

"She's never been able to do a whole lot of things."

"She can't help it, Matt."

"Sure she can, she just won't."

"No. After Daddy died, she finally agreed to try therapy, but she's kept everything bottled up for so long, I don't think she knows where to begin. Sometimes I think Kyle and Kenny will do it for her, but I don't know. She still blames herself."

"We all do. But she's the mother. It was her responsibility to get hold of herself and give a shit about us."

Sandra smiled an incredibly sad smile. "I'm a mother now, little brother. And I can promise you she gave a shit. And she still does. She just can't show it the way we want her to."

Matt knew he sounded like a petulant child, but he couldn't stop himself. "She wasn't the only one who lost someone."

"No, she wasn't." His sister slipped an arm up around his shoulder and squeezed. "And I don't think any of us ever really understood what it must have been like for you. But we all have our chosen method of coping." She placed a hand on his cheek and turned his face toward hers. "Or hiding."

"Olivia accused me of that very thing. Called me a Peter Pan and said I refused to grow up."

"Yeah, I know. I watched the show on the Internet. And I haven't been able to get you to utter her name all week. Obviously my attempts to make you talk have been too subtle."

Matt snorted at the idea of Sandra and the word "subtle" sharing the same sentence, and his gaze cut to the laptop he'd set up to monitor WTLK.

"Things were heating up between you right before we

left for Italy," Sandra said. "But we missed the remote. What happened?"

"You don't even want to know."

"Yes, I do. It would be nice to have some inkling why you've been moping around here all week."

"I'm not moping."

His sister just gave him that look she'd been giving him since she turned thirteen and decided girls were inherently superior to boys. "Well, as far as I'm concerned, she's on the air telling it like it is, while you're . . . ?"

Matt scowled at her.

Sandra just laughed. "I love her show. I keep picturing men in minivans trying to survive in suburbia."

Matt winced. It was hard to believe men and women could ever get together with that kind of condescension coming from the other side. He was just as capable of expressing his feelings and coping with everyday life as the next guy.

Sandra glanced at the clock on the wall and moved toward the computer. Both of their gazes traveled to the screen, and Matt reached over to adjust the volume. A moment later they heard, "This is Dr. Olivia Moore. You're on the air."

"So that's what you're doing here," his sister said. "You're hiding from Dr. O."

"Shhh." Matt raised the volume another notch and heard Olivia say, "I appreciate all the calls and support, but you can stop sending condolence cards. Nobody died. I told Matt Ransom how I felt and he didn't feel the same way. End of story."

His sister shot him another look, but Matt was completely focused on Olivia.

"Granted," she said, "most women don't expose themselves quite so publicly. But to my knowledge no one's ever actually died from embarrassment. I'm fine. Let's get on with your problems and issues."

Matt's gaze strayed to the cell phone lying next to the computer, then moved back to the screen.

Sandra stepped up beside him. "You'd have to be stupid to pass up a woman like Olivia Moore."

"I can't give her what she wants."

"Then give her what you can. She's a professional. She should be able to help fix your sorry ass, and she'd probably do it for free."

Sandra picked up the phone, flipped it open, and scrolled through the electronic phone book. When she found the number for WTLK, she hit the send button and handed it back to him. The door clicked shut behind her as Diane Lowe came on the line.

"Diane? It's Matt."

There was a silence and then, "Well what do you know, the schmuck calleth."

"Nice to talk with you, too, Di. Will you let Olivia know I'm on the line?"

"Probably, but not because I want to."

"Just put me through during the next break."

"Sorry, but as far as I'm concerned you can talk to Olivia on the air or not at all. You owe her at least that."

"All right." Matt took a deep breath and sat down in front of the computer screen, wondering what in the hell he was going to say to her.

A few seconds later they were on the air together.

"Hello, Livvy. How are you?"

At the sound of Matt's voice, Olivia's heart began to pound.

"Never better," she lied, as calmly as she could. "Where are you calling from?"

"Chicago. All the flights to Never Land were full. And I got voted out of my minivan."

She wiped sweaty palms on her pant leg and ordered herself to calm down. Apparently she wasn't prepared for the reality of confronting Matt on the air.

"Glad you've been catching the show. Are you having a good trip?"

"Yeah, everything's great."

"That's good," she said.

They sounded like two acquaintances who'd bumped into each other at a cocktail party. If they didn't watch out they'd be talking about . . .

"How's the weather down there?" Matt asked.

"Fine. It's a little dry, but there's a fifty percent chance of rain over the weekend."

There was a protracted silence.

"So. Are you calling about anything in particular?" she prompted.

"Yes."

He paused, and Olivia braced herself, having no idea what was coming next.

"I've been meaning to apologize for the fiasco during the remote," Matt said. "I have the greatest possible respect for your, um, professional capabilities. And I'm sorry I was partly responsible for compromising that professionalism."

"And?" she prompted again.

"And, uh, I've missed seeing you around. Maybe when I get back we could go out for a drink or something."

"You're asking me out on a date?" she asked incredulously.

"I think so. Is that a problem?"

"Matt, I went on the air over a week ago and admitted that I love you. You didn't bother to call. Now you're calling to ask me out on a date? As far as I'm concerned, we're a couple of light-years beyond dating."

She paused, trying to clamp down on her anger and disappointment; this was not the place to air either. "I don't know what you're doing in Chicago, but it doesn't seem to include getting in touch with reality or yourself. Even you should realize that this would be an ideal time for some self-exploration."

"Olivia, I'm on a vacation, not a spiritual quest. And in my world one person doesn't just blurt out their feelings and then demand that the other person do the same. Why the hell did you say you love me if you think I need so much work?"

His tone had that annoying edge of amusement to it, but Olivia could hear the anger and confusion underneath. At least they had that in common.

"Look," Matt continued. "When you're not trying to nail my ass to a wall, I really enjoy your company. We're good with each other. We have great chemistry together. I want to spend time with you. I have . . . feelings for you, but I am not looking to make declarations of undying love."

"But you do love me, Matt. And your inability to deal with it is an incredible waste." *For both of us.*

She could feel tears forming. Tears of anger and

frustration, tears for what could be if only she could make him see it.

She was a professional therapist in love with a man who refused to take so much as a poke at the cotton wool he'd wrapped around his feelings. And he wouldn't let her take a poke, either.

She scrubbed at her eyes with the back of her hand and blinked back the tears. There was no way she was crying over Matt Ransom. She hadn't allowed it in private; she sure as hell wasn't going to do it in public.

A glance at the digital clock confirmed she was close to sign-off, so she went ahead and brought her theme music in low.

"Oh, no, Olivia. We're not leaving it like this. I came to Chicago for a vacation, not to climb some emotional Everest."

"That's too bad, Matt, because that's exactly what you need to do. If you won't let me help you, then find someone who can. You're way too wonderful to spend the rest of your life as Atlanta's Bachelor of the Year."

"And you're totally incapable of accepting people the way they are. I don't think a psychologist's job is supposed to be changing people against their will."

She brought the music up a notch, but Matt didn't stop talking. "You heard the word 'vacation,' didn't you, Olivia? That means fun . . . friends . . . *women*. I'm not ready to give that up."

"Then we have nothing else to talk about. I'm sorry, Matt, but we seem to be out of time."

She brought her music up full, almost drowning him out.

"Olivia, I'm warning you. I've got my little black book with me, and I'm not afraid to use it."

"Knock yourself out, Matt. And then I'll just finish up getting over you. I understand it doesn't take anywhere near as long the second time."

And then with a great deal of unprofessional satisfaction, she dumped the call.

It took Dawg two days to choose the ring and another day to admit that JoBeth was actively avoiding him. He'd left messages, tried to catch her at work, even carried flowers over to her house, and each time, no JoBeth.

Last night at bowling he'd tried to pump Emmylou for information, but she'd been stubbornly closemouthed except to let Dawg know that JoBeth seemed to be seriously dating her old boyfriend—the accountant her parents had long ago given their seal of approval to.

A sense of urgency gnawed at his gut as Dawg climbed into the Jeep and drove to the Magnolia Diner. Enough was enough. Tonight he intended to get engaged—even if he had to browbeat a little gray-haired waitress to do it.

Noreen didn't look too happy when Dawg slid into the only empty table in her section. In fact, she looked downright ornery.

"Hey, Noreen."

"Hey, Dawg. What can I get you?"

"I need to know where JoBeth is. I want to talk to her."

Noreen stuck her pencil behind her ear and slipped the order pad into her apron pocket. "She doesn't want to talk to *you*, Dawg. She's pursuin' her dreams."

"With Middleton?" He shook his head. "I'm not buyin' it. It's me she loves."

"You know, sometimes that just isn't enough. She deserves a future and a family, and Middleton wants to give her both."

"She'll have to tell me that herself."

"She has told you that, Dawg. More than once. You just haven't been listening."

"Well, I'm all ears now."

The waitress folded her arms across her chest and stared stonily at him.

Dawg reached in his pocket and pulled out the small black velvet box. "You aren't the first person I was planning to show this to, you know."

Noreen's face thawed considerably. She lifted the box in her hand and held it up to the light, admiring the sparkle of the diamond. "That must be a whole carat."

"Well, it's not cubic zirconia, I can promise you that."

"It's right nice, Dawg. But I'm afraid you're a bit late."

Dawg snatched the box back and snapped it closed. "What do you mean?"

"JoBeth bought herself a fancy new dress for her dinner with Kevin tonight. If I don't miss my guess, she's expecting him to propose."

Dawg slid out of the booth and stood, towering over the waitress. "Where are they, Noreen?"

"Well, now, I'm not sure I should—"

"Noreen, I'm going to give you exactly one chance to tell me where they are, and then I'm going to pick you up and sling you over my shoulder and carry you out of this place. If you don't tell me where they are, I'll make you show me."

Noreen giggled like a teenager. "It does my heart good to see you finally realizing what you've had all this time. They're at La Parisienne. I just hope you're not too late. Their reservation was for seven."

Dawg looked down at his watch as he raced for the door. *Damn.* It was eight-thirty, and it would take him at least twenty minutes to get there. He tried not to run over anyone on the way into town, and while he drove he prayed that the service was bad at La Parisienne, or at least real slow.

Twenty minutes and a twenty-dollar bill later, he was knotting the loaner tie around his neck and squeezing into a dinner jacket made for a much smaller man. The maitre d' led him to a small linen-covered table in a secluded alcove, where Kevin Middleton sat alone.

"Where's JoBeth?"

" 'Lo, Rollins. Guess I shouldn't be surprised to see you here."

"Where's JoBeth?"

"You've been on every date we've had. Been a silent partner in every conversation. Might as well be here tonight."

"You're drunk, Middleton. Where's JoBeth?"

"Ladies' room, I think. Asked her to marry me, and she started crying. Said she had to go to the bathroom."

"But what did she say? Did she say yes?"

"Don't know. Couldn't understand a word she was saying. She was blubbering all over herself."

Heartened by Middleton's confusion, Dawg got directions to the ladies' room. After a warning knock, he opened the door and went inside.

JoBeth sat on a fancy sofa sobbing into a wet hanky. When she looked up and saw him, she cried harder.

"JoBeth? Honey?"

"Wh-wh-what are you doing here?" she sobbed. "Don't want to talk to you."

"Now, sweetheart." He plucked a big wad of tissues out of a gold-plated holder on the counter and went to sit next to her on the couch. "Why don't you tell me what happened?"

Her face crumpled, and a line of black gooey stuff streaked down one cheek as she cried. "K-K-Kevin asked me to marry him." She wailed even harder, as if her heart were broken. "Supposed to be the happiest day of my life. Wahhhhhhh."

He put an arm around her shoulder and drew her up against his chest. "Hush, sweetheart. It's okay."

"No, no it's not."

She sobbed until his shirt grew damp from her tears. Not knowing what else to do, he patted her on the back and rocked her like a baby. "Everything's okay, JoBeth."

"I wanted to fall in love with him. I tried so hard."

"I know, sweetheart. I know you did."

Her sobs lessened. She hiccupped, and he handed her another wad of tissue, taking the used ones and shoving them in the jacket pocket.

"But I already love you." She looked up at him, the tears rolling down her cheeks and carrying the last of her makeup with them. "I can't help it."

"I know, JoBeth. Me too." He used the pad of one thumb to wipe the tear tracks off her face. And then he bent down and kissed her.

"I'd rather just be with you than marry anyone else," she whispered.

Even tear-stained and without makeup, she was the most beautiful woman Dawg had ever seen. He wanted to make babies with her and grow old by her side. He'd buy her a gym membership, so she could help him around the equipment when he was old and doddering.

"But I want you to be married," he whispered back.

JoBeth sat up and sniffed. She looked at him in confusion. "You do?"

"I do."

He pulled out the velvet box and placed it in her hands, smiling at the way they shook as she opened it, reveling in the gasp of surprise and delight when she saw what lay inside. "As long as you get married to me."

33

Matt Ransom took out his little black book, the leather one with years of good times in it and a coded rating system so Machiavellian it had never been broken. Other guys had gone to Palm Pilots when the technology had presented itself, but Matt liked to see the possibilities right there in black and white.

He'd given Olivia fair warning. He didn't want to spill his guts, examine his motivations, or try to understand his family's dynamics. He just wanted to be himself again. And that meant going out and having some uncomplicated fun with women who weren't looking for more than he wanted to give.

He flipped through the book's gilt-edged pages and smiled over the memories they evoked. There were the Barrett twins, who'd insisted on doing everything together, including him. And Cindy Culpepper, who might have become a nun if he hadn't helped her discover how important it was to experience lust before confessing it.

In this book resided the phone numbers of all the women he had known, and while many of them were just pleasant memories at this point, others made ongoing guest appearances in his life.

Olivia Moore's was the only number he'd ripped out of the book and never intended to call again, the only woman he'd been unable to deal with on such a casual basis. She was too serious, too earnest in her beliefs, too determined to make him think and feel things he didn't want to think or feel.

He should have paid closer attention to how things had turned out eight years ago. At some point one had to learn from one's mistakes.

He flipped past Darlene Draper and Carly Feinway and stopped at MaryAnn Hightower, now a well-known television news anchor in Chicago. Olivia wanted him to explore his past? Fine, that's exactly what he'd do. And he'd make damned sure she knew how much effort he was putting into it.

Olivia entered the control room and found Di hunched over a morning newspaper. Her producer's shoulders stiffened, and she folded the paper and stuffed it into her handbag before turning around to acknowledge Olivia.

"What's in the paper?"

"Hmm?" Di looked guilty.

"Did you wrap something in that paper?" Olivia sniffed suspiciously. "Do I need to do a McMuffin search?"

"I'm clean, boss. Really. No back-sliding for me." Diane pushed her purse under the control board with her foot, never breaking eye contact.

"So what are you hiding?"

Di swallowed. "It's just *USA Today*."

Olivia held out her hand.

"It's nothing you want to see. Believe me."

That could mean only one thing. Olivia waggled her fingers at her producer. "Come on, give it up. Who'd he go out with this time?" Her tone was carefully nonchalant, but her stomach was clenched against the blow.

Diane pulled the paper out of her purse and passed it over.

Olivia unfolded it. "Oh, good, another picture."

Together they studied the grainy black and white photo of radio personality Matt Ransom "out on the town" with Chicago anchorwoman MaryAnn Hightower. Even shot through a restaurant window, Olivia noticed, Matt looked like an advertisement for tall, dark, and handsome. His companion, an angular blonde with perfectly styled hair, had the kind of cheekbones that belonged on the cover of *Vogue*.

Two days ago *People* had run an article headlined "Guy Dates, Will Doctor Wait?" accompanied by a photograph of Matt sandwiched between twin brunettes. Ever since they'd been caught on the Webcam during the remote, the paparazzi couldn't seem to get enough of him, and in every picture Matt looked happy as a clam. None of the women seemed to be complaining, either.

Olivia could hardly believe how much it hurt. Every headline, every picture that she shrugged off in public tore its own little piece of flesh. She'd taken so many direct hits that if she were a submarine, she'd be lying at the bottom of the ocean right now. And the more she shrugged off Matt's actions, the more frenzied his social life became—not exactly a healthy scenario for any of the parties involved.

"How many tall, beautiful, professional women do you think there are in Chicago, Olivia?"

"I don't know," Olivia responded. "Millions—and it looks like Matt intends to date them all."

She kept her tone flip, because admitting to the hurt would only make her an object of pity. But the time had come to end the psychological dance she and Matt had been doing.

As much as she wanted to believe Matt could deal with his baggage and come out the other side, her experience, both professional and personal, told her just how wishful that kind of thinking was. The time had come for her to cut Matt loose—not just on the outside, but deep down inside where he'd taken hold and wouldn't let go.

Gianelli's was mobbed. Customers stood three deep at the bar and elbow to elbow in the entrance. Those unlucky enough to be without reservations did their waiting out on the sidewalk.

Matt let the maitre d' escort his date to their booth while he went in search of his sister. He found her busing a just-vacated table.

"Wow. I've never seen it like this. What happened?"

"You did." Sandra shouted to be heard above the crowd. "Toss me a dishcloth, will you?"

Matt did as she asked, squeezing by a rowdy party of six to reach the other side of the table she was turning.

"The *USA Today* caption mentioned the restaurant, and the phone's been ringing off the hook since we opened."

"Gee, I guess you owe me."

"You're right. And because I'm so grateful, I'm going to give you some free advice."

"Oh, now there's a change."

"Cut out the shit, Matt. You're going too far and you're taking too long. If you keep waving women under her nose, the good doctor is going to write you off."

He broke eye contact with his sister to watch his date accept the glass of wine he'd had sent to their table. Like the others, she was beautiful and entertaining. She didn't have Olivia's keen intelligence, or her sincerity, and she didn't listen with the same kind of intensity, but then, who did?

She accepted him at face value and had no interest in turning him inside out and forcing him to grow as a human being. Being with her and the others was easy, restful . . . and surprisingly shallow and unsatisfying.

Matt frowned. "You don't really think Olivia has any interest in hearing from me at this point, do you?" he asked.

Sandra stopped shoving chairs into place. "That's it, isn't it? You *want* to scare her off. This whole public date-athon is your pathetic attempt to get out of having a serious relationship."

She shook her head in disgust. "Thanks for the free publicity, little brother, but I don't really want to be a part of this. If you can't see what you're throwing away, you're not smart enough to be a Ransom."

She gave a small nod toward the willowy redhead waiting for him on the other side of the room.

"Dr. O is right, you know. It's time for you to grow up. And way past time for you to stop playing with dolls."

Matt lifted his beer and drained it in one long gulp. It was 2 A.M. and he, Jonathan, and D.J. were firmly ensconced at their favorite table at Nick's. They'd shot pool with some of the old gang and consumed more than their fair share of alcohol. Only a handful of other tables were still occupied. It was time to start thinking about calling it a night.

"Are you okay, man?" Jon was one of Matt's oldest friends. He and his younger brother, D.J., had been Matt's carousing partners long before they'd been legally eligible to carouse. They were guys' guys, great to run with and no more anxious to settle down than he was.

"Yeah, I'm fine."

"I don't think you're as fine as you think you are." D.J.'s voice rasped from too many hours in a smoke-filled room.

"Why's that?" Matt's eyes felt like D.J.'s voice sounded. His head hurt, and something Dawg Rollins had said on the air about being bushwhacked by love kept teasing at his brain.

"Because you sent that redhead home in a cab at eleven o'clock. Eleven! And for the last two hours you've been totally ignoring the blonde over there."

Jonathan shook his head sadly. "There is something wrong in the world when Matt Ransom doesn't give a good-looking blonde a second glance."

Matt sat up and studied his friend. "You don't think I need to grow up and stop running around with women?"

D.J. motioned for another beer. "Hell, no. Why, that would be like Sammy Sosa refusing to hit another homer, or Tiger Woods giving up golf! It would disturb the natural order of things. What's got into you, anyway?"

Matt ran a hand through his hair and turned to look at the blonde. She was exceptionally well put together, and when she noticed him looking she shot him a silent invitation no man could mistake.

Matt didn't feel the slightest flicker of interest.

He cocked his head, gave her a slow once-over, and watched her run her tongue seductively across her lips.

Still nothing. He knew exactly who and what had gotten into him, and he didn't like it one bit. He considered getting up and taking the blonde up on her offer just to prove a point, but he was getting kind of tired of making the same point over and over.

He looked at the woman once more. Then he looked at his friends. Without intending to, he'd already taken a long hard look at himself. And he couldn't say he was too impressed with what he'd seen.

The following day Matt sat on a bench and watched the late afternoon sun glint on the lake. He tore the remnants of a hot dog bun into bits and tossed them to the ducks. A green mallard honked loudly before gobbling up the offering, his webbed feet paddling vigorously as he positioned himself in front of the others.

The boulder that had claimed his brother's life looked like nothing more than a random geological formation—just a big rock, not something that could change the course of a family's life.

He let his mind roam freely back to the summer days when he and Adam had raced around this lake with their friends and cooled off in its depths. Like he had every day for the past twenty-three years, Matt wished his brother were there to talk to. He also wished he hadn't argued with Sandra the night before, and that it wasn't time to go home and face Olivia. But wishing didn't make it so.

He heard soft footsteps on the grass behind him and looked up to see his mother approaching. Surprised, he moved over to make room for her, and for a time they both stared out across the lake, each lost in thought.

The bossy mallard honked loudly, and the rest of the flock fell into a loose V-formation behind him. They paddled toward the opposite shore as his mother began to speak.

"I've missed this lake." She paused. "And you."

Matt's gaze left the ducks to settle on his mother's face. The old pain was still etched clearly across it, and the lines that radiated from the corners of her eyes reflected years of looking inward. Or trying not to.

"I never meant to shut you and Sandra out. I never meant to do that."

"Mom, you don't have to . . ."

She turned away from the rock to face him . . . and, finally, their past. "Yes, I do. When Adam died, I was so stunned by the emptiness that I couldn't reach out. I couldn't make myself do what I knew needed to be done."

Her voice broke, and Matt waited silently for her to continue.

"When you and Sandra found the strength I couldn't, I was so ashamed. I knew you were hurting, I knew you needed me, but I just kept falling into that hole that Adam left."

He took his mother's hand in his and gave it a squeeze, knowing all too well the emptiness she described.

"Sandra's found her own way," his mother said. "She's got Dan and the boys and the restaurant. But I worry about you. You spend all your time sidestepping that hole, when what you really need to do is fill it in."

Matt smiled at the mental image. "So you're saying I need some emotional fill dirt?" Today's conversation with his mother would go a ways toward filling in the bottom layer of that hole; Olivia could probably dump in a whole truckload, if only he would let her.

He let himself really think about Olivia then. He thought about her sense of moral rightness, her desire to help others, and her determination to fight for what she believed in. She saw right through him and insisted on loving him anyway. Though he had no idea what she thought he had to offer in return, she seemed very certain he was worth having.

Wouldn't it be a pisser if she was right?

Across the lake the ducks changed formation, the mallard once again taking the lead. When they reached Adam's rock, they waddled ashore and shook themselves off in the fading light. A breeze ruffled their feathers and skimmed across the water to tease the branches of a nearby elm. There were good memories in this place, too, and a sense of comfort as well. With a new sense of purpose, Matt took his mother's arm and helped her up from the bench.

"Sandra said she thought you'd be heading home soon."

"Yeah," Matt said. "I have an appointment with my

agent tomorrow morning, and then I'm going to drive back to Atlanta. I've got some loose ends to tie up."

Matt's agent, Brad Hanford, pushed his half-eaten omelette aside and sat back in his chair. "Let me see if I've got this straight. You want me to tell Syntex Communications—the biggest syndicator of radio programming in the universe—that you are willing to consider their proposal for an opinion show with Olivia Moore. But you want them to lock her into the deal before you'll commit."

"Well, it does sound a little . . . unusual, but I have my reasons."

"Yes, I believe they're called fear and cowardice. The woman has already admitted she loves you, Matt. All you have to do is grovel a little. Men do it all the time. It isn't all that painful."

"But that's the beauty of it, Brad. I won't have to. Syntex is salivating to get us. It's their idea, let them do the courting. Olivia gets national syndication . . . and me. Everybody wins. We'll be working together and everything else will fall into place."

Brad shook his head. "You are one pathetic son of a bitch. Do you want me to keep talking to TLK?"

Matt shrugged. "It can't hurt to have a fallback, but there's no way they can match Syntex's offer."

Hanford picked up the check and gave Matt one last look. "You seem pretty sure of yourself. What if Dr. Moore's not interested? She told the world she loved you over three weeks ago, and you've been on a dating rampage ever since."

Matt shifted uncomfortably in his seat. He had screwed up the whole communication thing pretty royally, but if there was one thing he figured he could count on, it was Olivia's ambition.

As much as she'd hated the idea of the food bank remote, she'd gone along to protect her career. She might want to chew him up one end and down the other, but there was no way the Olivia he knew was going to turn down the offer of a lifetime.

"I may not know a hell of a lot about relationships, Brad, but I do know Olivia. This is exactly what she's been working toward since I met her; there's no way in hell she's going to turn it down."

34

"Work with Matt Ransom? I'd rather slide down a sharp razor and land in alcohol!" The faces regarding her from around the conference table registered shock and disbelief, which, Olivia suspected, made them mirror images of her own.

Unsure what to do next, she stood up and gathered her things. Her agent, Karen Crandall, stood more slowly, telegraphing her reluctance with every tortoiselike movement.

"Olivia," she said, "why don't we sit down and hear what they have to—"

"No, I'm sorry. I'd love to be a part of Syntex Communications, and a male/female counterpoint show is very tempting, but I can't do it with Matt. How do you argue thoughts and feelings with a man who won't admit he has any?"

"*Liv Live*'s a great show, Dr. Moore," Syntex's CEO, Edward Simms, said. "But we already have several call-in advice shows. You and Matt Ransom together eat up the airwaves. A star vehicle like *The Way We See It* doesn't come along every day."

Olivia looked Edward Simms straight in the eye. She opened her mouth, closed it, opened it again. She wasn't sure she had the strength to turn him down again.

This *was* the opportunity of a lifetime. And it was totally wrong for her right now. She needed to say no and mean it. Just as she should have said no when Crankower wanted to lock her in that apartment with Matt.

She'd known then that being in that kind of proximity and under that kind of pressure with Matt was an emotional disaster waiting to happen, but she had ignored her survival instincts because of her need to be the last talk show host still standing. Once again she was being forced to choose between emotional health and professional success. As she'd told her listeners over and over, a person was nothing more than the sum of her choices.

It was time to follow her own advice.

She nodded to Simms and his VPs. "Thank you very much for the offer. I'm flattered." She smiled. "And very tempted. But razor blades notwithstanding, I'm afraid I have to decline."

And then she was riding the elevator down twenty-two floors with her stunned agent beside her. Karen, who talked like others breathed, held her tongue until they exited through the revolving door onto Fifth Avenue.

"Olivia, think what you're doing here. Syntex will put *The Way We See It* in every major market in the country. If you want to counsel patients, you can build that into your schedule. You've done great with *Liv Live*, but the most TLK can do is put it on the twenty stations in their group. Why don't you let me go back and—"

"No. When T.J. asked me to do the food bank remote, I told myself they'd be holding the Winter Olympics in hell before I said yes. And then I gave in and did it. This time I mean it. The Devil will be doing a double axel on ice before I do *The Way We See It* with Matt Ransom."

Turning, Olivia strode up Fifth with Karen, the Syntex limo trailing behind them. She was trying very hard *not* to think about what she had just turned down. But she wasn't having much success.

Her feet pounded on the pavement as Olivia stared unseeing into the shop windows they passed. She had just turned down the biggest offer of her career, said no to the thing she wanted most. No to becoming a household name, no to reaching the pinnacle of syndication. No to more money than she'd thought to see in a lifetime.

And she'd done it because . . . ?

Olivia stopped in front of a display of Coach handbags as she examined the question more closely. She'd said no because she couldn't keep sacrificing her emotions in order to advance her career; because the quality of her life was more important than what she achieved professionally. Tired and out of time, she slid into the back of the limo beside Karen for the ride to JFK.

If she forced herself to work with Matt, given everything that was unresolved between them, what did that say about her? That she had learned nothing; that she would always subjugate and deny her feelings in order to succeed.

Life was too short to torture herself that way. And much too short to be manipulated. Taking her seat in the first-class cabin for the flight to Atlanta, Olivia realized how "off" the whole thing felt. If Matt Ransom was such an important part of the Syntex equation, where was he?

She sipped from the glass of wine the flight attendant pressed on her and thought about that for a while.

If the Bachelor of the Year wanted to do a show with her, he was going to have to tell her so himself. And he was going to have to tell her why.

Friday morning's *Liv Live* was chock-full of women dealing with unpleasant surprises, something Olivia could relate to after her own in the Syntex boardroom. For most of the morning she worked at ironing out the creases that wrinkled her callers' lives.

Sometimes those creases came in unexpected forms, like Melissa's husband, who had evidently been faking an interest in power tools.

"I just don't get it, Dr. O," a throaty-voiced Melissa said. "Every year since we got married, I've given my husband a power tool for his birthday."

"And?" Olivia asked.

"And the other day, while we were cleaning out the garage, he told me he'd rather have lingerie." Melissa's voice warbled. "From Victoria's Secret."

"And how do you feel about that?" Olivia asked.

"How would you feel? He used to rip my panties off at every opportunity. I didn't realize he was checking for a style number."

Olivia bit back a smile. She could hear the shock and confusion in Melissa's voice, but she detected no revulsion, which meant Melissa might be able to come to terms with her husband's predilection.

"Cross-dressers are almost always heterosexual,"

Olivia said. "If you love him, and you can live with the lingerie, it doesn't have to be a problem."

"But he's six feet two. His friends call him Bubba," Melissa pointed out. "And I already bought the table saw."

Olivia was well into the third hour of *Liv Live* when JoBeth called in, her voice vibrating with excitement. She too had experienced a life-altering surprise, but hers hadn't been at all unpleasant.

"You won't believe it, Dr. O. I'm getting married."

The rush of envy was completely personal and totally unprofessional. Olivia quashed it immediately. "Congratulations," she said. "That's fabulous."

"Thanks. I still can't believe it. Two men proposed to me in one night. It was the most incredible thing."

"Wow. Two proposals," Olivia marveled, unable to ignore the irony. The person she'd advised had received two marriage proposals, while the man she loved had put a monkey wrench in her career plans and was too busy dating to admit to any feelings at all.

"Was one of them Dawg?"

"Yes," JoBeth gushed. "It was so romantic. He came right into the ladies' room of La Parisienne to ask me. We're going to get married in the fall."

Dawg Rollins had stormed a ladies' room to propose. Okay, so it wasn't a scenario Olivia envied greatly. Still, he'd proposed; Matt Ransom had a recurring role on *The Dating Game*.

"Anyway, I just wanted to say thanks. If it weren't for you and Matt, this never would have happened."

Olivia couldn't bring herself to ask whether it was because of them or in spite of them. "Congratulations, JoBeth. Really. It's great that things worked out."

She was just trying to imagine Matt Ransom on his knees anywhere, let alone in a ladies' lounge, when she heard a strange noise in the control room. Olivia squinted up through the glass, but Diane had turned her back. There was some sort of altercation going on, but when no security guard appeared, Olivia shifted her attention back to her caller.

"Is Matt going to be back soon?" JoBeth asked. "Dawg's on a run out of state today, but he asked me to be sure to thank him, too."

Olivia heard raised voices on the other side of the plate glass. Craning her neck, she tried to see around Diane, but equipment blocked her view. "You know, I'm not really sure when he'll be back. In fact . . ."

Her producer turned around, and a moment later, Matt Ransom's head poked up above Diane's. While Olivia watched, he put his hands on Diane's shoulders and moved her firmly out of the way. The next voice she heard in her headphones was Matt's.

"Actually, JoBeth," he said, as if he hadn't just arm-wrestled Diane for his spot in front of the control-room microphone, "I am back, and I'm glad to hear things worked out so well for you and Dawg."

Diane popped her head out from behind Matt's shoulder and mouthed a silent apology, but Olivia was still trying to grasp what was going on.

"Oh, and JoBeth?" he said.

"Umm-hmm?"

"You were right to be pissed off at me the last time we spoke. I had no business giving Dawg advice when I was screwing up my own life so badly."

There was a stunned silence as Olivia, JoBeth, and,

Olivia was certain, every one of her listeners, shook their heads trying to unclog their ears.

"Gee, Matt," JoBeth observed. "You sure don't sound like your usual self."

"No, I don't, do I?" Matt replied. "I think we know who we can blame for that." He looked directly at Olivia, but it was impossible to read his thoughts through the glass.

Olivia imagined the whole station straining toward the nearest set of speakers. Somewhere in the bowels of the building Charles Crankower was undoubtedly jumping for joy. She didn't know why she was so surprised that Matt had shown up unannounced. Matt Ransom had always conducted his life by the seat of his pants. Too bad he filled them out so nicely.

"So, what brings you back to Atlanta?" She kept both her expression and her voice neutral, while she combated the glimmer of hope that stirred with a mental listing of Matt's many transgressions, including, but not limited to, compelling her to turn down her shot at national syndication.

"Well, I considered pretending I just happened to be passing by, but I came directly from Chicago, so that's a bit of a stretch."

Silent, she waited.

"And then I considered pretending I was a volunteer member of the relaxation police sent to evaluate your progress," he said.

Olivia braced for the expected punch line, but he surprised her. "But I'm getting real tired of pretending."

He sounded so unhappy about his admission that Olivia decided to test him with one of her own.

"I made the mistake of falling in love with you twice,

Matt," she said. "And then I felt the need to admit it to the world." She paused. "Only you didn't want to hear it."

"No, I didn't," he said. "I've been trying real hard not to listen to a lot of things."

Once again, Matt sounded less than happy about the revelation, but nonetheless, he'd made it. Three weeks ago this conversation would have sent him running for the emotional hills.

Olivia peered through the glass trying to see through it and inside of him. *Please, God,* she thought. *Please don't let him wimp out now.*

Matt stepped away from the plate glass. Olivia and her audience waited, collective breath held, while he left the control room and let himself into the studio. There he pushed her microphone up on its boom arm and leaned against the table where she sat, facing her.

Olivia looked up into Matt's eyes. There was something in them that hadn't been there before—a squeaky new grown-up thing that looked like it felt about as comfortable as a brand-new pair of high heels. But there was humor in them, too, and a willingness, she thought, to see this through. Her hope grew and began to multiply.

"Look, there's no way I'm getting down on one knee or anything, but I do have feelings for you. Real . . . feelings. With . . . depth behind them."

"Gee, Dr. O," chirped JoBeth. "He's starting to sound like a real live grown-up. Are you sure that's Matt Ransom in there?"

"It's not Memorex," growled Matt as he leaned over and dumped the call.

Olivia just nodded her head and reminded herself to breathe.

Matt cleared his throat. "I've been running from my emotions since my brother died, Olivia. I didn't want to feel that deeply about anyone again. But I feel that way about you."

The words were simply put, and they pierced her to the core. She thought about what it had taken for Matt to mention his brother so publicly and realized just how great a hurdle he'd just jumped.

"Thank you," she said softly. "That means a lot to me. But I'm not sure where that leaves us."

"You're the mental health professional. Isn't there a handbook you can look this stuff up in?"

Olivia smiled. "Well, some sort of demonstration of your feelings would be helpful."

Matt looked nonplussed for a moment. Then he reached into his back pocket and pulled out a little black book, presumably the one he'd threatened her with and put to such constant use in Chicago.

Barely flinching, he opened it and started ripping out the gilt-edged pages. He ripped them out two and then three at a time, littering the floor around them until all that was left was the leather binding, which he dropped in a nearby trash can.

"How's that?"

"That's ... good." Olivia found herself nodding her head, unsure how to continue, confounded by the utter Matt-ness of the demonstration.

Then he smiled, a sudden brightening that sent that damned dimple slicing through his cheek, and she couldn't help smiling back.

"It's the least I could do," he said. "I mean, now that

your reputation is completely blown, I may as well let go of mine."

He bent down then and kissed her, lightly. "I don't have a lot of experience with real relationships, Livvy. But if you're willing to walk me through it, I'm willing to give it a try."

As declarations of love went, it was somewhat lacking in hearts and flowers, but Olivia knew a breakthrough when she heard one. Happiness, love, and, okay, it was definitely relief, flooded through her.

Reaching up, she pulled Matt's mouth down to cover hers again. This time the kiss was deeper and definitely more thrilling and confirmed what Olivia had hoped: Matt Ransom might have left Never Land, but he still knew how to fly.

The sound of throat-clearing came from the control room and was followed by a tapping on the glass. Registering the silence in her headphones for the first time, Olivia opened one eye to peek over Matt's shoulder.

Diane stood in front of the audio board with a finger poised above it. While Olivia watched, her producer leaned forward and pushed a button on the console.

Smooching sound effects of the overdone cartoon variety went on the air and filled Olivia's headphones.

Before Olivia could blink, Diane leaned over the board again. A heartbeat later, the opening strains of the "Hallelujah Chorus" drowned out the cartoon kisses.

Still liplocked, but with both eyes wide open now, Olivia watched Diane adjust audio levels. Several long seconds of cartoon kisses and fervent hallelujahs followed.

Afraid that if she didn't do something, her show was

going to end with Porky Pig's rendition of "That's all, folks," Olivia unlocked her lips from Matt's and signaled Diane that she was ready to wrap things up. Leaning in to her microphone, she said with relish, "This is Dr. Olivia Moore, reminding you to get out there and live your life . . . *live*." After a last thumbs-up to Diane, she concluded, "Which is exactly what I intend to do."

When she was certain her microphone was off, Olivia removed her headphones and turned her full attention to Matt, who was still lounging casually against the table. Raising an expectant eyebrow, she waited for him to speak.

"So, are you ready to talk about moving to New York and arguing with each other for a living?" he asked.

"I still can't believe they want to pay me that much money just to disagree with you."

Matt smiled; they both seemed to be doing a ridiculous amount of that at the moment. "I knew that would be a major selling point," he said.

She cocked her head to one side and studied the face of the man beside her. "Yeah, but there's just one thing. What if we go ahead with this and one day we wake up and we're in such accord we can't think of anything to argue about?"

They looked into each other's eyes, looked away, and looked back again, their faces tight with barely suppressed laughter.

"You know," he said as he slung an arm around her shoulder and pulled her close. "I think we can start worrying about that right about the time world peace is declared." He brought his lips down to brush against hers.

"Yeah," she breathed. "Or when they go ahead and hold those Winter Olympics in hell."

About the Author

Wendy clearly remembers her first encounter with Dick and Jane. She's still unsure why this otherwise hip twosome were so preoccupied with their dog, Spot, but two seconds after reading "See Spot Run" she was hooked on words—and books—for life.

Despite efforts to control this addiction, Wendy—who has been unable to find an appropriate 12-step program—remains incapable of putting down a book once she's begun reading it, and has faced many mornings bleary-eyed as a result.

It wasn't long after leaving broadcast production for motherhood that Wendy realized reading just wasn't enough anymore. Soon she was writing every bit as compulsively as she'd always read. Once again, her mornings were anything but bright-eyed and bushy-tailed.

7 Days and 7 Nights is the author's first romantic comedy, and she sincerely hopes you sit up all night reading it—just like she did writing it.

Wendy lives in Atlanta with her husband and their two sons. You can write to her at 1401 Johnson Ferry Road, Suite 328/C-70, Marietta, GA 30062, or contact her on her website at www.authorwendywax.com.

Can't wait to join

Wendy Wax

in her next
hilariously sexy adventure?

Read on for a preview of
her new book . . .

Available summer 2004

———

Miranda Smith was looking for a stamp when she discovered just how good her husband looked in ladies' lingerie.

It was six-thirty P.M. on the coldest January 8th on record, and the Truro post office was already closed. But for Miranda—who was now conducting a room-by-room search—the stamp was no longer just postage but a symbol of every New Year's resolution she'd ever made. And failed to keep.

One week into the new year she'd already given up on becoming a better daughter and reading her way through the classics. She wasn't going to wimp out on the only resolution she still had a chance of keeping.

Somewhere in this five-bedroom, four-bath, six-thousand-square-foot home—which she'd just tossed like a petty thief looking for loot—there had to be enough postage to get her credit card payment in on time.

Miranda stood in the foyer outside Tom's study debating her next move.

With less than twenty minutes to get ready for Friday

night dinner at her parents', she should be heading upstairs to shower and change, not preparing to strip-search another room.

It was just a stamp, she told herself as she turned toward the stairs, not the Holy Grail. Paying an occasional late fee was not cause for shame.

Placing a hand on the banister, she took the first step and consoled herself with the fact that Tom's study had exceedingly low stamp potential, since she paid the household bills and he conducted all of his correspondence from the office.

On the next step, she decided that next year's resolutions would include buying stamps regularly, which would definitely enhance her chances of eliminating late fees in the future.

As if she'd be making any resolutions next year, when she'd folded so easily this year.

The thought stopped her in midstep, turned her around, and propelled her back down the stairs determined to find a stamp or die trying.

Miranda marched through the foyer and into the study, where she snapped on the overhead light and crossed to Tom's desk. Finding the desk drawer slightly ajar, she pulled on the knob, gritting her teeth in frustration when the drawer didn't budge.

Beyond impatience, Miranda wrapped both hands around the knob and yanked with all her might. The drawer sprang free and sent a packet of photos, which must have been holding up the works, spilling across the floor.

Still in single-minded pursuit of a stamp, Miranda crouched down to gather them up. She duckwalked across the floor, cramming the photos back into their envelope, muttering to herself and trying to figure out where else she could possibly find postage in the next thirty seconds.

Until she actually looked at the photo in her hand, the one of her husband, the former linebacker, in a red satin bustier and matching bikini panties.

Miranda's brain froze. Then it raced, sputtered, and ceased functioning altogether. Unable to think or move, she crouched on the study floor, staring at the picture clutched in her hand.

Her first clear thought was that there had to be some mistake. As president of Ballantyne Bras, her family's bra and lingerie business, her husband was expected to supervise the design and production of a comprehensive line of women's undergarments.

He was not supposed to wear them.

And yet here he was in a black lace teddy. And a fuchsia merry widow—with some woman's hand on his rear end.

Miranda squinted at the hand, hoping to recognize it, but except for its French manicure and obvious familiarity with her husband's derriere, it could have belonged to anyone.

The next photo revealed Tom in a cream-colored thong that looked as if it had been custom-made for him. Her head began to pound as she realized that it probably had.

Unable to tear her gaze from the sight of Tom's rugged torso sheathed in such feminine trappings, Miranda gathered up the rest of the photos and pulled herself up into the chair.

She thought of all the times she'd seen her husband smile and wink and say "Hi, I'm Tom Smith, and I'm in ladies' underwear," and never imagined he was telling the truth.

Or that he looked as good in lingerie as she did.

Drawing in one shaky breath and letting out another, she dragged her gaze from the photos to stare out the study window. Porch lights twinkled from the house across the cul-de-sac, and snow glistened in the arc of a streetlamp. It clung to the rain-slicked branches of the oak out front and coated the shiny layer of ice in the next-door neighbor's birdbath, though it was hard to fully appreciate the winter landscape with her brain occupied by the vision of Tom decked out in Ballantyne's biggest sellers.

Her thoughts moved slowly, and she felt strangely detached, as if someone had swabbed her with novocaine. There was no sharp, stinging pain, no specific point of impact, only a spreading ache of hurt and disbelief. And the sixty-four-million-dollar question: How could she not have known?

In this town, where her family's business had been the largest employer for more than a hundred years, someone should have known . . . and blabbed. And yet until a moment ago, she would have sworn her husband's interest in ladies' underwear was limited to manufacuring it.

The images ricocheted through her brain, bouncing off each other, raising more questions she couldn't answer.

Who had taken the pictures? Who did the female hand belong to? And how could a man who'd spent much of his waking life in a jockstrap and cleats look so good in a pale pink corset with tiny rosebuds down the front?

Miranda laid the pictures out on the desk. This was her husband. The man she'd met her first miraculous year at Emory University. The man her family had deemed perfect for her . . . and whom she'd married twelve years ago in the biggest wedding Truro had ever seen. The man with whom she'd been trying to have children for eight of those twelve years. The man who'd turned out to be somewhat . . . less . . . than she'd expected, but with whom she'd fully intended to grow old.

Icy tendrils of fear and dread wrapped themselves around her as she realized that no matter what happened next, her life would never be the same. If her husband wasn't who she thought he was, then who did that make her?

She fanned the photos out the way a card player might, forcing herself to look at them one more time. Lifting the last one to the light, she studied the disembodied woman's hand—with its flawless French manicure—resting so possessively on her husband's bare buttock, and a hot flash of anger melted some of the ice.

Another woman had fondled her husband's naked buns while he was dressed in women's lingerie.

Her stomach clenched, and she asked herself again how this could have happened. It was normal for married people to fall into their individual routines, normal for the excitement to dissipate after so many years together. It was not normal to miss something as big as this.

Had there been a "Gee, honey, I hope you don't mind but I really get off on dressing up in women's underclothes—which is really convenient, since I run your family's brassiere and lingerie business—and I especially like to do this with other women's hands on my butt"?

Had she smiled over the morning paper and her to-do list for the Ladies Guild and said, "That's nice, Tom. Can you pass the preserves?"

She sat, still numb, staring out the window, trying to see . . . something. Trying to imagine what in the world she was supposed to do now.

When she finally looked at the clock, it was eight P.M. and she and Tom were late for dinner. For a few long moments she tried to imagine where Tom might be—out being fitted for a new bra? Busy baring his butt to the woman with the long nails? Winking and telling people he was in ladies' underwear?

She dropped her head into her hands. There was no way she could face him right now—whatever he might be wearing—nor could she imagine what she would say to him when she did.

For a wild, wonderful moment she contemplated pretending she'd never found the pictures. Even with the grapevine in working order, the wife was usually the last to know. What if she just pretended she didn't?

She peered at the photos more closely but couldn't find a date. Maybe Tom didn't even dress up like this anymore. Maybe it had grown old for him, like the whitewater rafting and the iron-man triathlons. Who knew how long those pictures had been stuck in that drawer?

Experimentally, she picked up the photos and dropped them into the trash can. Then she turned her back on the trash can and leaned against the desk with studied nonchalance. Okay, so her husband liked to dress up in women's underwear. And he'd never mentioned this to her. And he did it with other women. Okay. Things could be worse. Things could always be worse.

Right.

Miranda bent over to retrieve the packet of photos, which now had strips of shredded paper clinging to it. She knew without thinking what her mother would say. "Make him give up Miss Manicure, Miranda. And do your best to forgive and forget."

Sure. Then they could get matching underwear made—they owned the company, after all—and ... and ... well, she wasn't sure exactly what you did once you were dressed up that way with your husband, but maybe it would be fun. Just because she didn't dress up didn't mean she didn't have an adventurous spirit.

Maybe her mother had a point. Maybe she could just show Tom the pictures and ask him to explain why he liked to do that. And why he'd never mentioned it. And who the hell the woman with the manicure was.

Right.

Miranda set the packet of photos in front of her. Idly, as she tried to follow that scenario through to its logical conclusion, she peeled the strips of shredded paper off the packet and began to shuffle them around the desktop. Words began to leap out at her. Words that pushed the images she'd just confronted right out of her mind. Words like "Ballantyne," and "receivables," and the truly alarming, "auditors to investigate."

No, no way. Desperately needing to see her glass as half full, Miranda stole a quick peek over her shoulder to check for a hidden camera, but there was no Allen Funt. And no one jumping out to shout, "Smile, you're on *Candid Camera!*"

With trembling fingers, Miranda retrieved more shredded pieces from the trash can and began to fit them together like pieces of a puzzle. They all appeared to be part of a letter from Ballantyne's primary lender, and though there were some gaps, the end result was every bit as life-smashing as the photos.

Not only did her husband like to dress up in women's underwear with other women helping, he had put Ballantyne—the company that had been passed down by the women in her family for generations—in a precarious position with its bank.

She couldn't seem to get any air into her lungs, and despite the snow outside, little beads of sweat popped out on her forehead.

The phone on the desk in front of her rang and she jumped. Heart racing, she brought the receiver up to her ear.

"Miranda, the pot roast is starting to resemble shoe leather. Your father and I were expecting you at seven-fifteen." Her mother, who rarely bothered with a greeting, sounded like her usual imperious self.

Miranda let out the breath she'd finally gotten ahold of. She tried to think lofty, composed, queenlike thoughts, as she'd been taught when she first started competing in pageants. She pictured the crown on her head and imagined Bert Parks asking her the inevitable question about world peace.

"I know, Mother. Is, uh, Tom there?"

"No, dear. I thought you were driving over together."

"Well, actually, I'm not feeling all that well." *Not exactly a lie.* "I think Tom may have misunderstood our plans."

And me. And our life. "Will you ask him to call me if he shows up there?"

"Of course, Miranda. But I want you to call me in the morning and let me know how you're feeling. You don't think you're . . ."

"No, Mother." Miranda winced at the raw hope in her mother's voice.

She doubted she was pregnant. She never was. And this was the first time she was glad of it.

As she hung up the phone, Miranda's gaze flitted around the study she so rarely entered. For the first time she noticed how bare the desktop was, except for her carefully laid out cache of evidence; how empty the drawer had been, except for the obviously overlooked pictures.

Miranda's mouth went dry. Not at all regally, she shoved back from the desk and stood, her knees wobbling.

Slowly, with the bad feeling in the pit of her stomach spreading bodywide, she forced herself up the stairs to the master bedroom. Stopping at the dresser, she drew a steadying breath and pulled Tom's top drawer open. Though she wouldn't have been surprised by satin or lace, she found neither. Nor did she find anything in white cotton. The drawer was empty.

Miranda opened each drawer in turn, but all of Tom's clothes were gone. Trying not to hyperventilate, she moved to the walk-in closet and found more of the same. Or was that none of the same?

Like a zombie, she turned and walked back into the bedroom stopping at the king-size bed she'd shared with

Tom Smith for the last twelve years. A man she'd evidently never known nor understood.

There, propped on her pillow, sat a small square envelope. Miranda sank onto the edge of the bed and reached for the envelope. Maybe it was an invitation to some event somehow gone astray. Or instructions to smile because she was, in fact, on *Candid Camera*, not watching her life swirl steadily down the toilet.

Murmuring a small prayer, she picked up the envelope and pried it open with clumsy fingers.

The message was brief and to the point. Once again some part of Miranda's mind cried "foul," because after this many years a woman deserved some warning. And she definitely deserved an explanation.

In a firm hand, with well-formed curves and crisply dotted *i*'s, Tom had written: "Dear Miranda, By the time you find this I plan to be out of the country. Sorry things turned out this way. Have a nice life. Tom."

Miranda balled up the note and threw it at the dresser mirror while the pressure built behind her eyelids. Soon tears were streaming down her cheeks, puffing up her eyes, wreaking all kinds of havoc on her face.

She and Tom had loved each other once, she was sure of it. Maybe not with the searing intensity you read about in romance novels, but enough—she had thought—to weather the ups and downs of a lifetime. And when the initial excitement had worn off, she'd told herself that it had been replaced by something mellower and longer lasting.

She'd thought they had mutual respect and a certain amount of caring. But in fact they had cheating, and cross-dressing, followed by a very definite running away.

The tears were freefalling now, and Miranda didn't bother to wipe them away. She pictured the horrified look on her mother's face, but for once she was too miserable to care how puffy her eyes got or whether every last stitch of makeup was washed away. With a sniff, she wondered if it was like the tree falling in the empty forest. If no one was here to see her cry, did that mean that she wasn't?

As if loosened by the thought, the tears fell faster. Miranda let the hot salty drops make tracks through her makeup, licking them away only when they reached the corners of her mouth.

She felt like a wounded animal, battered and bruised, with spears sticking out of its hide. But even in her misery she recognized that her heart, though it hurt, wasn't completely shattered. This realization made her cry even harder.

She lost track of how long she cried, but when she finally looked into the mirror a pitiful woman stared back. Miranda sat up straighter and squared her shoulders, but the woman still had tears streaming down her face.

Plucking a tissue from the nightstand, she blew her nose, loud, since there still wasn't anyone in her forest and might not ever be again.

At last she sniffled and hiccupped her way to a stop. Reaching for something to cling to, she grabbed on to the pageant instruction her mother had been drilling into her since her fifth birthday.

Okay, then. Sometimes you didn't win the crown. Sometimes, though she didn't have prior personal experience with this, you didn't even make the final five. You could still put on the smile, and you could still walk the walk. If there was anything she knew how to do, it was that.

Tom didn't want her? Fine. But he was going to have to tell her so in person. Right after he fixed whatever damage he'd done to Ballantyne. Then he could go off and dress up in some other company's lingerie to his heart's content.

All she had to do was find the lying, cheating, cross-dressing S.O.B. Yes, that would be her first step. She'd get started just as soon as the woman in the mirror stopped crying.